TAMARA'S STORY

To Ann & David -
In remembrance of our
pleasant dinners together
on the Cacouna, June 03.
Tom Berry

TAMARA'S STORY

---

*Of Love and Intrigue
at the Russian Court*

Tom Berry

CONTENTS

TO VALIA

CHAPTER 1

Tsar Alexander I annexed the Kingdom of Georgia in 1801, but many tribes of the mountainous areas were never fully subjugated. Savage incidents kept dashing Cossacks busy in the rugged canyons where the Terek River flowed out of the high snow-capped peaks. Georgian warriors, agile as devils, were legendary and Russians long esteemed their riding prowess. Anyone who dreamed of mystery and adventure thought of the Caucasus.

For centuries the wild Kura River cascaded through the gorge dividing the capital city Tiflis. Old Georgian houses defied gravity by protruding out on their railings from the cliffs above the splashing torrents. A unique architecture developed with stucco exteriors and wide, ornately decorated verandas where the warm climate allowed much outdoor living. By 1900 the ancient part of the city contrasted greatly with the European mansions built by the conquerors on the other side of the Kura. The river symbolized the division between the Georgians and the Russians, two cultures combined, but not blended.

At the beginning of the 20th century Tiflis was a very cosmopolitan city. Travelers were amazed at the sophisticated cultural activities and fashionable tree-lined boulevards. It was known as the Paris of the Caucasus. Society at balls and the opera was a mixture of Russians and Georgians, but ancient families such as the Zhorzhadze and Rustavelli remained aloof from close contact and continued their ancient customs. They wanted pure blood lines and considered a marriage between a

Russian and a Georgian a mesalliance. Such was the fate of the Princess Tamara Borisovna Zhorzhadze. Her father, a dashing Georgian general, conquered the heart of the Countess Trushinsky. Their

happy marriage ended in a tragic motor accident and their two
orphaned children, Tamara and Valery, were put under the care of
their aunt and uncle in the European section of Tiflis.

In July, 1913 Princess Tamara looked through the curtains
covering the large French windows of the salon in her aunt's mansion. She saw three camels in single file, each burdened with rolls
of oriental carpets, walking slowly behind a carriage. At that moment a stroll through the Georgian markets flashed through her
mind. She loved walking with her old governess through the narrow streets in the ancient part of the city. Marvelous woven rugs
lined the walls of silver and brass shops where merchants gave her
a chance to speak Georgian, the language of her father's noble
ancestors. Suddenly her thoughts were changed when a smart carriage with four horses passed on the street below. The vehicle
brought back memories of St. Petersburg and she wondered if a
servant's whispers were true. Was she really returning to that splendid northern city so far away? The question thrilled her and she
started waltzing around the ornate salon.

"Princess," a maid politely called, stopping her in an awkward
pose. "The countess wants you." Tamara thanked her in Russian
and began straightening some disheveled curls in the mirror of a
girandole hanging on a wall. Realizing that she would soon be
with her aunt, the Countess Zita Ivanovna Trushinsky, she started
thinking in French. Early in her youth, after the death of her parents, when she and her brother, Prince Valery Borisovich
Zhorzhadze, had first come to live in Tiflis, she learned that certain languages pertained to certain people. While the blood of the
ancient kings of Georgia ran in her veins, her father's marriage to a
Russian had been considered a mesalliance by both sides of the
family. Consequently, she spoke Georgian with her paternal grandmother, French with her aunt, and Russian with her uncle, Count
Vadim Igorevich Trushinsky.

Leaving the salon, she crossed the hall and started up the stairs
which reminded her of the grand staircase in the St. Petersburg
palace of the Dashkovs, her wealthy relatives who had connections

at court. Her aunt, Princess Lidia Dashkov, was a Lady in Waiting for Her Majesty, Tsarina Alexandra. It was known that the Empress favored the princess among her ladies at court because she often visited the notorious monk Rasputin at his apartment and allowed him visiting rights in her own mansion on the Fontanka. Through marriage she was related to the famous Princess Dashkov who was a friend of Catherine the Great and helped her ascend the throne of Russia. With such a prestigious background and position in society the Princess Lidia was a formidable figure in St. Petersburg society. Her son Vladimir was a Page of the Tsar and her husband, Prince Dashkov, was an Aidede-Camp of his Imperial Majesty, Nicholas II. Tamara had visited the Dashkovs only once, but the grand scale of their world had become the major theme of her daydreams. Through their influence she could become a Maid of Honor to the tsarina: another dream Tamara remembered as she knocked on her aunt's door.

"Entre," resounded and she quickly opened the left portal. Her aunt was lying on a chaise lounge, brushing her dyed thinning hair while a seamstress was working on a dress-maker's model. "Madame Dubnov," the countess said in a brusk tone, "Let us finish this tomorrow." The woman did not want the delay, but the countess waved her away with a long lace handkerchief. Showing her displeasure, the seamstress curtsied, but as she left she mentioned Tamara's beauty because she knew it would upset the countess. When the door closed, Aunt Zita remarked, "What one puts up with these days! If that woman wasn't the best seamstress in Tiflis, I'd send her packing!" After straightening herself on the lounge while she searched in a mirror for a blemish in her makeup, she continued. "Ma chere, come closer. I have news."

Tamara smiled faintly and sat down quickly beside her on a boudoir stool. She carefully looked around to see if her aunt's lover, Count Bagrov, was in the room. He wasn't, and she was thankful because she disliked him immensely.

Aunt Zita adjusted her lace frock and put down her mirror. A loose hairpin was adjusted and an eyelid rubbed. It was obvious that she must communicate something she didn't favor. Folding her hands and looking straight at her ward, she stated with great preciseness that the Princess Dashkov had prepared Tamara's introduction to society in St. Petersburg even though she would not be eighteen until the end of the season. Therefore, she would travel with her aunt and uncle to the capital city.

"Oh, auntie," Tamara blurted out, jumping up.

"Don't be so Georgian," the countess criticized, wrinkling her face as if she disapproved of such a display of emotion. English reserve was in fashion and the countess had to keep up with the belle monde. "As if we Russians weren't mad enough, your mother married a Georgian!"

Tamara smiled and sat down again. She was proud of her royal Georgian ancestry and knew that her aunt was jealous. While Russians looked down on the Georgians and liked to remark that every decent household had a Georgian prince for a cook, Tamara's ancestors had once ruled the country and her dark eyes and white skin reflected the best qualities of her Russian and Georgian blood.

"You know that Lidia Constantinovna has been interested in you for some time and that she has the means of helping you greatly. Her country estates alone must be worth a fortune. She can do anything; and now she's asking for you."

The princess began waltzing around the room.

"Stop it! That's no reason for behaving like a Georgian horseman. You're beautiful, it's true, but conduct is just as important!"

Realizing that she had perturbed her aunt, Tamara said something that would please her, "And you'll get to meet that Holy Man!"

Aunt Zita looked at her nails, but her face showed her satisfaction. The Princess Dashkov had promised to introduce her to the Siberian monk Rasputin, who had won the tsarina's favor in spite of rumors about his scandalous debaucheries. While the thought appealed, the countess avoided showing her eagerness by changing the subject, "Perhaps taking you to St. Petersburg will eradicate that wild cousin from your mind."

Tamara did not respond, but the remark hurt her feelings. She and her second cousin Prince Shota Zhorzhadze had fallen in love, but the family had not allowed the relationship. She still cared for him, but was forbidden his company. She wondered if a conspiracy was separating them. Leaving him at the country estate near the ancient city of Mtsety would be difficult, but perhaps the distance would help take away the pain in her heart.

The countess's brow slightly wrinkled. "You Georgians want it all, don't you. Isn't it enough to be a Maid of Honor to Her Majesty? Oh, who could ever understand the wild blood that flows in your veins?" The countess sighed before continuing, "Whatever made my dear sister marry that father of yours I'll never know!"

Such remarks hurt Tamara's feelings, but there was no point in an argument. Her lineage gave her the opportunity to be a Maid of Honor to the Empress whereas the countess's background did not. When servants made snide remarks about the lady of the house, Tamara either pretended that she did not hear or shook her head and did not reply. She listened only when old Luda the cook whispered, "She's jealous of you." Yet Tamara knew that time was on her side. So, she waited.

Waiting had paid off in Russian history and she knew it. Had not Catherine the Great waited seven years for her husband to consummate their marriage? He played with dolls and toy soldiers during the night while she befriended him, knowing that the alternative was a return to the poor German principality from whence she had come. Then the Empress Elizabeth brought to court the handsome Saltykov and Catherine succumbed. It was still an unsolved mystery whether Peter the Third or Saltykov was the father of her son Paul. Tamara was curious about Catherine's behavior, but she could only discuss it with her friend Nina Evgenievna Cherkessky.

At that moment Count Igor Constantinovich Bagrov entered. The tall bald colonel was her aunt's lover and Tamara hated him. Not seeing her in the corner, he said, "Ma chere, have you decided about this evening?" The countess winced, flashing her eyes toward

Tamara. Showing no concern that he was caught in the mistress's boudoir, the count greeted the princess.

Tamara smiled. While she detested Count Bagrov, she strove for politeness. He was her brother's commandant in the Cadet Corps, but he was impudent and took liberties that were improper. He often tried petting her arm or pinching her when he greeted her. He was also so careless with his comments and actions that it was common knowledge among the servants that he was having an affair with the lady of the house. Tamara had heard the maids' gossip and hated him even more. The liaison seemed unfair to her uncle whom she adored. She also felt unkindly toward her aunt for deceiving her uncle; but at that time she knew little about the behavior of high society. The complexities of love in the household were as difficult to understand as the perplexing behavior of Catherine the Great in the historical past.

THE COUNT AND COUNTESS BEGAN TALKING ABOUT THE SEANCE THEY WOULD ATTEND THAT EVENING. TAMARA KNEW THAT HER AUNT HAD A GREAT INTEREST IN SPIRITUALISM WHICH WAS THE RAGE IN ST. PETERSBURG SOCIETY. SHE ALWAYS READ THE JOURNAL *The Rebus* as soon as it arrived. Tamara was not sure that her aunt believed in mediums and seances; her fascination with the "other world" was possibly a quise for her evening excursions with the count.

On her way downstairs Tamara did not notice things that usually took her attention. She walked by a large bouquet of flowers in the alcove of the stairwell without stopping for a sniff of their aroma and she paid no attention to a cleaning lady on the lower steps of the winding staircase. She was in a hurry for a chat with her beloved Luda, the one servant who had been with her since her childhood and who knew so much about the family. So there was no surprise when she opened the kitchen door and heard the wrinkled old cook say, "Good afternoon to our Maid of Honor!"

Tamara ran into the short, heavy-set woman's arms for a hug. The old cook had always been her solace in times of need, as when a tutor scolded, or her brother teased, or the countess reprimanded. "Oh, Luda, I shall miss you so."

Luda's eyes were immediately moist with tears, but after kissing the princess on a cheek, she quickly went back to preparing cheese dumplings. Realizing that the servant was too busy for questions about Count Bagrov, Tamara left.

Entering the library, she found her uncle Count Trushinsky sitting behind his desk. Since she knew that Count Bagrov was upstairs with her aunt, she asked with apprehension, "Vadim Igorevich, what are you doing home?"

The count looked up from the papers he was reading and brushed his grey streaked hair with one hand as he said, "My dear, how are you?" His wrinkled face smiled with benevolence.

"Fine," but her face must have kept its look of amazement because her uncle laughed. At that moment that she realized that he knew why she was apprehensive and, even more amazing, it also seemed that he did not care that the count was with his wife.

"Come here, Tamarochka, my dear," he said, continuing to smile and motioning with his hands. When she approached, his brown eyes seemed full of compassion as he said, "Now I believe you've something to tell me? Something very wonderful?"

Tamara laughed. Everyone seemed to know her good fortune.

"So, you are to be a Maid of Honor to the Empress!" The count stood up and opened his arms for a warm embrace. After he kissed each cheek and made the sign of the cross over her, she began telling him about her hopes and joys for the future. He listened intently, watching her radiant smile which reflected her warmth of heart and the youthful enthusiasm of her inner spirit.

He admired his niece's beauty. Her Georgian blood had given her very long eyelashes and thick black hair, yet her Russian lineage had made her skin lustrously fair and her features perfect in form. He wanted only the best for her.

During their talk, her brother Valery entered and she ran and threw her arms around him, forcing him to circle with her two times as if they were dancing. Finally he was able to throw off her arms and regain his composure. "Have you gone mad?" he asked, straightening his long dark hair. The glint in his sparkling eyes, which always attracted people to him, shone brightly.

"Yes, I've gone deliriously mad," she rapturously responded and told her news. The prince congratulated her and kissed her forehead, but his own mind was too preoccupied with events he had heard at the Cadet Corps. Before she could continue with details, he had turned toward their uncle.

"Vadim Igorevich, have you heard that Grand Duke Michael has warned the tsar that the Austrians are increasing their military expansion?"

"Yes, it's ominous. I do hope the tsar will listen."

"Surely he will. Surely his own uncle can convince him."

"I don't know. There's been so much—"

Tamara quickly interrupted them. "Oh, you men! Is that all you think about?" When they turned toward her with a look of surprise, she ran out of the room.

In the hallway she saw Aunt Zita and Count Bagrov descending the stairs. It was an awkward situation but Tamara knew that they had seen her. The countess stopped on the lower stairs and said, "Count Bagrov is leaving, Tamarochka. Would you see him to the door?"

"What an honor," the count commented with a sly grin. He turned and kissed his companion's hand, winked and started walking toward the princess. She hated his pretensions, but there was no choice but to accept his arm and escort him toward the door. "And have you done your lessons for the day," the count asked, condescendingly. Tamara didn't answer. "So you don't care to talk with one of your admirers?" he asked and gave her a wink while looking at her well formed breasts. She slipped her arm out of his and walked ahead.. After checking if his mistress had entered the library, the count bent toward her and whispered, "Someday you might be glad for my favors."

Not looking at him, Tamara opened the door and stepped back. Bagrov laughed and went out as she closed the door and stepped away from it quickly. Tamara had experienced the count's insinuations before, but she had never mentioned them to the countess. Her aunt had the habit of misinterpreting remarks and might accuse her of inviting the man's attentions.

When the countess entered the library, she joined the conversation about the possibilities of war. Since they would all be going into dinner in a short while, Tamara decided that she would wait until that boring subject passed. She picked up a book on Greek vases and began paging through while her brother expounded on the great victories that would take place. "We've got more airplanes than any country in Europe," he bragged, "and I'm thinking of applying for training."

"You'll do no such thing!" the countess calmly commented..

Valery laughed, but the countess squinted her eyes and said slowly but firmly, "As your guardian, I would never allow it."

"Awww, Aunt Zita," Valery replied kindly, realizing he had overlooked the attention she required at all times, "It's the future in warfare."

The countess stood up. "Enough of this madness!"

"Besides," the count said, "While we might have more planes, we don't have the parts to run them. Our air force is just a collection of planes on loan from private owners. They're French, English and American planes, but where are their parts?"

"We'll make them!" Valery enthusiastically replied.

"I said, 'Enough!'" Aunt Zita interrupted. "Now, take me into dinner! I have a fascinating story to tell from *The Rebus*."

No one said anything because they were accustomed to the countess's enthusiasm for spiritualistic events. The family merely fell into its usual routine: the count escorted his wife and Valery, Tamara. She was still amazed that her uncle acted as if nothing had transpired. He knew that Count Bagrov had been in his wife's boudoir yet he was kind and polite. Did he really not care? or could he possibly have someone else, too? The thought astounded her, especially when her aunt and uncle started talking in the most casual manner.

"There was the most remarkable event at a seance at the Grand Duchess Marie's the other day. The Rebus gave some details, but I can't wait to hear more from Lidia Constantinovna."

"How do you know she was there?" the count asked his wife.

"But of course she was. She and Marie are very close. Oh how glad I shall be to leave this land of crafty Georgians. I miss society so."

Tamara and Valery were used to their aunt's remarks about Georgians and did not give them any attention. They had learned early that being critical was part of her nature. The count did not approve of his wife's sarcastic remarks, yet he merely frowned and changed the subject. "Calm yourself, you'll soon be in St. Petersburg. We should be thankful that we can spend part of the season in the capital; most of our officers are not so privileged."

The countess looked at the ceiling and sighed. "Are you ever going to be transferred back to civilization?"

Frowning again, the count did not answer. Instead, he asked Tamara and Valery, "Is this the weekend that you've been invited to your grandmother's?"

Before either of them could answer, the countess said, "Yes. Ivan is taking them on Saturday; it's all arranged. And that cousin will be in the mountains." Then she added in a tone that showed her usual sarcasm when speaking of the Georgians, "I've even sent word to the old princess that they're coming. I hope she appreciates it."

No one said anything. Tamara and Valery knew that the countess hated their grandmother because the old lady would have nothing to do with her. There was also the delicate matter of the dashing second-cousin Prince Shota Zhorzhadze. Some time ago he had decided that he wanted Tamara for his wife and had let his feelings be known among the family. When Tamara realized his intentions, she was overwhelmed. What girl would not be taken in by his physical grandeur? Georgians were known for their handsome looks, but Shota was almost beyond description. Her brother's eyes had the shinning glint typical of Georgians, but his did not match Shota's. A look from him expressing his desire was so powerful, she trembled just thinking of it. Naturally she had fallen madly in love. However, their grandmother had not approved and Shota had not been allowed to see her for over a year. When she would visit Mtsety, her cousin would either be on a hunt in the mountains or taking riding lessons in Gori.

The count continued the conversation and asked if his niece and nephew would be back on Sunday? It was a matter of the automobile. The count knew that his wife was irritated because the weekend excursion to Mtsety caused a delay in the family's trip to their summer dacha on the Black Sea at Gagra.

Again there was a brief silence until Uncle Vadim changed the subject. "What are we doing this evening? Anyone for whist?" Valery immediately accepted the challenge, knowing that his uncle was probably depending on him or he wouldn't have asked. Tamara mentioned that her friend Nina was coming and the countess said that she was attending a seance. Tamara and Valery both looked at their uncle as if they were expecting some kind of reaction. There was none.

Nina Evgenievna Cherkessky was one of Tamara's few social acquaintances, yet they saw each other rarely. Their families were on the same social level since Nina's father was also an officer in the Cadet Corps, but the countess did not care for Nina's mother whom she considered, as she did most people, too boring and pious.

Tamara knew that Nina was enamored with Valery and sometimes wondered if she pretended friendship so that she could see the cadet of the family. Yet she enjoyed her friend's *joie de vivre*. Nina could relate amusing incidents and had worldly knowledge far above the other young ladies in society. Tamara wasn't sure that she believed all that Nina told about herself, but she liked listening and talking with her.

When Nina and her governess arrived, it was evident from the expression on Nina's face that she was bursting with excitement and could hardly wait to tell some interesting news. Tamara escorted them into the music room where they left the governess with her knitting.

On the way up the stairs to Tamara's room, Nina pointed to the library and asked in a whisper, "Is Valery in there?" Tamara could not help but smile when she nodded. Nina tried looking through the rails of the banister, but could not see into the library. "Oh, later," she said and waved her hand as if her feelings for Valery could wait. When they entered the boudoir, Nina closed the door and said aloud, "He loves me!"

Tamara looked at her friend in amazement. She was sure her brother would have told her if he was in love with Nina, but he had said nothing. Since her sibling kept little from her, she felt somewhat disappointed and asked, "Valery?"

"Oh, no!" Nina laughed. "Not him. Oh, sure I like him, but he doesn't pay any attention. No, I mean my new love!"

"Heavens, Nina, what are you talking about?"

Nina burst into raptures about the new man in her life. At a reception for the new governor-general of the city, she met a dashing government official and had a secret meeting with him.

"How do you know that he loves you?"

A coy smile came on her friend's face and she whispered, "Because of what we did."

"What do you mean? Did he violate you?"

Nina laughed. "What a conception! No, he did not violate me, but he loved me."

Tamara was speechless. A girl in their society could not allow such a thing. Many questions came to mind, but her timidity restrained her. Nina expounded on her marvelous experience until her governess entered for their departure. "Don't worry," Nina whispered in leaving, "Your turn will come someday!"

As Tamara followed her guests down the stairway, she did not hear the trivial remarks that Nina was making merely for the sake of conversation. Her thoughts were concentrated on the comment in her room: that her turn would come.

The next morning the family's enormous Renault was waiting in the portico of the house when Tamara went down for breakfast. Her brother and uncle were already eating and, of course, talking about the coming war. That subject bored her and she asked, "Did grandmother give a reason for inviting us this weekend?"

"Yes," her uncle answered, interrupting his comments on a new German gun. "Seems there's a horse riding exhibition in the valley."

Tamara was delighted. She envisioned the Georgians riding wild horses in stunts and races. Also, she knew that Shota would not be away because he was one of the best horsemen in the family. If there was a competition, he was sure to be there and it would give her a chance for a farewell.

After Ivan the chauffeur cranked the car, the engine roared and Tamara and Valery put on their goggles and dust jackets. Soon they were moving along the famous tree-lined Rustaveli Street in the European section of Tiflis. Since very few people in Tiflis owned a car, it was always quite an attraction as it noisily dodged carriages and frightened horses. Once they drove out of the area of the Western-styled mansions, the car drove along the beautiful Kura River. The famous ruined Fortress of Narikal came into view above the city. How many times had Tamara's imagination envisioned herself being saved from the burning fortress by her cousin Shota. With his great strength, he would tear her out of the arms of some vile Chenchen and carry her over the parapet while arrows flew around them. Since Shota was always having some sort of silly mishap, he would slip on the ladder during her rescue, but his strength would save them. Such were her thoughts as they drove below the ancient fortress. The Turks had destroyed the castle and walls long ago, but even yet the ruins dominated a high crag in the heart of the metropolitan area.

Finally the car drove out of the mountains onto a high uneven plateau. The barren hills emanated a sense of mystery and fear because of the bandit gangs of Circassians and other tribes that once inhibited the area. How many unsuspecting Russians rode their horses or coaches around a bend only to be suddenly confronted by robbers who had stealthily come out of a bushy crevice in a hillock. History was also envisioned as the car drove past ancient fortresses and churches that stood on many high tors and precipices. How many invading armies had swept through the area since the early times! There was even a theory that Georgians had Egyptian ancestors.

Tamara spent most of the ride thinking of her cousin Shota. She knew that their meeting would probably be the last for some years. Possibly forever. Would she not stay in St. Petersburg and serve the Empress? When would she ever come back to Mtsety? Suddenly the car was driving up to the famous Fifth-century Dzhvari Church and she knew they were on the cliffs above the ancient Georgian capital of Mtsety.

It had been a custom in the family ever since she could remember that they would stop at the Dzhvari Church and offer a prayer for their ancestors. Dzhvari Church, one of the oldest in the world, stood on a precipice overlooking a wide valley that was rimmed by two mountain ranges. Below in the distance was the ancient capital of Georgia. Mtsety stood on the point of land made where the wild Aragva River poured into the Kura. Their strong, ferocious currents met and, after fierce entanglements that created many water eddies and small whirlpools, blended into a savage Caucasian river that made its way down the valley and eventually through Tiflis. Through the large, open cave-like portals of the church ruins, one looked down on a valley that stretched past Mtsety and into the bluish distant mountains.

Tamara and her brother crossed themselves in the Russian fashion and said a short prayer for their ancestors. Since the famous medieval Queen Tamara was from her family, Tamara always mentioned her. Grandmother Zhorzhadze liked to remind her that she had Tamara's legendary beauty and maybe even her strong will. Tamara's twelfth-century reign was a great period in Georgian history because of her successful military campaigns and her encouragement of the arts. Tamara was proud to be her descendant and to have her name.

Coming out of the church, she looked up the valley toward the area where her grandmother's estate was located. The great

Georgian homes were really compounds where an entire family lived. The architecture was completely different from the homes in Tiflis because of the cold winters. Each large house had a tower that gave a view over the family's lands. For that reason, looking down on all those roofed towers from the heights of the precipice, Mtsety had an unusual appearance and a visit at the Zhorzhadzes was like entering another world. The widowed Grandmother Zhorzhadze lived in the old style. She wore long elaborately embroidered caftans over a dress of fine cloth. A bejeweled toque sat on the top of her head with a beautiful scarf attached to it which covered her hair except for the long, thin curls that were allowed to fall along the sides of her face. Save for the quality of her apparel and the manor of her bearing, she could have passed for a gypsy to the uninformed. She stood tall and prepossessing. Her eyes spoke as readily as her voice and she ruled the household with strength and wisdom.

When the car drove into the courtyard of the great stucco house, servants and relatives quickly came out with smiles and waving arms. Tamara looked for Shota, but he was not in the group. Stepping from the car, she was instantly kissed and hugged by cousins, aunts and uncles who yelled their pleasure and cried out details about the afternoon's zhigitovka or horse riding competitions. Suddenly they all cleared aside because grandmother had appeared on the steps of the main house. While the old lady was smiling, even at that distance Tamara could see her piercing eyes. When she ran into the waiting arms, the family matriarch made the sign of the cross on her forehead and greeted her in Georgian. When Valery joined them, the ritual was repeated before they entered the house.

News of the Zhorzhadze clan dominated the conversation, yet Tamara noticed that Shota was not mentioned. When the head of the family finally retired, cousin Somi grabbed Tamara's hand and rushed her into a back wing of the house. In the entrance way of a large veranda, they confronted Shota. The brilliance of his dark eyes shone and his curly black hair seemed fuller than ever. His strong arms took hold of Tamara's shoulders and he gazed at her with passionate eyes. "So, my beautiful little bird, you have flown back to your Shota?"

Tamara's fear of their grandmother and her joy at Shota's profession of love brought on such conflicting emotions that she was speechless. His burning eyes hypnotized her. Suddenly she sensed that he was bending down toward her. A kiss was out of the question, especially with Somi there. She quickly turned and slipped out of his arms. "Shota!" she finally said, "How wonderful to see you!"

He grabbed her again. "Then prove it! Kiss me!"

"Shota! What would grandmother say?"

"She'll never know."

"But she knows everything."

Somi spoke up. "She's right, Shota. You know the servants spy for her."

"Then before I go, tell me. Are you still mine?"

Tamara looked into his ardent face. His large dark eyes bore into her soul. For a few seconds her own eyes pleaded for mercy and then she started crying.

Shota released her and quickly slipped across the veranda. Somi took Tamara into her arms and let her cry on her shoulder. Since childhood they had been friends; yet both realized that their grandmother had Somi in mind for Shota because her blood was pure Georgian. She did care for him, but carefully hid her feelings.

Lunch was served on two long tables spread across a wide veranda in the courtyard of the manor house.. There were about forty relatives since others had come from neighboring estates for the afternoon horse racing. Shota and some other male cousins took seats near Tamara. She enjoyed the moments when their eyes would meet. Unfortunately, their little intrigue was noticed.

Mounds of khachapuri or cheese bread were served with a special Kekhetinsky wine. In no time the group was in a cheerful mood. Since Tamara had not seen some of the relatives for a long time, it was amusing to note who had gained weight, who had grown taller and the other changes that age brings. Several told her stories from the past regarding her mother. It was a jubilant occasion.

After feasting on roasted lamb, the family rested before attending the horse riding competition. It was at that time that Tamara was summoned to grandmother's room, which was located in the large right wing of the main house. Since it was one of the older parts of the compound, it was dark and had an odor of dryness. She entered the long, low ceiling room, dreading what the old lady would say.

From a dark corner of the room Tamara heard the familiar scratchy voice. "Come closer, my child." Grandmother Zhorzhadze was seated on a tall, elaborately carved wooden chair. Tamara took a seat and listened. "I did not like the way you and Shota looked at each other during our repast."

"But I—

"No, do not interrupt. You must remember that our family is one of the oldest in Georgia. We are honored and respected. Our blood line must be kept pure. While you are very appealing and I understand why Shota admires you, there is no question of a union. Besides, I know men. His feelings are just an admiration for your beauty and no more. Men feel better about themselves when they have conquered a lady like you, but that does not mean that they love you. No, it means that they are serving themselves. You must understand that. Shota does not know you well enough for what he is thinking; he wants you for the jewel you would be in his milieu. Would you want to be neglected when your beauty fades?"

"But grandmother, he—"

"No, don't try to speak about things that you do not understand. Just promise me that you will refuse him his pleasures should he ask them of you."

Tamara was shocked. Her grandmother was surely referring to the forbidden subject and she could hardly believe her ears. Did she possibly think that she would do that? "But grandmother, Shota has never—"

"I know that, my child. But he is reckless and adventurous.

There is no doubt but what he is enamored of you; so, we must help him overcome his infatuation."

Tamara did not know how she should respond. She merely nodded and let her old relative speak. Again the grandmother went into the family history and told Tamara how glad she was that the famous Princess Tamara's beauty had once again appeared in their family. It was a compliment, of course, but Tamara had heard it many times and did not listen. Her mind was occupied with what actions her grandmother might take.

Finally the matriarch ceased talking about the historical past and began focusing her dark eyes on her grandchild. "You must discourage Shota. Only you can help him now. So promise me that you will."

Tamara nodded. There was no other recourse. She nodded every time the question was repeated. At last the old lady finished and Tamara was given an embrace and a kiss.

The Zhorzhadze clan gathered in the courtyard for the march to the meadow behind the Samtavriskaia Cathedral. It was a glorious setting with the ancient ruins of the Dvzhari Church on the precipice in the distance across the Kura River. A great many Georgians had gathered on the plain and beautiful horses were being led to and fro all over the grassy fields. Finally an ancient horn blew and resounded through the valley. It was time for the zhigitovka!

Rider after rider performed amazing tricks on their horses as the crowd roared its approval. Incredible feats were performed. Some horsemen were capable of touching the ground before flipping their bodies back up on their horses and continuing their acrobatics on the backs of the racing animals. Others changed horses at breakneck speeds. Many of the performers were noted horsemen who often participated in tournaments where they played the famous tskhenburti, a ball game played on horseback. However, it was Shota who won the prize of the day. Whether he did his dangerous stunt for her sake, Tamara did not know, but the crowd was stunned when he stood on his head on his saddle as the horse galloped past the cheering audience. Tamara was almost paralyzed with fear when he began his ascent on the wobbly saddle, but she watched with fascination as he carried it out with such aplomb. It was as if there was some kind of communication between him and the horse that no human could possibly surmise. The animal obeyed his commands and seemed to glide more steadily as he did his amazing feat. The crowd went wild and he was proclaimed the hero of the competition. The Zhorzhadzes were delirious and the cousins of the clan carried Shota off the field on their backs. He was cheered by all. As he approached the family group, Tamara could tell that his eyes were searching for her. It was thrilling; and when their eyes did meet, she received a message from his soul that he had performed that stunt for her. However, just seconds after she sensed what Shota had wanted her to know, he lost his balance from leaning too far in her direction and had the usual mishap that his enthusiasm and haste always brought on. He fell amidst the relatives, but was quickly raised again amid cheers and laughter. Tamara was proud and pleased; however she could not tell Shota at the time because her cousins carried him on their way back to the family compound.

Back in the courtyard, Shota was toasted many times with fine wine. Valery could not let him out of his sight; he was too thrilled by his cousin's feat. How handsome the two were together. Valery's lighter skin contrasted with Shota's, but it was obvious they were Georgian cousins. Shota joked and talked with everyone, except Tamara. He would look at her occasionally, but it was obvious that he was being careful not to show his interest. She did congratulate him, but he did not hug and kiss her like he did most of the relatives. Still she had the feeling when their eyes met that he was telling her something. She wasn't sure, but she felt as if he were indicating that he would see her yet that evening. There was a tension between them that spoke of a desire that needed fulfillment. She couldn't imagine how they could meet before she left the next day, but Shota could never be underestimated. They did come together, but in a way she could have never guessed.

In the moonlight that evening the family sang old Georgian songs and visited. When grandmother joined them, candles were brought and placed around her as everyone seated themselves near her. It was time for the reading of the famous Rusthaveli epic, "The Knight in the Tiger's Skin." No other people on earth had such a literary piece. It was Georgian and seven hundred years old, written during the period when the Zhorzhadze clan was strong and glorious. For that reason, it was traditional for the head of the household to read parts of it aloud on special occasions. Since Shota had brought honor to the house, the performance would be in his honor. A special pillow was placed by grandmother's chair and Shota was led there by Valery and other cousins. Grandmother read tales about the great hero Tariel who was like a tiger and whose ruddy face was graced with lips of ruby and skin of crystal. Shota matched the description and at times became the hero of the tale in everyone's imagination.

Since Shota was seated by grandmother, it gave him a chance to look at his love; however, it became obvious to some, such as his cousin Davar, that Shota's eyes were gleaming at Tamara. As for her, hearing the heroic deeds of the famous literary hero and gazing at the handsome Shota made the evening in the moonlight most enjoyable, but it was what happened later that made it quite memorable.

When she went to her room, Tamara was very happy. It had been an exciting day and being with the Georgian side of her family had given her a feeling of belonging. The strangeness that she always felt in the beginning when she visited had dissipated and she was again Georgian. She looked at the moonlight streaming in through her window and thought that perhaps she should stay in Mtsety. Her ancient lineage meant more to her than her Russian background and her Georgian family, save for grandmother, was much more enjoyable than her sophisticated Russian relatives, save for uncle Vadim. Why not just stay and become more Georgian? Perhaps then grandmother would relent and she could marry Shota.

Tamara undressed and put on a short sheer gown. Thinking of Shota she lay back on her bed and watched the moonlight in the window. Suddenly the light was partially blocked and she saw a dark figure in the aperture. Before she could call out, she heard Shota whisper. "Little bird, come here!"

It was horrifying, yet thrilling. It was so dangerous and so unbelievable. He stepped into her room and came toward her. She slipped from the bed and whispered, "Shota, you cannot stay!"

He grabbed her and pulled her to him. In seconds she was in the power of his great arms. He lifted her face toward him in the moonlight and she saw his great shining eyes. "Shota, no! No! You mustn't."

Yet he did. Their lips came together for her first kiss of love, a kiss she remembered all her life. His moist lips blended into her mouth and in seconds they were one. It was for her an emotion felt only in paradise. She was also aware of something hard pressing against her; she could not think, she only wanted that closeness and firmness. Her arms embraced his powerful body and her right hand went up into his curly black hair. His tongue stayed in her mouth, refreshingly and enjoyably. How long they stayed in that embrace, she did not know, but she knew then that she wanted to be his wife.

Suddenly Shota put a hand into her sheer garment and lifted out one of her well—formed breasts. In seconds he kneeled and kissed it. An instantaneous current of incredible joy swept through her body and she jerked from the delight. Uncontrollably her hands went into his hair and pulled his head closer, burying his face into her breast. However, at the same time an impulse of great control forced her to begin pushing him away. She stepped back quickly and, breathing heavily, said, "No, Shota, No!"

He whispered kindly, "You are my queen!"

Realizing that he was coming toward her and that nothing could stop him from doing what he wanted, Tamara stepped back. Grandmother's warning flashed through mind, yet something would not let her call out.

At that very moment a rock came in through the window. Shota immediately leaped forward like a wild leopard, kissed her lightly and went out through the window. Another cousin, Alek, had stood guard in the patio below and had warned him. She realized what might have happened if that had not occurred. By the time she reached the window, her cousins were out of sight. Sleep did not come for a long time after the incident. Shota's beautiful eyes pierced the darkness and she imagined his great muscular body in her bed.

The next morning she entered the dining hall with great trepidation. Did the family know about the incident? What had caused the warning from the cousin? Was Shota caught? Somi waved from one of the tables and she joined her and another cousin, Davar, who was not trustworthy. Ever since their childhood Somi and Tamara had avoided her whenever possible. Davar had always been a tattletale and a jealous type. The Georgian aspects of her face were too strong, her nose too long, her eyes too large. Those features that created beauty in most Georgian women were overdone in her face. Consequently, with Davar there, Tamara could not ask Somi anything.

During breakfast of pomegranate juice, left over cheese bread and milk or coffee, the cousins talked about trivial events which gave Tamara some reassurance that nothing was known about the incident in the night. However, when Davar went for oranges, Somi smiled and said, "I know." Tamara stared. "Don't worry," Somi whispered, "We can trust Alek. He likes you and he's devoted to Shota."

Fortunately that Sunday morning, it was Davar's turn to help grandmother dress for church. Servant girls did most of the preparation, but a member of the family was always at hand for the adornment of jewels and religious ornaments. The old lady always looked as if she would topple over from the weight of the decorations she wore at church ceremonies, but such refinements and dress during religious ceremonies were a Georgian custom among the nobility.

While Davar was busy with grandmother, Somi led Tamara into a grotto near the house and revealed an incredible message from Shota. He was planning an elopement.

Tamara's eyes showed her amazement. "When?" she asked.

"Shota knows that you're going with your aunt to their summer place at Gagra next week. He will come for you there."

Tamara;s lower lip went under her teeth. "Oh, Somi, what should I do?"

"You do love him, don't you?"

The young ladies embraced. "Oh, Somi dear, how does one know? Grandmother told me that he was in love with my looks, not with me."

"But that's part of love. Be glad. An ugly girl like me couldn't think of attracting someone like Shota. He's a warrior! A hero! A god!"

Tamara stepped back. "Somi, you love him too!"

"No! No, I don't."

Tamara embraced her saying, "You do; I sense it. Oh, forgive me, Somi."

"Tamarochka, my darling. If I love Shota a little, you can understand, can't you? I live here and see him all the time. He is so handsome and strong; and I love it when he blunders or has a mishap because of his rambunctiousness. What girl as plain as me would not think of him?"

"Oh, Somi, you aren't plain."

"Compared to you, I'm ugly! But will you go with him?"

"Did he send you for my answer?"

When Somi nodded, Tamara slipped away and seated herself on a bench and breathed deeply of the fresh air that poured into the grotto. "My God, Somi, what should I do?"

"Go with him only if you love him."

"But Somi, we've all loved each other ever since we were children. Even in our games I was always Princess Tamara and he was Ashoka, our Conqueror. We were always teamed together."

"And how I envied you!"

Tamara stood and embraced her cousin again. "Oh, forgive me, Somi. I didn't know."

"How could you? You are so beautiful, it was only natural that you should be his queen; but that didn't keep me from wanting him, too."

Both young ladies were silent for a few moments. Finally Tamara continued, "What misery his plan would cause!"

"Yes, it would cause many problems. Grandmother might even disinherit him."

Tamara's lip went under her teeth! "What should I do?"

Somi replied quickly, "Tamarochka, in your place I would go with Shota no matter what happened."

"Does Shota know that I'm going St. Petersburg to become a Maid of Honor?"

"Yes, he knows that, but feels he should save you from it. We Georgians do not think much of the royal family. Our blood lines are older and nobler in our opinion. Consequently, he wants you before you are contaminated."

"Contaminated?"

"Yes, the Petersburg court has many degenerates in it. Look at that so-called holy man, Rasputin. It's a disgrace."

Again her mouth opened in disbelief. "My aunt plans on meeting him in St. Petersburg."

"But the rumors are so disgusting. Even here they're known."

After a few seconds, Tamara said, "Somi, I must talk with Shota. How can I see him alone?"

Somi contemplated. "That would be very difficult. Our schedule today is so full. This morning we all march to church. After the service we come back here for a feast and you leave in the afternoon. When could you possibly talk with him?" After some reflection, she continued, "Grandmother always stands at the front of our clan with our aunts and uncles behind her. We grandchildren are behind them. I'll tell Shota that you will slip into the vestry during the service and he can join you there."

Oh, thank you, Somi, but what should I tell him?"

Grandmother Zhorzhadze's large carriage was the first out of the gate of the estate for the grand procession to the cathedral. It was followed by everything from splendid tarantases and droshkys to simple carts and wagons. Tamara rode with Somi, Davar and Asmath in a droshky. While her cousins chatted, Tamara thought of Shota. At the cathedral the family assembled in the square along with many other families from the region: the Drazhvilis, the Bardriashvilis, the Bagrationys, and so forth. When a family was complete, it marched into the edifice and took its customary place. As the Zhorzhadzes marched in Tamara was conscious of people staring at her. Word had spread through the clans that the Zhorzhadzes had a new "Princess Tamara" and curiosity caused the young swains to seek her out. However, Tamara could not have cared less; her thoughts were of Shota.

When the line of girl cousins formed in the courtyard, Somi and Tamara took places at the end for the sake of their plan. After they marched in Tamara found herself near an exit to the side wing of the church. Shota was behind her somewhere and she dared not look. When the singing started, she slipped into the vestry.

Walking over by a pillar, she turned and saw her dashing cousin coming toward her. She could tell by the look in his eyes and the speed of his gait that he was planning an embrace. She put hands out in front of her and whispered as he came near, "No, not here!" It was pointless. He took her into his arms and kissed her lightly before letting her go. She quickly looked around. The hall was empty.

"Do you love me?" he asked, giving no time for a reprimand.

"Yes, Shota, I love you."

"Then you'll marry me?"

"Yes, but not now."

His eyes seemed instantly wild. "Why?"

"I have to go to St. Petersburg."

"Never! That place is bad!"

"Shota, don't make it difficult for me. I told you that I love you and that I will be your wife."

"Then why wait?"

"Because of grandmother. Maybe she will change her mind after I become a Maid of Honor."

"That will only make her more against us. You know how we Georgians hate the tsar!"

Tamara nodded. Her remark had been ridiculous. It was evident that she was grasping for any excuse possible.

"I'm coming for you at Gagra."

"But Shota, where can we go? What can we do?"

"I'll be head of our clan someday. You'll be my queen!"

"Oh, Shota, grandmother will disinherit you."

"Then we'll leave the clan."

Tears filled Tamara's eyes. "Shota, you'd give up so much? Oh, don't make it so difficult for me."

A priest entered from the back and stopped when he saw them. It was awkward; they had to part. "Till Gagra," Shota whispered and walked away.

When he was out of the hall, Tamara, not looking at the priest, slowly walked back into the cathedral nave and took her place by Somi. Davar whispered, "Where did you go?"

Somi said, "Later!"

Everyone in the family quickly knew about the incident and during the family repast Tamara kept seeing faces turned toward her, some with smiles, some with frowns. Threatening eyes seemed all around. Too many family members were afraid of grandmother and were always waiting for a chance to be in her good graces. Someone did inform the matriarch; so after the feast there was another summons. Grandmother demanded all the details of the conversation that transpired in the church. Naturally Tamara could not reveal the intimate aspects of the talk, so she passed the event off as merely a final meeting before her departure for St. Petersburg. Whether the old lady believed her or not, she could not discern; however, later when she and her brother were putting on their travelling gear and saying goodbye to the family in the courtyard, grandmother did not appear for a long time. When she did, her countenance was severe. She bade them farewell and blessed them without a smile. The family waved and cheered as the guests entered the automobile. It was a joyous departure, but the journey back to Tiflis was filled with apprehension about what the matriarch might demand of Shota and what he might do in revenge.

Returning to the Trushchinsky mansion in the European section of Tiflis, Tamara and Valery found that the countess was in a peevish mood and consequently the entire household was on edge. She was upset from all the packing and planning. It was the same old story: the countess often dreamed up grandiose arrangements, but she could not be bothered with fulfilling them. In fact, she considered it an impertinence if it were suggested that any inconvenience she might have was her own fault. Tamara believed that her aunt actually enjoyed such periods of confusion because it increased her opportunities for scolding and ordering the servants about. Countess Zita truly loved being in command and took advantage of any chance she had for putting down anyone no matter what their rank. However, if she were attacking a member of her own class, she always did it with savoir faire.

Since packing for two different trips was in progress, the disorder in the house was two fold. Aunt Zita and Tamara were going to the family's seaside villa at Gagra on the Black Sea for a week before leaving for St. Petersburg. They had already visited Gagra in the early summer, but the countess had decided that she must go for another stay before her departure for "cold St. Petersburg!" Tamara thought it odd that they would go without Uncle Vadim and her brother who were busy at the Cadets Corps, but she should have known that the countess had an ulterior motive. However, since they all loved Gagra, it did not seem unusual that they would spend time there before heading north. Besides, summer was a glorious time on the Black Sea.

Another matter was bothering the countess. The Princess Lidia Constantinovna Dashkov had sent a list delineating the dresses that Tamara would need for the fall season and, most importantly, for her presentation to the Empress. Aunt Zita was clearly jealous.

She summoned her dress maker and humiliated the poor woman in every way possible while they measured and discussed materials for the dresses. Tamara put up with the countess's irritability as kindly as possible because she was terribly excited about all the finery that was being created for her. However, just before the seamstress started on the dress for the presentation to the Empress, Princess Lidia Ivanovna sent word that she would have the dress made in St. Petersburg. The countess was furious because the material had already been purchased, but she knew she could not contradict a Lady-in-Waiting to Her Majesty.

With all the preparations, the week before their departure for Gagra passed quickly. Tamara had hoped for a visit with her friend Nina Evgenievna but it never happened. The travelers caught the train for the ride over the mountains to the seashore at Batumi where Ivan would meet them with the car for the ride up the coast to Gagra. Aunt Zita talked mainly about St. Petersburg and Tamara realized how drastically her life was changing. Shota seemed farther and farther away as she thought of the palaces and balls of the Russian court. Because of all her preconceived ideas about St. Petersburg, she was again divided between her Russian and Georgian heritage.

The train ride was uneventful save for the beautiful scenery, especially when the train came over the highest ridge and the Black Sea shimmered in the distance. When they arrived at Gagra in the early evening, Aunt Zita's scheme was revealed. A wire was waiting for them from Count Bagrov. He would arrive the next day. The countess pretended indifference, but Tamara knew otherwise and slipped out on the long porch of the Swiss Chalet the family had built after a visit in Switzerland. The view toward the sea from the bluff where their dacha stood was quite magnificent. She paused there looking at the beauty, but thought about her aunt's deviousness.

An old Russian couple, Zahar and Arina Grobin, lived in the chalet year round and served as servants when the family was in residence. They were kind people and for some reason seemed in awe of Tamara. She was sure that they did not like her aunt, but they never complained about her. While Tamara was standing on the porch, Arina called out that dinner was ready and she joined her aunt in the large open room that had a raised dining area on one end and a parlor on the other. An enormous window of medium-sized glass panes filled each end of the long, spacious enclosure. Arina served her delicious stuffed quail, but Tamara was the only one who complimented her because the countess was not in a talkative mood.

The next day, when Tamara returned from a walk down the winding road that led to the foot of the bluff on which the chalet stood, Count Bagrov was sitting with the countess on the porch drinking tea. While he greeted her kindly, she could tell from his attitude and from her aunt's expression that something was wrong. It was quickly revealed. A telegram had arrived in which Uncle Vadim related a message from Grandmother Zhorzhadze. She warned that Tamara was planning an elopement with Shota, who had disappeared from Mtsety. The young princess denied the accusation, but she might as well have remained quiet. There had already been enough time for preventive measures, in other words, she was to be confined to the chalet. Count Bagrov, jumping at a chance to show his authority, was actually making himself her protector; but she knew that he had ulterior motives.

According to the count's plan, the prisoner was required to report daily activities. If she wanted an outing, Bagrov would accompany her. Even Ivan the chauffeur and the Grobins were instructed to spy on her. She was to be watched every moment of the day. At night her room would be locked and the trellis outside her bedroom was to be removed. Tamara was amazed at the preparations, and Zahar regretted destroying a beautiful rose bush that had climbed so high along the menacing trellis.

Fortunately for Tamara, there was a small library off the center room of the chalet. While most of the books were old, she lost herself in French poetry of the eighteenth century, especially Andrea Chenier's poems before the French Revolution.

On the third day of their stay, Aunt Zita and the count were
driven into town by Ivan while Tamara was left under the watchful
eye of the Grobins. She felt sorry for the old couple and could tell
by the fearful look in their eyes that they were anticipating something dreadful. She tried her best to relieve their anxieties, but no
matter how casually she continued her daily routine, they were
apprehensive.

When their "highnesses" returned, Aunt Zita had some interesting news. At a reception on a neighboring estate, she had met a
niece of the tsar, Princess Irina, daughter of Grand Duke Alexander
Mihailovich, a brother-in-law of the Emperor. She was visiting
from the great Yusupov estate called Ai Tudor near Sochi. Aunt
Zita's eyes and expressions implied that she had been with the
highest of society. She mentioned that the Princess Irina was not
only a niece of the tsar himself, but also engaged to marry Prince
Felix Yusupov, the wealthiest man in Russia. During a conversation with the princess, Aunt Zita had mentioned that her niece
was to become a Maid of Honor to the Empress. Princess Irina
expressed her delight and invited Tamara for tea at Ai-Tudor the
next afternoon.

Since their "highnesses" were waiting for some sort of joyous
reaction from her, Tamara smiled and thanked them as kindly as
she could; however, her response did not satisfy the countess who
said, "I should think you would realize how important this contact is for you!" Tamara assured her aunt that she was most pleased.
The countess relaxed a little, but she could never be fully satisfied.

That evening as Tamara lay in bed in her locked room, she
thought of Shota and wondered if he would come. She couldn't
help but be amused that Count Bagrov thought he could keep
Shota away from her. The count was all talk; Shota was all action.
Of course he sometimes had mishaps because of his haste, but
nothing could stop him if he was determined. She was sure of his
prowess and courage.

The next day the three vacationers drove along the Black Sea
to the outskirts of the famous resort Sochi. During the ride the

countess told Tamara about the Yusupovs. Evidently the marriage between the niece of the tsar and Prince Yusupov was not exactly a love match. Irina was known for her tolerance and Felix was known for his pederasty which the countess referred to as 'ungodliness.' Tamara did not know what she meant, but she noticed that her aunt winked slyly at the count. She also told her about Felix's parties and his friendship with the tsar's cousin, Grand Duke Dmitry. It was evident that the scandals of the royal family were quite well known in society.

Arriving at Ai-Tudor Tamara was dropped at the gate of the estate where a guard informed her that a carriage was ready to take her to the mansion. During her visit with Irina, the count and countess would visit in Sochi. It was obvious that her aunt had not made the best impression on the Princess or she too would have been invited. A charming little coach drawn by two donkeys that had pink ribbons on their necks took the visitor through flower lined lanes up the hillside. Ai-Tudor was a beautiful place. The old house was smothered with flowers. Roses and wisteria covered the walls of the veranda that surrounded the edifice. Servants in quaint outfits lined the stairs when her coach stopped at the main staircase. It was like living a role in a fairy tale.

Inside the large, airy entrance hall, a servant motioned with his hand and she followed him onto a beautiful stucco veranda that overlooked the sea in the distance. In seconds a thin, lovely young lady in a most charming dress came toward her. She was pretty and her face was so serene and placid that Tamara felt at ease with her immediately. It seemed incredible that a person of her social position could be so modest and demure. She was a most gracious hostess and their chit-chat soon became an earnest and sincere exchange of personal feelings. The more they talked the more Tamara felt that her hostess was lonely. She was by herself at the estate since her fiance was at the Yusupov estate outside Moscow, Archangelskoie. They would both soon be back in St. Petersburg and she informed Tamara that she was at home for visitors on Tuesdays—an open invitation.

During their conversation, Tamara mentioned that her Aunt Zita was hoping to meet the famous holy man Rasputin through a relative, the Princess Lidia Constantinovna Dashkov. No sooner had she mentioned the monk's name than the Princess Irina's face took on a strange expression. Tamara knew that she had mentioned something unpleasant and, since they had been speaking rather frankly to each other, asked most sincerely, "Do tell me what's wrong. I really know nothing about him."

Irina smiled, but said, "Be careful of that man."

"Is there something I should know?"

A troubled expression again came over Irina's face. "Just be careful."

After an hour of pleasant conversation, a servant came and informed Irina that the coach was ready. She expressed her regret that the delightful tea had come to an end and asked Tamara if her aunt might allow her to stay over night. A driver could return her to Gagra the next day. Tamara didn't know whether she should accept, yet because they had been so truthful with each other, she quickly told Irina about Shota and the apprehension in the family. The hostess nodded knowingly when she finished and began escorting her through the entrance hall. When they were away from the servant, she whispered, "Love is more important than all the honor and palaces of the world." Her remark astounded Tamara and she wanted desperately to talk more with her, but they had reached the front entrance and Irina resumed her role. "Please do not forget that you have promised to visit us in St. Petersburg."

"As if I could ever forget!"

The reply touched the hostess and she came close and kissed Tamara on each cheek before she waved her away. The ride down through the manicured lawn and bushes was spent thinking about the afternoon conversation. Their "Highnesses" were waiting at the gate and during the ride back to the chalet, the countess enquired about the Yusupovs. When Tamara revealed that Princess Irina had invited her to visit in St. Petersburg, the countess said, "Oh, those Yusupovs have hundreds of guests," but her down-playing the invitation only revealed her jealousy.

That evening the family gathered at the dinning table that faced the large window at the far end of the parlor. Aunt Zita and Count Bagrov were at the ends of the table and Tamara in the middle. Suddenly the count and countess noticed a look of fright on Tamara's face. She was staring, wide-eyed toward the large window. They looked and saw in the bright moonlight of the early evening a rider approaching on a horse. It was Shota and he was heading straight for the window. When it seemed he would actually crash through, he abruptly stopped and jumped off his horse. In seconds he was pounding on the door. Count Bagrov realized who it was and rushed over to the entrance way. In a loud voice, he yelled, "Leave at once!"

Shota did. He came back to the window, broke out a pane in one of the glass sections and slipped through. Before anyone could do anything, he had run across the room and jumped over the table by putting one hand on it and flipping his entire body over. Unfortunately, a silly mishap took place which at the moment was frightening. Shota's movement of the table when he went over it caused Aunt Zita's plate of creamed mushrooms to fall on her lap. Her screech was terrible and Tamara didn't know whether to look at her or at Shota. When she did gaze at her abductor, she had never seen him looking so magnificent. Yet his action had been done so quickly, no one could react. In seconds he had picked her up and was carrying her back toward the window. By that time Count Bagrov had come back down into the parlor and had begun shouting, "Put her down! Put her down!"

Shota did. He stood her on her feet and with his right fist knocked Count Bagrov onto an overstuffed chair. As his victim fell, Shota rushed Tamara up to the door, yelling back as he opened it. "Leave us alone!"

In seconds the young couple was outside and moving quickly to the edge of the bluff. By the time Count Bagrov and Aunt Zita were outside Tamara and Shota were standing on the edge of the precipice. The countess was still wiping sour cream from her dress as she and the count started going toward them. Shota suddenly called out, "I only want to talk with her; come close and we'll go off the cliff!"

The count and countess stopped immediately. Tamara heard her aunt say, "Stop! He's just mad enough to do it!"

Never had a moonlit evening so enhanced Shota. He stood silently before her with his eyes blazing and his huge frame ready to carry her off to the ends of the world. She was completely in his power and he knew it. With a look in his eyes she could never forget, he slowly took her in his arms. Finally he whispered into her ear, "Will you come with me now and be my queen?" Having said it, he loosened his grip so that he could look at her. She never forgot the love and desire that his face expressed, yet she was so fascinated and hypnotized by his eyes she couldn't answer. When he started to kiss her, she softly uttered, "Shots before God, I love you, but I cannot go now."

"If you love me as you say, then you must come."

"And dishonor our family? You could never do that!"

He hit his fists together and grabbed her again. "There is no dishonor in our marriage."

"But without our family's blessing there is no honor. either!" She began crying.

"We're alive! We love! We can overcome it all!"

"Shota, don't make me cry anymore. Of course I love you and I shall be yours, but not now."

Bagrov in the meantime had run into the house for his gun. He was slipping toward the couple when they saw him. In disgust Tamara cried out, "No melodrama from you! Go back!" The look that came on the count's face showed that he was offended. She had not respected his attempt at saving her. That realization caused her to laugh, further insulting Bagrov. She did not care. Her emotions were raw. At any second she might run off with Shota. It was a moment of incredible tension and resolve.

"You invoked God," Shota said, "Let Him be our judge!"

"Before God, I say that I love you, but please not now."

"Then when?"

"When I come back from St. Petersburg."

Shota looked downcast. There was anguish in his face, yet his great frame relaxed. He felt and showed his defeat. Slowly he said, "They will change you. I will lose you."

"Shota, my darling, never! I shall love you all my life. Where else could I find such a falcon, such a hero? You are my Tariel; I am your Nestan!"

The mentioning of the lovers from the great Rustavelli epic made an impression on Shota. He raised his eyes and took her into his arms. "As God is my witness, you are my queen!" He kissed her hard, but she could not enjoy it because she knew that it was goodbye. When they broke, he jumped onto an abutment sticking out from the precipice below and leaped from crag to crag until he circumvented the chalet. Naturally he had another mishap. On his last jump, he misjudged the distance and landed on the edge of the embankment; however, because of his great strength, he was quickly up on the overhang. Uncannily, his horse was waiting at the place where he came out on the road. Tamara was sure that Shota could communicate with horses and that proved it. It was simply part of his wild nature. How she loved him at that moment.

Three days later the travelers were back in Tiflis and the countess and Tamara, accompanied by a maid, boarded a train for St. Petersburg. The long train ride gave the princess time for much contemplation. She was sure of only one thing: Shota was wrong; the majestic capital city could never change her. girl the last time she traveled to the fabled capital and had not observed the Russia that passed before her. She watched sunburned peasant boys and old men bent from constant labor sowing in rows over enormous fields. Young girls in brightly embroidered dresses drove herds of cattle to pastures and badly dressed villagers streamed out of gold-domed churches. It was different from the Georgian countryside; it was another world. "How poorly they live!" often came to her mind and she thought of herself: a young girl traveling to become a Maid of Honor to the Empress of Russia.

Arriving in St. Petersburg the countess and Tamara took seats in a landau or open carriage while the count hired porters for their luggage. Their bearded coachman wore a long reddish coat reaching past the calves of his high boots. A brightly colored sash was tied around his waist and his lozenge-shaped hat had feathers on its side. Soon the travelers were going at a swift pace through the area of cheap-looking vegetable and merchandise markets that surrounded the station. Horse-drawn cabs and an occasional automobile filled the streets and the coachman shouted loudly at the approaching carts and vehicles. Soon the streets grew wider and the city resembled a European city. Entering the most famous street in Russia, the Nevsky Prospect, the plate glass windows had gold lettering advertising expensive furs, jewels and apparel which could be seen in the brilliant shop windows. Reaching the Fontanka Canal which flowed through the heart of the residential quarter the scene was again

CHAPTER 2

Velvet lined train compartments and fine dining car facilities did little for the ennui that the countess experienced during the five day train trip from Tiflis to St. Petersburg. The count was occupied with papers from military headquarters. The Peace of London in May between Turkey and the Balkan states was causing turmoil between Serbia, Rumania and Bulgaria. Their greed in carving up the land granted by the Porte was leading them to war. "Would Russia interfere?" was a popular question of the day and Count Trushinsky was greatly concerned. None of the political entanglements of her husband interested the countess, so the couple had little for discussion through the trip.

Tamara usually spent afternoons in her relatives' compartment and that gave the countess an opportunity for counselling. She informed her niece that correspondence with Shota was forbidden and that she must remember that her aunt was still her guardian. The count usually interrupted the advising by changing the subject or by pointing out an interesting view through the train windows. Tamara tolerated the countess's chatter because she knew that her aunt and uncle would only stay two weeks in St. Petersburg; then she would be free.

Once out of the beautiful Caucasus mountains, the countryside turned into vast open spaces punctuated with peasant villages. The change in scenery only aggravated the countess, but for Tamara it was a rewarding experience. She had been a small quite different: ornately designed iron gates and balconies decorated mansions with tall columns supporting marble canopies. Suddenly the carriage turned into the courtyard of such an edifice. It was the palatial home of the Dashkovs.

Old Russian customs were followed in the Dashkov palace. When the visitors entered the large marble foyer they were greeted by a servant holding a tray with the customary bread and salt, one of the oldest Russian traditions. Each guest pinched off a piece of bread and touched the salt before placing it in their mouths. The hostess, standing a little back from the servant, then opened her arms and greeted them with three kisses each. She led them into a salon where they exchanged greetings. Tamara was amused that Lidia did most of the talking instead of the countess. The hostess was in full command of her establishment. Her background had given her the confidence to be a reigning queen in society. Her own family had been Rurikovichi, the ancient titled princely families dating back to the beginnings of Russia. Her maiden name, Eletskii, had a long history of noble figures in great Russian enterprises. One Eletskii general had been a hero at the Battle of Kulikova in 1380 when the famous tartar chieftain Mamai was routed. When she married Prince Dashkov she inherited another famous name from Russian history. Lidia was very proud of her prestigious ancestors and accepted her position as Lady in Waiting to the Empress Alexandra as a proper way for her to continue her family's service to the tsar. However, her close relationship with the tsarina was due more to the monk Rasputin whom she and the Empress favored.

Lidia was petite with grey hair and walked leaning forward so that she always looked as if she were going to run into the person she approached. In the salon she advanced toward Tamara and gave her an inspection from head to toe. The girl was amused, but Lidia studied her most studiously. "She certainly has turned into a beautiful young lady. I knew it. I could see it when she was a child. Oh, those eyes. What I couldn't have done with those eyes!" She turned to the countess. "Tomorrow we must order her things at Maison Worth-" she abruptly stopped. "No, I have court duties tomorrow. The next day we'll go there."

The hostess's attentive behavior toward Tamara bored the countess, so she sat down on a settee and waved the count over by her.

Sensing the countess's mood, Lidia mentioned that she would take Zita for a ride that very afternoon and introduce her to the famous monk Rasputin. Tea was served before the guests were escorted by servants to their rooms. Going up the grand marble staircase Tamara remembered playing on it four years before. Now that she was a young lady, she tried walking erect and poised. After entering her cream-colored rococo room, she even felt more grown up. She looked into a large gold framed mirror near her writing desk and thought, "Oh, Shota, if only you could be here."

Count Trushinsky soon left for military headquarters and did not stay for lunch, which was served in a glassed-in tropical garden, Princess Lidia Dashkov's enthusiasm over the Siberian monk Rasputin became evident. She expounded on his amazing relationship to God Almighty and how he had helped the tsar and tsarina. She did not mention, which only showed her naivete, that he was treating the tsarevich when he suffered from his hemophilia; she considered that a great secret between herself and Their Majesties. She did not accept the fact that many in society did know about the boy's affliction and doubted the monk's healing power. Lidia was adamant that Nicholas and Alexandra did not deserve the rebuke so popular among certain members of society who claimed that Rasputin had a hypnotic power over the rulers. "Why the tsar's own niece, the Princess Irina, criticizes the holy man. If only she knew how he helps Them!"

The countess looked at Tamara with a glance that indicated she should not reveal at that time her relationship with the Princess Irina:

A fine landau covered in red leather carried the ladies through the streets and canals of the Northern Venice. Rasputin lived on Gorohovaia Street in a working class neighborhood, an area the princess did not like but necessity prevailed. She went there for the sake of the tsarina and considered her visit a sacred honor. After leaving the area of fine mansions, the carriage traveled through run down apartment buildings and entered an archway that led from the street to a courtyard. The foyer had a tiled floor and two staircases: one decorated with a rusted, wrought-iron banister and the other hidden behind a door in the corner of the hall. The princess was allowed usage of the back entrance because she often brought messages from the tsarina. She led the countess and Tamara up the staircase to the monk's third floor flat. Hearing steps on the stairs, a kitchen maid opened the door. She recognized the princess, bowed and backed out of the way. Lidia led her guests past a steaming samovar in the dining area to the drawing room where several seated ladies immediately stood up when she entered. Several bowed. The princess condescendingly nodded at them and continued into the study. The apartment consisted of six rooms which were filled with massive oak furniture and decorated with poorly made icons of various saints and cheap lithographs of Tsar Nicholas II and Empress Alexandra. The dark walls, badly in need of paint, gave the flat a somber atmosphere.

Suddenly the ladies were startled by the entrance of the monk himself. All that Tamara had heard about the so-called holy man did not seem true. He did not have an imposing figure and merely seemed like a disheveled peasant in an unkept kaftan. Yet she suddenly noticed how his pale blue eyes radiated magnetism. His gaze was at once piercing and intent. Tamara uncontrollably stepped back when he looked at her and her movement caused him to laugh. He went to the princess, kissed her hand and asked if she had a message from their friend, which meant the Empress? She did not, but she would be going to the Alexander Palace the next day, implying that she could deliver something from him. He thanked her and turned to the others. Looking at Tamara, he blurted out,

"How beautiful!"

The princess introduced her relatives and the monk invited them for tea. Going back through the salon, several ladies stood up and ran to their host, begging that they be allowed a visit. He briskly shoved one away and tightly embraced another whom he invited into the dining room. When others approached him, he waved them away and said that their turn would be later. Tamara was embarrassed and confused. The monk seemed humble and sincere, yet his manners were uncouth. She could not imagine that a man would treat a woman as he did or that a lady would tolerate his conduct. She remembered the rumors her friend Nina had told her about Rasputin. She didn't understand exactly what an orgy was, but she was sure that it pertained to the forbidden act. Still she could not discern whether she was in a holy man's grotto or a wolf's lair. She wondered how Lidia and the countess permitted such behavior in front of them, but was again confused when the woman he had brought in said to the ladies, "Father Gregory has proven that God still sends guardian angels to help us."

The kitchen maid served tea from the samovar and brought in some small cakes that a bakery had donated. Rasputin did not bother to introduce the lady he had invited in with his guests and seated her on his right side while the princess was on his left. While the maid was passing out tea, the monk suddenly plunged two fingers into a pot of jam and told the lady to humble herself by licking them clean. The countess and Tamara were speechless, but the princess leaned toward them and whispered, "His Holiness is only testing her. Pay no attention." She then whispered for a few moments with her holy man while his companion cleaned his fingers. Once she finished, he made the sign of the cross on her bosom in a most indelicate manner. Tamara looked at the countess, but she seemed engrossed in the man's actions. The princess remembered that her tutor of literature had given her works by Tolstoy in which he stated that "God is life!" and watching Rasputin's behavior, Tamara wondered if the writer mean that flesh and faith were the same?

As Rasputin was drinking his tea, he started a discourse: "The ancient Celts always chose for their leader a man who had known all sins. Their wisdom was based on observance of mankind's nature. Our Holy Christ also had to know sin in order to judge us all. Only through sin can one be redeemed. Salvation is there for those who love God and want his blessings. This lady wishes to be purified and by God's mercy she has come unto me. Oh, Lord, help her to realize her path to salvation." Falling silent, the monk stood and escorted the lady into a bedroom. The tea party was over. The countess was ecstatic; Tamara, aghast and confused.

When the three ladies left by the front entrance, two policemen stood on each side of the door with note pads. The princess walked past without a word and waved her companions on with her. As they descended the stairs she said, "The guards are for his protection. The tsarina insists on it. You can't imagine the ugly things that are being said about him. And I'm glad you witnessed such a glorious session. That lady is now in prayer with His Holiness and I am thankful for her salvation."

The countess, cunning as ever, assumed that there was more than prayer taking place between Frather Gregory and the woman, but she refrained from commenting. She was thinking of a means of meeting the monk herself. Suddenly she noticed that her niece was staring at her as if she was waiting for her opinion about the occasion, yet she remained silent and let the Princess Dashkov talk. The latter chatted on about the amazing things the holy man had done for the royal family and that she was expecting absolute revelations from his obvious relationship with God. Finally she asked the countess how she enjoyed the session and heard the most complimentary phrases, ending with a request for another visit during her stay in St. Petersburg. The princess agreed, but was a bit perturbed by Tamara's silence. "Weren't you thrilled, ma chere?" Tamara smiled and thanked the princess for the visit, but did not commit herself. She was perplexed and saddened by the experience.

When the ladies returned from visiting "His Holiness," they found Prince Vladimir Dashkov and his friend Count Pavel Voroshilov in the salon. They had a free evening from their duties as pages of the tsar. Vladimir, the Princess Dashkov's only son, was practically a stranger to Tamara. When she had visited four years previously, he had been busy at the corps and she had met him only once. Now he was a graduate and spending his year of service for Their Majesties. Tamara did not recognize him as the boy she had known in their youth. He was now tall with blue eyes and light brown hair and seemed very haughty. His friend, Count Voroshilov, was just the opposite. He was of medium height with dark eyes and blonde hair and most pleasant. The princess did not give them much chance for conversation as she was excited about the visit at Rasputin's. Tamara could sense that her son was not pleased by her enthusiasm and wondered if his attitude might be the cause of his aloof behavior. The pages explained that they could stay for dinner but had duties at the Anichkov Palace that evening.

Vladimir had entered the Corps des Pages, located in the former Vorontsov mansion behind the Imperial Library on the Nevsky Prospect, when he was twelve. His entrance into the exclusive school had been arranged by his great uncle, Count Gradekov, a Governor General of Siberia in the 1880s. Vladimir had all the requirements: five generations of aristocratic background, wealth and a splendid mind. During his six years he had excelled in his studies and was second in his class at graduation. The rank gave him the honor of serving the Empress Alexandra at court. Since his mother was one of her few trusted friends, he also had the advantage of the Empress's patronage. It was obvious that a brilliant career awaited him.

Count Pavel Voroshilov was a descendant of an ancient family of landowners who served as generals and diplomats through several centuries of Russian history. His family owned linen factories near the city of Orel and his mother kept a literary salon in their mansion in Moscow. The family received the aristocratic title in 1718 when Peter the Great awarded a certain Ivan Voroshilov nobility for government service. Pavel entered the Corps des Pages as a boy with Vladimir and they were good friends from the beginning. Pavel finished the corps as valedictorian, giving him the honor of serving the tsar while his friend Vladimir served the tsarina. Both pages were in a most privileged position and were expected to make brilliant marriages. When Pavel heard about Tamara's background, his interest was immediate. She noticed how he stared at her and smiled when she caught his gaze. There was no chance for talk, but his eyes told her what his lips could not say.

At last in her room, Tamara sat down before the mirror of her vanity table and looked at herself. Everything seemed to be happening too fast. The city of St. Petersburg had thrilled her; the visit with the so-called holy man had frightened her; and now she had the attentions of a handsome young page of the tsar. Her thoughts ran from one theme to another and she continually asked herself, "What does it all mean?"

In Russian fashion, the first course was drinks and hors d'oeuvre. At the Dashkovs they were served either in the salon, the study or the glassed in terrace. The princess chose which room and sometimes changed it just before guests arrived. For that pleasant summer day she had chosen the salon. Tamara had not really given the room much thought when they had arrived, but waiting with the princess for the others gave her a chance for observation. The rococo stateroom was filled with exquisite 18th century French furniture. The princess explained that the famous Princess Dashkov who had been so close to Catherine the Great had benefitted from their relationship. When Catherine seized the throne, the Winter Palace had just been completed. While it was being built, the Empress Elizabeth had built a 100 room palace on the Nevsky Prospect for her living quarters. That palace, since it was temporary, was made of wood. When Catherine had it dissembled, she gave priceless furniture to friends who had helped her become Empress, mainly the Princess Dashkov and Gregory Orlov. The latter placed his rewards in Gatchina, the summer palace the ruler gave him for services rendered. "And here you see what the Dashkov's received," the princess exclaimed, waving her small thin arm in the air without moving her head. Tamara looked at the black and grey striped Louis XV chairs sitting on the cream colored rugs. She admired the French bombe chests and ornate mirrors at each end of the large room. Shelves were filled with priceless porcelains, and French paintings by Boucher and Fragonard filled the wall panels lined in gold leaf.

The host of the mansion, Prince Svyatoslav Dashkov, had just returned from diplomatic duty in England. He had been brought out of retirement by the Department of Foreign Affairs at a time when there was a strain in Anglo-Russian relations because of England's military activities in Persia. The prince was recalled because he was noted for his charming personality and excellent conversational skill in English. The short, white mustached old prince proved the correct choice for the mission because he quickly soothed the difficulties between the two countries. His recourse had mainly been elaborate receptions at the Russian Embassy in London. In actually he had brought about amelioration, not solution. When he entered the salon, the princess greeted her husband whose sprightly gait quickly took him to her outstretched hand, which he kissed. Since it was not proper to kiss an unmarried girl's hand, he bowed to Tamara and then extended his arms out as if surprised, exclaiming, "Mon Dieu, is this beauty the little princess we used to know?" Compliments and chatter followed until everyone had gathered.

Once again Russian diplomatic affairs were the center of conversation. Because the young pages and Count Trushinsky were eager for news about Prince Dashkov's trip to London which at the time was considered very successful, they bombarded their host with questions. Why were the Turks securing the services of French, English and German specialists? Is it true that the Turks are allowing Von der Goltz to infuse Prussian discipline in the Ottoman army? Can Minister Sazonov keep the Dardanelles open to the Russian Black Sea Fleet? As the conversation grew more intense, small glasses of vodka were drunk and caviar devoured. Servants were kept busy filling glasses and passing hors d'oeuvre to the men as they stood talking. The women, seated in an arrangement of Louis XV chairs away from the men, drank champagne and either listened to the men or talked about Rasputin. Tamara was bored by the concentration on military matters and amazed at the sincere belief of the princess and the odd interest of the countess in the holy man. Yet she did notice how the young princes often looked at her when there would be a lull in their talk. The countess and princess also noticed the attention they gave her and they did not approve, but for different reasons.

When dinner was announced, Prince Vladimir offered to escort Tamara, but the princess interrupted and insisted that her son and husband both lead her into the dining room. Prince Pavel was left as Tamara's escort, a duty he accepted with pleasure. She thought it strange that the princess would interfere as she did, but accepted Pavel's arm with a smile. While dining, Tamara again became the center of attention when a ball at the Shuvalov palace was mentioned. Both pages proposed taking her, but again the princess interceded and reminded Vladimir that he was taking the Princess Zenia Trubetsky. Her son did not object out of propriety, but the look on his face showed his displeasure. His friend Pavel would take Tamara to the ball.

The haute monde of St. Petersburg society was fragmented. There was a very conservative group which usually centered around the grand dukes and their families. The tsar and tsarina rarely attended such functions, preferring to stay in the Alexander Palace in Tsarskoe Selo, thirty miles from the capitol. The tsarevich's health, their relationship with Rasputin, and the tsarina's fear of intrigue had caused the royal family to withdraw from social activities as much as possible. The Dashkovs were privy to the family's attentions, but also participated in activities of the conservative group. A second group of society, which included the Shuvalovs, were very liberal in their views, very cosmopolitan, and gave very splendid parties. The young pages participated in both sections of society as "young men about town" or, in truth, very eligible bachelors.

The Countess Elizabeth Shuvalov, who was called "Betsie" by her friends, and she considered everyone her friend even though she had some society dragons as enemies, was noted for her extravagant fetes and masquerades. Her mansion on the Moika Canal had recently been renovated to its original eighteenth-century style by the best architects and decorators in the capital. Society was expecting a splendid festivity for the opening of the mansion's restored ballroom and the occasion was finally planned for the First of October. Since the countess had chosen the day that began the fall social season, her greatest rival, Madame Brianchaninov, the former Princess Kudashev, sent invitations for a grand masquerade on the following Saturday, October 7. The 1913 season would be off to a grand start with two resplendent balls in one week.

When Tamara returned to her boudoir, a maid, who introduced herself as Louise, was removing a satin bedspread. She was one of the many servant girls the Princess Dashkov had hired in Paris. While she was helping Tamara brush her long, black hair and telling about her life in Paris, the countess entered. With a wave of her hand, she sent the servant out of the room and sat down on a chaise lounge. She had just had a talk with the princess and had some excellent council for Tamara. The latter expected it. The Dashkovs admired and loved Tamara, but there was no possibility for a match between her and Prince Vladimir. Tamara grimaced. The thought repelled her, but before she could speak, the countess waved her hand and continued with some explanations. The Dashkovs were arranging a brilliant marriage for their son with the Princess Dolgoruky. It could not be a more advantageous union: two of the most noble and ancient families in Russia.

"And not Georgian," Tamara interjected, knowing the real reason. How strange it seemed. While she had no feelings toward Prince Vladimir, she could not be his wife because she was not purely Russian, whereas she could not have her love, Shota, because she was not purely Georgian. The countess objected, but Tamara did not want an argument and assured her aunt that she had no interest in the prince.

The next morning Mlle Louise brought the princess a breakfast tray and informed her that a coachman would take her to the Maison Worth for a fitting at ten o'clock. She thought she had enough dresses, but the princess had decided that she should have something extraordinarily special for the coming season. She could not object. Her reception at the St. Petersburg branch of the famous French couturier was a bit uncomfortable because of the abundance of attention she was given. Tamara thought it was because the Princess Dashkov had made the appointment, which was partly true, but she didn't realize that her own beauty aroused much interest. The shop girls whispered among themselves and one by one they casually walked by the fitting area where Tamara was being measured. When Monsieur Depre, the manager of the store, also heard of the princess, he arranged a chance meeting. Tamara left the establishment somewhat embarrassed by the compliments.

The countess was waiting for the carriage when Tamara returned to the Dashkovs. Aunt Zita did not explain where she was going, but gave a vague suggestion about some legal business that needed tending and quickly left. The Princess Dashkov was at the Winter Palace for a formal reception with the Empress, so Tamara had lunch by herself in the garden terrace. When Mlle Louise brought her a bowl of leek soup, she looked around as if checking for alien ears. Tamara noticed and asked her for an explanation. The maid whispered, "You've been so kind. Would it be an imposition to ask a small favor?" Tamara shook her head. "The princess is planning a month in the country before the fall season starts and I am scheduled to go as your maid." Tamara's face showed that she didn't understand. "Oh, I want to be your maid, but I don't want to go to the country." The princess asked why, and Louise explained that she had a friend who was a student and they had plans.

Tamara smiled. "Oh, Louise, how wonderful. I'm so happy for you. Marriage?"

An odd expression covered the maid's face for a second, but she quickly said, "Sort of."

Tamara didn't grasp what she meant, but said that while she couldn't promise, she would tell the princess that she didn't need a maid in the country. Louise thanked her very much and left. Tamara was amused by the incident. She didn't know about the trip to the country, but she realized that the mansion was run just like the one in Tiflis: the servants always knew more than the inhabitants.

Tamara was walking across the main foyer when a servant opened the front portal. The countess entered rather flustered. Seeing Tamara she waved and called, "Ma chere." Such a pleasant greeting informed the princess that her aunt wanted something. It was true. The countess had arranged a meeting with the so-called holy man and wanted Tamara with her. The princess objected in as kind a manner as possible, but the countess was adamant. In an hour the two ladies were on their way to Green Pea Street.

Ever since Tamara had been at Rasputin's she had been asking herself, Is he a man of God? If so, why does he seem so shameless and uncouth? She remembered his sweaty hands and shuddered. She had learned that he was a pilgrim, not a priest and that his fame was based on his association with the Empress. If Her Majesty believd in him so sincerely, surely there was more to him than she had seen. Tamara decided the holy man should be given another chance.

Not knowing whether she had the right to use the back stair case, the countess led her niece up to the main entrance of Rasputin's apartment. There weren't any policemen at the doorway that afternoon and they entered without knocking. No one was in the sitting room. The kitchen maid came and explained that Father Gregory was not there at the moment which explained why the police were absent. The ladies were sent into the study. Before they were seated, Rasputin came rushing in, his hair dishevelled and his eyes gleaming. He kissed the countess's hand and bowed to Tamara. When he tried caressing her face in his hands, she backed away, appalled at his repugnant and loathsome appearance. He let out a cynical laugh. Turning to the countess, he found her much more receptive. He put his large rough hands on her shoulders and looked into her eyes, saying "Let the warm current of my whole being flow into your heart." His large eyes became two penetrating phosphorescent beams of light that melted into a luminous ring which at times drew nearer her face and then

moved farther away. She seemed transfixed. He made the sign of
the cross over her head and began making strange passes in the air
with his hands as he launched into an incoherent diatribe about
God and brotherly love. Tamara could not understand what he
was talking about, but the countess drank in every word as if his
talk had some profound mystical meaning. Suddenly he took her
hands in his and raised her arms. Staring intently into her eyes, he
pulled her to him, enclosing her in his arms which slid down the
curves of her body. She did not protest. Tamara was aghast and
slowly backed farther away. She could not believe that her aunt
would allow him such liberties and she wondered if he had hypnotized her? The holy man began talking about purification
through sin, untroubled by the gnawings of conscience. The countess rested her head on his shoulder and the monk led her into the
bedroom that had a sign on its door, "The Holy of Holies." In that
shrine she received her salvation through sin.

For a few days after the incident at Father Gregory's, the countess
was very affectionate with her niece. When they had driven back
to the Dashkov mansion, she had given no account of her experience with the holy man and Tamara had not asked. She knew
about her aunt and Count Bagrov, but her behavior with Rasputin
had shocked her. Still, she dared not speak any rebuke; so she
accepted her aunt's kindness, knowing that the countess would be
leaving for Tiflis in the near future and hoping that she might take
a letter for Shota with her.

On Sundays a priest performed the Russian orthodox service
in the private chapel of the Dashkov mansion; however, on days
dedicated to some special religious observance, the princess
attended mass at the Alexandro-Nevskaya Lavra which Peter the
Great built on the spot, as the legend says, where Alexander Nevsky
defeated the Swedes in 1241. The relics of the famous Russian
hero were brought to the monastery in 1721 and the church was
completed in 1753. However, cracks in the walls developed and
the Empress Elizabeth ordered the edifice torn down and rebuilt.
It was completed in 1790. Princess Dashkov liked the cathedral

there because the choir sang from both ends of the huge edifice. Since Russian churches never had musical instruments, the choirs were famous for their chants, some even written by Ivan the Terrible in the 16th century.

Princess Dashkov led Tamara through the mausoleum of the monastery and pointed out the exquisite engraving on the burial stone of Count Felix Perovsky. She confessed that she had taken that route so that Tamara would know the name Perovsky. It had a remarkable history and the Perovsky's she knew had a son whom she thought Tamara would like. The latter could not help but smile and the princess winked at her as she continued. "The Perovsky name stems from the lover of the Empress Elizabeth, Razumovsky. His brother had an affair with a married countess and they gave their nine children the name Perovsky after one of her estates." Tamara was amused and embarrassed. The princess had never spoken so openly about such a subject with her before. She was glad that she did, but wasn't sure how she should respond.

Before she could say anything, they entered the cathedral.

Great sonorous sounds filled the air as the princesses walked down the center of the massive building decorated with enormous icons. The chants sung in Old Church Slavonic rang out, sometimes from the back, then from the front and then together. Tamara was deeply touched and followed the princess to the area before the huge iconostasis. They kneeled and prayed. When Tamara stood up, she saw the tsar's niece, Princess Irina, standing near the large silver tomb of Alexander Nevsky. They smiled at each other and quickly walked over to the side of the church where they could talk. It was a fortunate meeting. Tamara was invited for tea at the palace of Grand Duke Alexander, Irina's father.

Princess Lidia Dashkov knew most of the royal family very well, but she did not approve of the conduct of several members, including the Grand Duke Alexander. He was considered a liberal and his detestation of Rasputin was known in family circles. Consequently, he and his wife, the Grand Duchess Xenia, were rarely in attendance at functions with the Tsarina Alexandra. Since Xenia was Nicholas II's sister, it was an awkward situation in the royal family. When the princess was informed about the invitation to Irina's, she was not pleased. She felt that if Tamara was to become a Maid of Honor of Her Majesty, she should avoid people who offended the tsarina. However, she also believed the young princess should have every opportunity in society that was possible, so she consented. However, when she told Tamara about her decision, she also felt it necessary to reveal a brewing scandal in the Imperial family. The Princess Irina was engaged to Prince Felix Ususpov, a known pederast. When she said that word, Tamara remembered hearing it from the countess, but her face must have shown her lack of comprehension, causing Lidia to say, "It's an ungodliness that men do! Felix even dresses in his mother's clothes and goes to restaurants! And his own brother was killed in a duel. A strange fate follows those Yusupovs, so you must beware."

The Grand Duke Alexander and Grand Duchess lived in a palace on the banks of the Neva, not far from the Winter Palace. When Tamara arrived, she was escorted by servants up a marble stairway to an ornate, predominately rose colored 18th century room that had sweeping views of the river from its windows. To the right she could see the Funstkammera of Peter the Great next to his columned Academy and to the left the Imperial Academy of Art built by Catherine the Great. Tamara stood entranced. Princess Irina entered and greeted her guest, complimenting her on her appearance. They squeezed each others hands and sat down on a small divan.

Princess Irina's engagement and forthcoming marriage to Prince Yusupov was again the subject of conversation. While Irina was discreet, Tamara could not tell whether she wanted advice or encouragement. She had never met the prince, but had only heard strange references to him and she did not know Irina well enough for any questioning. So, she let her talk. Suddenly the Grand Duchess Xenia entered and Irina introduced her mother who displayed grace, modesty and kindness of heart. She complimented Tamara on her extraordinary beauty and the two had an immediate liking for each other. When Irina and her mother found out that Tamara was going to the Dashkov estate, Radnoe, near Moscow for the rest of the summer, they invited her to their summer palace in Tsarskoe Selo for a few days. Tamara could take the train to them and they would arrange transportation to Radnoe after their visit. The Grand Duchess even said that she herself would ask permission from the Princess Dashkov. Tamara thanked them both and accepted kindly. It seemed that the whole world was opening up for the Georgian princess whom no Russian prince could marry.

The Countess Trushevsky became a frequent visitor at the apartment of the notorious Father Gregory. Saving her soul evidently took considerable effort. However, she also attended many seances during the two weeks the Trushevskys were in St. Petersburg. Spiritualism had been the rage in society since the 1880s and seances were held in many of the royal palaces of the grand dukes. Spiritualistic journals with names like "From Dark to Light" multiplied. Even the royal family had been influenced by spiritualists. In 1904 Grand Duke Peter Nikolaivich and the Grand Duchess Melitsa introduced Dr. Phillipe, a French charlatan, to Nicholas and Alexandra and they were quickly under his spell. The French spiritualist conducted many seances in which he supposedly contacted the spirit of Alexander III, the tsar's deceased father. The royal couple lost faith in the doctor when he persuaded the Empress that she was pregnant, though she wasn't, and when he prophesied that Russia would have a quick success in the war with Japan. However, before leaving Russia, he told the Empress that she would soon meet a holy man who would bring her a message from God Almighty. Fatefully, Rasputin soon came into her life and the royal family was quickly entrapped in his mysticism.

When the Grand Duchess Melitsa invited the Countess Trushinsky to a seance at her palace on the Moika Canal, Zita asked if she could bring her niece. The Grand Duchess was delighted because she had heard rumors in society about the girl's phenomenal beauty. Tamara was leery of accepting the invitation, but she knew that cooperation with the countess would be the only way she might take a letter to Shota. She agreed without condescension.

The Grand Duchess Melitsa was known for her great interest in spiritualism and write ups of her seances were often published in the journal "Rebus." Several relatives objected to Militsa's so-called "advertising" of her spiritualistic meetings because they thought it showed a lack of propriety. It gave the false impression, in their opinion, that the entire Romanov dynasty believed in spiritualism. Such diverse opinions were another indication of the divisions developing among the members of the royal family.

Arriving at the Moika palace the countess and princess were escorted into a small room filled with overstuffed furniture. A round table in the middle had eight chairs where the hostess was busy seating her guests. When her attention turned to the newcomers, she loudly complimented Tamara on her striking good looks. All eyes turned toward the princess to the countess's chagrin. The noted spiritualists Mr. Fox repeated the compliments to Tamara and others agreed. Tamara was amused and did not dare look at her aunt.

Mr. Fox asked that all present place their hands on the table. The gas lights were dimmed and the seance started. The spiritualist requested that everyone close their eyes while he tried contacting any spirits in the room. Silence reigned. After a few minutes the table moved slightly. One woman gasped, but Mr. Fox asked that all remain quiet. He then asked, "Is there anyone there?" Across the room a curtain rustled. The same woman gasped again. "Do you wish to speak?" Mr. Fox asked the air. There was no reply. His efforts continued for some time until he finally confessed that there were no vibrations that afternoon and he considered the seance finished. The Grand Duchess explained that many seances go unfulfilled for one reason or another and they should all return the next afternoon. Disappointed in the failure, the guests began telling about successful seances they had witnessed. Tamara could only doubt most of the accounts, but the countess was fascinated. On their way home she again expressed her desire to live in the great capital where so many interesting events were taking place.

Throughout 1913 the Austrian and German armament expansion was the major topic of conversation among Russian military personnel and leaders of society. Many were confident and even welcomed a war. Russian pride in its enormous resources of men and materials; greatly exaggerated, led them to believe that there was no great cause for alarm. Russia, in their opinion, could vanquish any aggressor. The mistakes of the Russo-Japanese War were forgotten because of the good relationship that had developed between the two countries since the 1905 debacle. Still many were greatly troubled because they did remember the past: the lack of transportation facilities, the millions of ill equipped soldiers and the disruptive political activists among the general population. Count Trushevsky believed war was certainly possible and would be disastrous for Russia. He spent his time in St. Petersburg at the headquarters of the Cadet

School seeking a transfer from the same academy in Tiflis. He felt that if war did come, he could serve his country better if he were nearer the scene of action. Such a move would also separate the countess from Count Bagrov, whom he considered unworthy of her affection, and fulfill her wish for residency in the capital. Prince Dashkov did not agree with the count and held to the theory that the Kaiser, being a cousin of Nicholas II, would never attack Russia. Diplomacy, in his view, was the only answer and it was only a matter of time before disagreements between the two countries would be worked out. Their opposing views reflected Russian attitudes throughout 1913.

Dinner conversations while the Trushevskys were in St. Petersburg moved back and forth from the nadir to the sublime. The gentlemen talked of war, the Princess Dashkov elucidated the activities of Father Gregory and the countess recounted events from the seances she attended. Tamara felt uneasy when the princess rectified Rasputin's actions and elaborated on his holy mission in Russia. It was evident that she did not know about the countess's visits to the so-called holy man. The countess avoided talking about Father Gregory and eluded the subject by interjecting the name of some grand duke or famous diplomat whom she had met at a seance. The mentioning of a noted personage always brought forth a diatribe about the person from both of the Dashkovs. The ritual continued until the Trushinskys' departure.

Before leaving for Tiflis the countess and count discussed several family matters with Tamara. Her estate was in trust and under the supervision of the count. He had made arrangements for her expenditures while she was in the capital, but did inform her that the Dashkovs were taking care of her living expenses by their own choice. When the count was called away by a servant in regards to their luggage, Tamara produced a letter for Shota. To her surprise, the countess accepted it and said she would see that it was delivered. They parted with much show of affection, keeping the secrets they held in common.

The Princess Dashkov received a hand written note from the Grand Duchess Xenia Alexandrovna inviting Tamara to Tsarskoe Selo. Propriety would not allow a refusal and that distressed the princess greatly. Her allegiance was to the Empress and she knew that Her Majesty was not pleased with the criticism the tsar's sister had made about Rasputin. Also, her daughter, the Princess Irina, was engaged to Felix Yusupov, the pederast. Lidia shrugged just thinking of the word. Yet, after she had contemplated all the reasons Tamara must not accept the invitation, she acquiesced, remembering that it could not be refused.

Arrangements worked to the advantage of the maid Louise. She would accompany her mistress the short distance to Tsarskoe Selo and then return to St. Petersburg. She was delighted with the news. Since the Dashkovs would be away, it meant that she could spend time that August with her close friend, the student Ivan Ivanov. She always avoided questions about her free time and Tamara respected her privacy. Her curiosity was finally satisfied at the train station when the young ladies were departing. Just before boarding, a rugged looking, but attractive blonde young man came running up, handed Louise a packet and ran away. It was obvious he embarrassed her for she blushed, but said nothing. They entered the first class compartment and sat down. When Tamara looked out the window, she saw two policemen running along side the train and noticed that Louise put the packet behind her. The princess glanced at Louise, but she looked away and seemed to be holding her breath. The train slowly left the station. Little was said between the two young ladies as they rode through the Russian countryside. Tamara did not pry, but she was sure that Louise's friend was being chased by the police and she wondered what was in the packet. The short ride to Tsarskoe Selo went quickly and the ladies parted at the station where Princess Irina was waiting for Tamara in a handsome landau.

Riding into Tsarskoe Selo was like being transported back into the 18th century. The Grand Palace, designed and built by Rastrelli for Catherine the Great, was a baroque masterpiece and the major edifice of the village of palaces where many of the famous noble families of Russia lived in the summer. Irina and her mother were staying at a Louis XV style pavilion built by Felix Yusupov's grandmother. The mansion was white inside and out. It had a large oval room in the center with six doors leading to drawing rooms, dining-areas and gardens. The furniture in all the rooms was painted white and covered with flowered cretonne. Long curtains of the same material were lined with buttercup-yellow silk and when light glimmered through them the rooms seemed filled with sunshine. It was a fairy-tale palace.

On the third floor of the white mansion, Felix Yusupov had arranged a small apartment for himself. He referred to it as his lair and used it as his base in the summer. His close companion that summer of 1913 was the Grand Duke Dmitry Pavlovitch who was a member of the Royal Horse Guards and was living with the Empress and Emperor at the Alexander Palace, not far away. Dmitry was a very handsome elegant young man. He was well-bred, but easily gave into his impulses if an escapade aroused his interest. He found Felix Yusupov amusing and was familiar to a certain extent with his scandalous life. Practically every evening they would drive into St. Petersburg to gypsy establishments and carouse into the early hours of the morning.

When Tamara appeared on a garden terrace for dinner, she met the two noted revelers: Felix and Dmitry. They were both dazzled by her beauty and both greeted her with complimentary phrases. When Dmitry exclaimed, "She is perfect concinity!" Everyone laughed because they knew his habit of trying new words on the unexpected.

Felix interrupted and said, "What he means is, you're very beautiful."

Tamara was just as taken by them. Everything she had heard about Felix was true: he had inherited his mother's ethereal beauty. The Princess Zenaide Yusupov was known as the most beautiful woman in Russia as well as the richest. Her son had inherited her finest features. Tamara was amazed at the length of his eyelashes and could hardly refrain from staring.

During the dinner Tamara was questioned for some time about the Caucasus. All present had been in Tiflis, but they had not seen the ancient capital, Mtsety. During dessert Princess Irina announced that she had a surprise for Tamara. She asked her if she would be a bridesmaid at her wedding in February? All agreed that the idea was splendid and the princess readily accepted, but she wondered if there would be a marriage. Felix was undoubtedly the most eligible bachelor in Russia, being heir to the Yusupov fortune, and Princess Irina was one of the most eligible maidens, being the niece of the tsar; yet Tamara was puzzled by the match. He was certainly spectacular in appearance: tall and splendor, almost too handsome with dark melancholy eyes and ivory skin. Yet if he was doing "ungodliness," maybe even with Dmitry, why would he marry her? and why would she accept him? Was it possible she didn't know?

Suddenly Felix stood up holding a glass of champagne and said, "Let's go to the gypsies!'" Dmitry seconded the suggestion, but Irina refused. Felix persuaded her by promising that they wouldn't stay too late. A limousine was ordered and the four took off for St. Petersburg, leaving the Grand Duchess Xenia. On route Dmitry mentioned that he was leaving the Alexander Palace because the Empress objected to his activities. His comment led to Rasputin, but Tamara remained silent, not wanting to expose her Aunt Zita.

The gypsy night clubs were in a suburb of St. Petersburg called Novaya Dresvnya which was located in an area known as "The Islands," because many canals of the Neva made it into an archipelago. When the two couples entered, a cry resounded and several gypsy girls with cooper-colored skin, ebony hair and blazing eyes came running forth. It was obvious that they knew the men of the group and ushered them into the hall with hugs and kisses. The gypsies wore brightly colored, long full skirts with shawls over their shoulders. Gold, silver and sequin necklaces hung on their necks below long shiny earrings. They each had a special beauty of their own and gave the impression of being very free with their charms. It was just the opposite. They did not allow obscene behavior and were always under the eye of their men who wore brightly-colored Russian blouses covered with long-sleeved black caftans embroidered in gold and silver. Their baggy trousers hung over brightly shining black boots and they wore wide-brimmed black hats. Tamara felt she was entering another world and it all reminded her of her beloved Georgia and Shota.

Gypsy voices were pouring out a melancholy melody when the habitues entered the major hall which had overstuffed divans and rows of chairs with small tables. Bright lights showed the singers to their best advantage, causing their ornaments to shine. Once seated Felix ordered the best champagne and requested some songs he especially liked. The gypsy master bowed to Felix when told of his choices. The music swelled, sometimes sad and sentimental, sometimes in a frenzied gaiety. Dazzling gypsy dancers appeared at times and dominated the stage, sometimes with flashy dart-like movements and sometimes with slow, studied motions. The music and dancing stirred the soul and the atmosphere created by all the activity and emotion caused everyone to fall victim to its spell. During the ride home Felix and Dmitry sang gypsy songs and made Tamara sing some Georgian melodies. They brought back thoughts of Shota and she felt sad, both from memory and champagne.

The Yusupov private railway car which contained a suite of rooms full of overstuffed furniture carried Tamara to Moscow where she was met by the Princes Vladimir and Pavel. They drove off into the holy city with its innumerable golden-domed churches, high walled monasteries, and stately dwellings. The threesome had lunch in the old Dashkov mansion near the Kremlin. Many aristocratic families retained their ancient domiciles which reflected the styles of old 17th century Moscovy: vaulted rooms, walls elaborately decorated with frescoes and many narrow passageways. The Dashkovs kept the residence out of family pride and used it only when court duties required their presence in Moscow. A two hour motor ride into the countryside brought the threesome to the Dashkovs' summer place, Radnoe, a great columned mansion with spacious lawns and large oak trees. Vladimir and Pavel, on vacation from court duties, entertained Tamara during the ride with news, songs and society gossip.

A month in the country! Horse rides in the mornings, picnics in the pavilion by the lake, afternoon walks in the beautiful gardens. Dinners on the terraces and evenings in the salon with music, cards and games. Days passed in summer bliss. Callers from neighboring estates, the Shuvalovs, the Olsofievs, the Scherbatovs and Cheremetievs, dropped in for visits with the Dashkovs and departed leaving invitations for horse riding, picnics, walks and dinners on terraces. It was all the same as at home, but different.

On Sunday afternoons Princess Lidia Dashkov received the estate peasants and their families on a terrace in the courtyard. Refreshments were served and workers were allowed to present their requests and grievances. Tamara sensed a most sincere warmth between the mistress and the peasants. They seemed like children, listening attentively to her every word and always agreeing with her. Occasionally they held rural festivals with singing and dancing so delightful that everyone became enthusiastic. Plow hands who were usually clumsy from walking on uneven ground in their work would dance nimbly and maidens who never sang at their chores would join in the choruses. Many love matches were made at the festivals when the peasants were free to mingle among each other.

From the beginning of her stay at Radnoe, Tamara had noticed that Prince Pavel Voroshilov had watched her very closely. She would catch him staring at her during the various activities of the leisure days; yet when they would sometimes find themselves alone, he would not make any overtures. She was glad because she considered herself bound to Shota; still she was curious about his behavior. One day in the pavilion at the lake, Vladimir was called away by his mother. Pavel sat down on the bench beside Tamara and said, "You have the most entrancing eyes imaginable and I have fallen completely under your spell." Tamara leaned away. "Pavlick, I—"

"Don't say anything until I have finished. You know that I have chosen a military career and you know what that entails. However, I could promise you a life of ease and comfort."

She could not help but smile and noticed that it offended him. She quickly explained that his kindness had made her smile and that she was greatly honored by his proposal. However, she did not feel that her aunt and uncle would sanction a marriage at her age.

"Then you would marry me if they agreed?"

She smiled again and said, "They won't agree."

"But there's no hurry. Please say that you'll be mine."

Her grandmother's warning came to mind—Shota wants you as a jewel in his milieu. Tamara stood up and sat across from Pavel. She looked into his brown, pleading eyes. After a brief silence she asked if he would allow her some time. It was, after all, a surprise. He had not given any indication of such feelings. At that he protested and said, "You know that I've been eyeing you ever since we came."

"Yes. But Pavlick, let's become better acquainted. You might change your mind."

"How could I not love you?"

Tamara thought of Shota. If he were in Pavel's place he would have embraced her by now and showered her with kisses. Such a difference between the two men! She again asked for time and they slowly walked back to the manor house. That evening Pavel did not show up for dinner and Tamara was told that he had left for his parents estate on important business, but would return in two days. While he was gone, the Princess Dashkov often looked into Tamara's eyes as if she were discerning whether she was the cause of Pavel's quick departure. Her casual question, "Is anything troubling you, ma chere?" implied more of a request for information than a concern. Tamara did not feel she should jeopardize Pavel's reputation and said nothing. However, when he sent word that affairs would not allow his return, there was much speculation among the Dashkovs. Tamara remained silent and wondered if her Georgian blood had again caused a rejection?

By the middle of September the leisure summer days had ended and the fall season was approaching. Back in St. Petersburg the Dashkovs were involved in their usual activities: the Princess and Vladimir were busy with court duties and the old Prince was serving as a consultant in the Department of Foreign Affairs. The Treaty of Bucharest had been signed on August 10 and Russia was helping Serbia regain territory lost to Bulgaria. Prince Dashkov was delighted that his services were still appreciated in the upper echelons of the government, particularly since he was invited to advise the Russian delegation that went to Turkey in September for the signing of the Treaty of Constantinople in which Adrianople was restored to the Porte. Tamara was usually the only person in the Dashkov mansion during the morning hours and she kept busy with preparations for the Shuvalov ball. Since it would be her first appearance in society, it was deemed by Lidia as a most important occasion; especially since she had arranged for Igor Perovsky to be Tamara's escort. Final fittings on the special dress from Maison

Worth were made and there seemed to be an aura of excitement developing about the coming out of the princess.

One morning at the end of September, Louise rushed into Tamara's bedroom and blurted out a strange request: "Mademoiselle, may I speak openly with you?" Tamara had grown up with servants and tutors and one cardinal rule was to avoid entanglements in their personnel lives. Aunt Zita had been adamant on that point. Still, Tamara liked Louise and could see from the expression on her face that she was very worried. When she asked what the trouble was, Louise fell on her knees before her and started crying. Tamara felt sorry for her dutiful maid and helped her stand up, asking again what was wrong. Louise begged Tamara's help in a serious matter. Her friend Ivan was in prison and only Tamara could save him.

A frown of disbelief wrinkled the mistress's forehead. She was confused. Louise realized how vague she had been and revealed the plan she had for saving Ivan. She knew that the princess had been to Rasputin's with the countess and it was well known that the so-called holy man could arrange anything in the government because he was under the Empress's protection. Therefore, Louise begged the princess to ask Father Gregory's help. Tamara sat down on her boudoir stool. She was speechless. How could she ask help of that horrible man? What would he expect in return? How could she interfere in a police matter? The latter question made her ask, "Why is Ivan imprisoned?"

The question opened another world to the princess so long sheltered in mansions and villas. She knew the history of the revolutionary university groups in the 1870s and how they had assassinated Tsar Alexander II in 1881. The aristocrat Sophia Perovsky and her peasant lover Andrey Zheliabov had been hanged in a public square in St. Petersburg for the crime. She also had heard members of society speak of police actions against illegal printing presses and student agitators. Grand Duke Serge had been blown to bits outside his mansion in Moscow by such malcontents. Yet for all that Tamara knew about revolutionary activity, she had never confronted it until now. She stared at Louise in disbelief. Her maid was involved in criminal pursuits.

Louise again fell before the princess and sobbed. Tamara said nothing. She wanted an answer and could think of none. How could she dare participate in such an affair? Yet she was too kindhearted to refuse. She thought of her religious upbringing. Helping others was a Christian principle. So she concluded that by helping Louise, she might save her soul. Suddenly the event seemed worthwhile. If Louise would promise to reform and not participate in any more revolutionary activities, she would carry out her plan. Louise cried from relief and gratitude. She eagerly promised that she would never do anything wrong again and would make Ivan leave his underground group. Tamara naively felt that she had done something very fine. It was an indication, in her opinion, of her new maturity. She would save through service.

Feeling secure in her mission, Tamara had the Dashkov's coachman drive her to Rasputin's apartment on Green Pea Street. She decided on the back staircase and entered the kitchen where the cook was cleaning potatoes. She asked if Father Gregory was at home? The old servant nodded and without saying a word indicated with a shrug of her head that the princess should continue into the apartment. Tamara thanked her and walked on. The dining room and main salon were empty, so Tamara opened the door of the study only to freeze in horror. Rasputin was seated in a chair with his legs open and Felix Yusupov was kneeling before him enclosed by the holy man's legs. Both men turned their heads toward her. After only a momentary look, Tamara closed the door quickly and ran out of the apartment. She was horrified. Why would Felix be there and what was he doing? She concluded that he was praying, but why would he pray before Father Gregory and not an icon? Then she realized that maybe she had seen more. Was this the ungodliness the Princess Dashkov had mentioned? Was that what men do? Did Irina know? Disillusioned and confused, Tamara returned to the Dashkovs and informed Louise that Rasputin had not been at home.

Clever as Tamara had considered herself, she forgot that the coachman would certainly report his activities to the head of the household. The Princess Dashkov immediately called Tamara to her private study and demanded a full explanation. In tears the princess revealed what had occurred and to her further sorrow, Lidia dismissed Louise, saying that Godlessness must be stopped in Russia and that she was astounded that a princess of royal blood would even consider aiding one of those disgusting rebel outlaws who were causing so much disruption in Russia. "How could you, a noble lady, permit yourself such license? It's beneath your personal dignity and contemptible. There's obviously a sentimental streak in you that will only cause you grief." Leaning ever more forward in her awkward stance, Lidia started walking away but then turned and said in an entirely different voice and mood, "Ma chere, one must always guard oneself from the world. Your kindness has not served you well. Remember that and be cautious in the future. You were born a princess and shall die one. It's your fate as it is mine." Tottering a bit, Lidia left Tamara to her thoughts. She was disappointed that she had harmed Louise and ashamed that she had forsaken her own values for those of her maid. She recalled how enthusiastically she had embarked on her mission and how infatuated she had been with the noble idea of saving Louise. Princess Dashkov was right: Louise deceived her and would have never kept her promise. Her naivete had harmed them both.

The 1913 fall social season commenced with a grand ball at the Shuvalov palace on the Fontanka. The Shuvalovs had long been leaders of society. They received their title during the reign of the Empress Elizabeth when Peter Shuvalov III was rewarded for supporting her during the monarchial crisis in the night of November 17, 1741 when the Empress seized the throne from the infant Ivan VI. Since her reign, Shuvalovs had held many high government positions and the Countess Elizabeth Shuvalov, known as Betsie to her friends, had inherited her wealth and position from her husband's distinguished relatives.

Dressing for her first ball, Tamara felt delirious from excitement.

She was sure her long, full white dress would muss up her hair when she put it on, but it didn't; she knew her white satin shoes would be too tight, but they weren't; and she assumed that her diamond necklace would not be long enough for the decolletage of the gown, but it was in perfect proportion. Her fears were pointless, her joys only beginning. When she appeared on the stairway and began descending, the Prince and Princess Dashkov were standing below and began applauding. Tamara flushed pink, but continued her descent because she noticed several young men applauding with her benefactors.

Prince Vladimir introduced the princess to a few of his friends from the Corps des Pages: Prince Kochubey, a thin, tall young man with a small moustache; Count Sheremetiev, a short, chubby chap; and Prince Vadim Gagarin, a smart looking fellow with a charming smile. Tamara wondered why Pavel Voroshilov was not among the guests, but she refrained from inquiring. The princes greeted her most kindly and asked for dances at the ball. The Princess Dashkov interrupted by saying, "You must wait till she has her dance card. Now Tamara, I want you to meet Count Igor Perovsky."

A handsome brown headed young man with side whiskers advanced and bowed. He expressed his delight for the opportunity of escorting her to the ball. Riding with him in the carriage made the princess think of Cinderella. The compliments she had received on her dress and beauty from the Dashkovs and the young princes had gone to her head. The world seemed to belong to her and, perhaps for the first time in her life, she felt truly royal—not from her ancient bloodline, but from the ceaseless attention. She looked at the count and wondered, "What other miracles will there be tonight?"

Her escort, quite enamored by her loveliness, continued his compliments during their ride. To divert him, Tamara recalled that the Princess Dashkov had shown her his relatives tomb in the Alexander Nevsky Monastery. Count Igor proudly recounted aspects of the family history, mentioning the family's connection to

Russian literature. The mother of the noted 19th century writer A.K. Tolstoy was born a Perovsky and her brother Andrey was famous for having introduced Hoffmanist fantasy into Russian literature under the pseudonym Pogorelsky. Tamara noticed that he did not include the famous revolutionary Sophia Perovsky who was hanged by orders of the tsar. By the end of his tirade, she wasn't sure she liked her escort. His laugh seemed affected and he was continually looking at her breasts. She was glad when they drove through the iron gates of the Shuvalov mansion.

Entering the main foyer with its great gilt-edged panels the princess noticed how heads and staring eyes turned her way. She felt exhilarated. There was no worry about being asked for a dance, she had an escort; there was nothing to take attention from her as her dress was the prettiest in the hall; and there was no reason not to be happy, she was the belle of the ball. When Count Igor introduced her to Countess Shuvalov, the hostess remarked very sweetly, "They have not lied about you. You're gorgeous!" Tamara's heart was beating so fast she could only smile and walk by. It was all too much of a dream.

Rainbows of color filled the ballroom from the splendid uniforms of so many elite schools and regiments. His Majesty's Cossack bodyguards were in bright scarlet tunics with rows of silver cartridges on their chests and silver belts holding daggers in silver sheaths; they contrasted with the Hussars in flaming red; the Streltsy Regiment, dating from the time of Peter the Great, wore bright blue coats over raspberry colored blouses; the Pages of the tsar were in smartly tailored tunics decorated with gold braid down the front; silver and gold epaulets decorated the officers from the calvary regiments stationed around St. Petersburg; naval officers from the Baltic Sea fleet were in white with gold and navy blue trim; and diplomats were in tuxedos called "smoking." Since most of the dresses were white, the colors of the various uniforms were very distinctive.

As Tamara and Prince Igor passed a table holding a huge bouquet of roses, the Maitre de Ball handed Tamara a dance card. Her companion took it from her hand and signed for the first and last dance. By tradition it was assumed that the young man who requested the mazurka was planning a proposal at the end of the dance. Tamara looked at him and he winked. Suddenly she was surrounded and her dance card was filled. When the music started for the grand polonaise which always started a ball, Igor proudly led her into the slow processional march. He was delighted that his partner was the most beautiful young lady in the hall and it showed in his expression. Tamara remembered her grandmother's words, "He only wants you for the jewel you would be in his milieu."

Prince Gagarin, the heir of an ancient Russian family, appeared for the cotillion when colored favors and fancy rose corsages were passed out. He helped pin her flowers to her dress and escorted her onto the floor as the master of ceremony called out commands in a great stentorian voice: "Grand Rond!" "Balancez vos Dames!" "Allez a gouche!" Count Sheremetiev, almost as rich as Yusupov, claimed the next dance, a quadrille, and because he was shorter than Tamara, she tried unsuccessfully to stoop a little. Prince Kochubey, another scion of a historic family, came for his turn, a waltz. The couple floated around the ballroom and Tamara felt senseless as she gazed at the brilliantly shining gold chandeliers and the beautifully colored uniforms flashing around her. One dance followed another until suddenly a trumpet quartet sounded out quite loudly. When it ceased, the Master of Ceremony announced, "Grand marche a diner!" Couples began forming for the procession into the dining hall.

Suddenly Pavel Voroshilov took Tamara's arm and put it in his own. She was speechless and turned toward Igor. When he noticed what had happened, he objected, only to be told that Tamara was taken. As indiscreet scrimmage was about to occur when the Countess Shuvalov, having been warned by Prince Vladimir that his friend Pavel had arrived for a particular reason, interrupted the two competitors. "Mes amies," she calmly and sweetly exclaimed, "I think the princess should chose her partner, n'estce pas?"

Her question placed Tamara in an awkward position, but it avoided an unpleasantness. She amazed herself by saying, "Igor, since you had the first dance, do you mind if Pavel escorts me?" As a gentleman, Igor stepped away. The countess whispered to the princess, "Ma chere, your first ball and already a duel. C'est magnifique!"

Tamara and Pavel moved into the procession line behind Prince Vladimir who introduced the Princess Olga Vorontsov, an unattractive young lady wearing a Maison Worth gown in a Grecian style. Her figure was not well proportioned so the dress, which was undoubtedly very expensive, appeared to be hanging on her rather than fitting her body. She looked at Tamara 's dress with a critical glare and said, "Princess Dashkov told me that she was helping you choose your dress. She has such old-fashioned ideas, don't you think?" Tamara merely smiled, but she was amazed at the Princess Dashkov's choice for her son. True, the Vorontsovs were famous: the Emperor Peter III had chosen a Princess Vorontsov as his mistress and wanted to make her his tsarina, deposing Catherine the Great; but how could a scandal in the past make for a happy marriage in the present?

After the banquet, during which Olga displayed even more of her haughtiness, Pavel finally managed a few minutes alone with Tamara in an alcove of the long hall. After starting with a few awkward phrases showing his nervousness, he apologized for not returning to the Dashkov estate, but offered no excuses. He stated that because of his career his parents demanded that he put off any thought of marriage at this time. However, he assured Tamara that he still loved her; his main concern now was whether she would wait for him?

Tamara's lips twisted a bit as she made her uncontrollable smile. "Pavel, you dear!" she said tenderly, and explained that since they had made no plans, he was not under any obligation to her. She preferred that they think of each other as good friends and let the future decide their fate. Her answer saddened Pavel, but he realized that he was in no position to ask for more. He escorted her

back into the dance hall and surrendered her to Count Perovsky
for the mazurka. Tamara noticed that Pavel stood by a column and
sadly watched her dance.

Princess Dashkov entered Tamara's bedroom the next morning
with an impish grin on her face. She exclaimed, "You were a triumph! I know all about it and I am so proud of you! Now, tell me
about Igor! Did you like him?"

Tamara sat up in bed, rubbed her eyes and said what was
expected of her, "Yes, I liked him."

Lidia emitted a joyous cry, "Wonderful!" She was relieved and
satisfied that her match making had been successful and continued babbling about Igor's career possibilities and family influence. Tamara hardly listened until Lidia said, "And he will take
you to the Kudashev masquerade!" She referred to Mme
Brianchaninov, the former Princess Kudashev, whose second marriage had brought her great wealth. She was known for her extravagant parties and society always referred to them as Kudashev affairs. Tamara did not want Igor as an escort because of his boring
conceit, but she could not refuse.

Count Perovsky did escort Tamara to the Kudashev masquerade, but dressed as a fairy princess she captivated many others.
Invitations poured into the Dashkov mansion. Prince Gagarin, who
had impressed her at the Shuvalovs, gave her a thrilling evening at
the Marinsky Opera when Chaliapin sang Mousoursky's "Boris
Godunov." Count Sheremetiev, in spite of being shorter, took his
chances and Tamara saw Chekhov's "Sea Gull" when the Moscow
Art Theater toured in the city. Of course, Prince Pavel Voroshilov
wanted a monopoly of the princess's time, but he didn't succeed;
all society had become aware of the dazzling Georgian beauty and
the invitations never ceased. Princess Dashkov, however, arranged
meetings between Count Perovsky and Tamara whenever possible.

One morning in the middle of December, Lipa, Tamara's maid,
brought in a letter from the Countess Trushinsky. It was most
welcome and the princess tore it open quickly. The countess reported that Valery had successfully completed the academic work

of the Cadet School and would spend the final semester in military maneuvers. Count Trushinsky was still trying for a transfer to St. Petersburg and felt it would be finalized in the spring. Luda was continually asking about Tamara and somehow had it in her mind that the princess was visiting the tsarina. Tamara couldn't help but laugh. Then the fateful blow fell. "Your grandmother is not well and Shota has married his cousin Somi." Tears immediately filled Tamara's eyes. "Oh, how cruel," she thought. The countess knew it would hurt and had tacked it on the end of the letter as if it were merely matter of fact. The princess fell on her bed and cried. She would never again feel those great arms around her or those eyes beaming into hers. She would never again be his Nestan or he, her Terial. She would never again feel his lips on her breast or know such love. "Oh, God, why?"

CHAPTER 3

1914

The Yusupovs annual New Years Ball was held in their great palace on the Moika. The affair usually started in their 18th century rococo theater where a light opera or humorous French play would be performed. After the splendid dinner that followed, the party would dance in the grand ballroom. Several grand dukes and duchesses would attend with la creme de la societe. It was the ultimate social affair, famed for its extravagance and distinguished guests. To welcome in 1914, the Dashkovs and the Princess Zharzhadze were invited. Tamara had seen Princess Irina several times since the incident with Rasputin, but she had not seen Felix. She had met Irina at Maison Worth's for fittings on the bridesmaid gown and she had been to tea with Irina and her mother, Grand Duchess Xenia, but Felix had never been there. In a sense, she dreaded facing him because she was embarrassed for having witnessed him in such a compromising situation at Rasputin's. There had been no one with whom she could discuss the matter and she had avoided thinking about it. However, when she was with Irina, she did think about it and would have liked to talk with her, but she did not dare. She had heard much more about Felix since that incident: how he dressed in women's clothes and sang in a night club; how he brought back a polar bear at great expense from Murmansk; and how the Dowager Empress Maria Fedorovna had objected to his marrying Irina. Yet Tamara could not discuss such things with the demure and pleasant princess.

Going up the grand marble staircase of the Moika palace, Tamara saw Grand Duke Dmitry on the landing between the double stairs. A soft smile appeared on her face as he walked around two generals to greet her. He bowed and asked if he could escort her into the theater. He was very formal, not at all as relaxed as he had been at Tsarskoe Selo. She took his arm and he whispered, "As soon as we're away from those two, we'll talk." Tamara learned that the younger grand dukes held the elder ones in awe. Past the generals, Dmitry asked the princess if she minded his escort?

"I'm delighted," she replied, looking at him with her usual pleasing smile.

Suddenly Felix Yusupov and a beautiful woman came out of a drawing room. Seeing Tamara, he walked over and bowed, asking if he could present her to his mother, Princess Zenaide Yusupov. The young princess beheld the richest woman in Russia wearing the most enchanting lavender and gold dress Tamara had ever seen. Zenaide expressed her regret for not being in Tsarskoe Selo when Tamara visited and said that she was pleased at last to meet her. The four went through the long art gallery where Rembrandts, Poussins and Tiepolos were hanging, part of the remarkable Yusupov collection. Entering the rococo gold and red velvet theater, they met Princess Irina, who greeted Tamara warmly. Once they were seated in the center box, the world renown singer, Amelita Patti began a short concert of opera and art songs.

After a splendid dinner of creamed squid and smoked pheasant the was presented on a gold service, the guests went to the ballroom. During the dancing Tamara noticed that there were no pages of the tsar in attendance. Instead her dance card was filled mainly by visiting elderly French aristocrats: the Duc de La Rochefoucauld, the Conte de Castellane, the Duc de Rohan. A few wealthy financiers of the "haute bourgeoisie" also asked to partner her. The well-known industrialist V.G. Morozov even invited Tamara to his mansion in Moscow to see his outstanding collection of modern art. In spite of the famous beauty of the hostess, Tamara was again the belle of the ball.

Just as the mazurka started, a woman's cry resounded through the hall and the music stopped. Somehow Princess Irina had badly twisted her ankle and was in great pain. Many crowded around her as a doctor examined her foot. It was deemed quite serious and she was carried off the floor. The hostess asked for the continuation of the dance, but the brilliant mood of the evening had been disturbed. Soon after the New Year was toasted with champagne, people began leaving.

The next day the Princess Zenaide Yusupov called on the Princess Dashkov. It was unusual. While they kept up the pretense of friendship, they could not be close because Zenaida did not support Father Gregory and Lidia did. However, Lidia was pleased to receive the princess and walked her into the salon. Zenaida explained that Princess Irina had to see a famous foot specialist in Paris and they wanted Tamara along as her companion. The only objection Lidia had was that there were soon to be fittings for the dress for Tamara's presentation to the Empress. Zenaida assured Lidia that the dress could be made in Paris and that she would personally supervise it. While Lidia was concerned about the reaction the Empress might have, she finally consented: Tamara would accompany Irina to Paris.

The Yusupov private railroad car for long distance travel had a vestibule which was used as an outside veranda in the summer. It contained an aviary so that the songs of the birds would drown out the train's monotonous rumble. The salon had mahogany panelling with green leather chairs and yellow silk curtains. Three bedrooms decorated in chintz followed and then several roomettes for guests. The kitchen and compartments for the staff and servants were in the rear. Tamara had always known a comfortable life style, but the extravagance of the Yusupovs amazed her, especially when they arrived at the Russian border station Verzhbolov. Russian railroad cars were double gauged, so for the continuance of the trip into Europe, another private coach of the Yusupovs with narrower wheels awaited them. While the servants moved their things to their new quarters, the family waited in the station which was full of odors: wet straw, strong tobacco, sheepskins, tarred boots and wood-burning stoves.

Several times during the trip through Germany and into France, Princess Irina mentioned a French duke whom she knew very well. The coy smile that would appear on her face suggested that she was plotting something. Finally, as the train was entering Paris, she confessed that her friend, the duc, would meet them at the station. "You will like him, and I KNOW he'll like you." Her emphatic "know" told Tamara everything. And the princess proved correct. When the train stopped in the station, Irina was being wrapped in a sable cloak when she suddenly started waving at someone through the window. A very distinguished looking gentleman was nodding at her. His elegant top hat and formal morning clothes made him appear very debonair. Irina called her companion and said, "There he is, the Duc de Chevreuse!"

Tamara looked through the window into the grey eyes of a face endowed with fine features. Looking at her his eyes opened wide and his small moustache curled with his lips as he made a flirtatious grin. Tamara's modesty took her eyes away. At that moment the servants began carrying Irina out of the train. On the platform she introduced the duc who bowed and grinned again. They were joined by the Yusupovs swathed in fur: Felix in bear and Zenaida in chinchilla. They embraced their friend the duc and soon the party was off to the Ritz.

Since Princess Irina required several weeks of therapy, she insisted that the duc escort Tamara around Paris. He was most willing and in the course of some time conducted her on tours of the Louvre, the Tulleries, Versailles and Napoleon's tomb. If they didn't go sightseeing in the daytime, he would take her for an evening at the Chatelet. The impresario Diaghliev was in town with the famous ballet stars Nijinsky, Pavlova and Karsavina. Tamara marveled at the bright colored scenery by Bakst and Benois. Whenever she expressed regret about leaving Irina, the princess would not listen. Tamara began wondering if Irina was encouraging a liaison between her and the duc. He certainly was trying. His compliments on her beauty had reached far heights; his courteous, yet

flirtational behavior had become routine; and his witty talk had
made her look forward to their daily meetings. Irina also eagerly
awaited a full report after each outing.

Evenings were usually spent in the salon of Irina's suite. The
family would have dinner brought up from the dinning room and
then play cards. The duc often came, entertaining everyone with
society gossip. One evening he asked if he could drive Tamara to
his family estate, Dampierre, with his cousin, the Marquise de
Guise, as chaperon. Without asking Tamara, everyone agreed that
she must go see the famous chateau which was one of the major
17th-century achievements in architecture outside the royal or
public domains. The fortune that paid for the edifice came from
Colbert, Louis XIV's economic minister and a relative of a former
Duchesse de Chevreuse.

Wearing dust coats and goggles the duc himself drove Tamara
and his cousin through the lush green countryside to the Valley of
Chevreuse where the stately chateau stood perfectly integrated with
its surrounding park. Since the weather was mild for January, the
roads were not full of ruts or muddy. Entering the valley the car
drove through a long wooded corridor with the mansion visible in
the distance. It was a superb edifice and had served the aristocratic
family for centuries. One duc even stayed in the chateau during
the French revolution while his peasants protected him.

The Marquise de Guise envied Tamara her beauty, but she was
amused at her naivete. As a member of a group of aristocrats noted
for their liberal views and actions, the Marquise enjoyed scandal of
a polite nature more than anything in the world. She considered a
scandal "polite," if it didn't cause lawsuits or break up a marriage.
Knowing her cousin the duc since childhood, she often helped
him in his escapades. When she first saw Tamara she knew what
the duc had in mind and played along. Whenever possible she
enumerated to the princess the duc's fine qualities and how he had
long searched for a proper mate for his distinguished heritage.
Tamara was complimented, thinking that the Marquise was actually
suggesting that she should be the future duchesse.

After dinner in a room of white and gold carved paneling, the marquise excused herself, saying that she was tired from the trip and would retire. The duc led Tamara into a small study where a two-seated divan stood in front of a roaring fireplace. It was very warm and cozy. The duc was very interested in history and asked many questions about the Caucasus area and the background of the Zharzhadze family. After some time, he slipped closer and put his arm on the back of the settee. She wondered what she should do? Shota was now out of her life and if the duc really liked her, should she not consider such a liaison? Then he asked, "You know that I adore you, don't you?"

Tamara turned, looked into his eyes and said, "You've been so kind, but you hardly know me."

"There is nothing more to know. I want you."

"You want to marry me?"

The duc stuttered something as he stood up and walked over by the fireplace. He was blushing. Tamara realized what his intent had been and she too blushed. The whole escapade had been a set up for a tryst and she had been so utterly naive. She could hardly find words, but finally said, "It's late. May I retire now?" Without speaking, the duc led her down a hall to her bedroom. He bowed at the door and left.

The Marquise du Guise suppressed a smile when she met the princess the next morning. She invited her into a small dining room where they had tea and petit pain with preserves. During the repast, the marquise explained that the duc had been called away and that a driver would take them back to Paris that morning. Tamara agreed, but she dreaded riding with the smirking companion. She went to her room and looked in a mirror. "Seems you're not to be a duchesse!"

The Yusupovs and Princess Irina were surprised when Tamara returned after only one day in the country. They knew something was wrong, but pretended that everything was fine. When the two young ladies were alone, Irina broke her protocol and asked the reason for the quick return. Tears came to Tamara's eyes, but she felt at ease and told her everything that happened. Irina was amazed and disappointed. She assured her friend that the duc had always conducted himself most courteously and apologized for placing Tamara into such an awkward situation.

Since they were discussing discreet matters, Tamara felt that she could ask Irina about her relationship with Felix. The princess looked at the floor and said, "You've heard the rumors, haven't you?" Tamara nodded. Irina looked away and related her feelings on the subject. She loved Felix because he was so kind and gentle. If he did those things, it was because he had a need. She did not hold that against him, but loved him more for his weaknesses. Tamara squeezed her hand, deciding not to mention what she had seen at Rasputin's.

Two days later the Marquise du Guise appeared at Irina's suite, requesting a meeting with Tamara. Princess Zenaida Yusupov denied the request unless she could be in attendance. The marquise agreed and joined the ladies for tea. She related some astonishing news: her cousin, the duc, had received permission from his father, a Marechal of France, to propose marriage to Tamara. Everyone was speechless. Zenaida asked why the duc himself had not come. The marquise explained that the duc was ashamed of his behavior at the chateau and was sending an apology through her. Would Tamara see him?

Zenaida, feeling responsible for Tamara, informed the marquise that while she was delighted with the thought of the coming together of two such distinguished families, Tamara was only 17 and her aunt and uncle in Tiflis were her guardians; such an important matter could only be decided by them. However, the duc was welcome if Tamara wished it. She nodded. The marquise smiled cunningly and said, "Ma chere, I must tell you that my cousin shocked me with his revelation. He has truly fallen in love with you. I know him too well for it not to be true." A meeting was arranged for the next afternoon.

Princess Irina was thrilled and saddened by the news. She confessed to Tamara that she had once loved the duc, but was afraid that he was not serious about her. Now he had found love and she was happy for them both. "You do love him, n'est-ce pas?" Tamara couldn't answer immediately. She smiled and nodded her head once, but it was obvious that she wasn't sure. If Irina had rejected him for his libertine ways, how could she be sure he would cease after their marriage. She did not want an arrangement like Irina was entering with Felix. It was all very complex and Tamara waited anxiously for the meeting with the duc.

The Duc de Crevreuse was 26 and had a reputation in society for giving in to extravagant pleasures. His philandering had caused many mothers concern about their daughters. They would have liked him for a son-in-law, but he enjoyed his freedom and avoided all entrapments. Well-known for his wit and charm, the handsome and rich bachelor was the favorite of hostesses who needed an extra gentleman at their table. When the duc met the Princess Zhorzhadze he desired adding her to his conquests, but during the days he spent with her, he discovered that she possessed more than a title and beauty. She interested him; she understood him; and she captivated him. He realized that he loved her when she embarrassed him at the chateau. He wanted her.

Tamara met the duc in Irina's salon by herself. Zenaida and Irina had earlier discussed with her the implications of such a marriage and they knew she would respect their advice. It could not be at once and approval was necessary. The duc bowed when he met the princess and expressed his regret for his behavior. Tamara avoided the subject and said, "You have paid me the greatest of compliments." He went down on one knee before her and asked if she could consider being his wife. Her knowing smile crossed her face and she said, "Yes. Yes, of course, I would." The duc stood up, took her into his arms and kissed her.

In the days that followed, Tamara went for fittings at Maison Worth, examined jewels at Cartier, and won the approval of the duc's mother, the Countess de Chabrillan who was known for her fabulous fetes. The duc introduced her to Parisian society and at one soiree the Marquis de Bailleul, after commenting on Tamara's beauty, asked her, "Have you read Merezhkovsky?"

"I only know the name. He's creating a new religion, I believe."

"Yes, he's doing the world a favor by combining carnal paganism and ascetic Christianity."

Tamara could not respond, and realized that she was not well read in contemporary philosophical currents. The duc interrupted and said, "We're too much in love for philosophy!" The marquis's thin lips twisted into a smile and he bowed.

At a reception for the Spanish Ambassador, the Duchesse d'Aumale gazed at Tamara and remarked, "What a jewel!" The princess remembered the comment of her grandmother, 'a jewel in his milieu.' She wondered if the duc really loved her or was she just another beautiful acquisition. Shota came to mind, but she tried not to compare him with the duc. The old life was over and the new was beginning. She would forget Shota and enjoy being the belle of the ball. Invitations came from the nobility and wealthy financiers. She lived a dream without end only to be awakened by a telegram from the Princess Dashkov: "Countess requests your immediate return."

Princess Irina's sprained ankle had recovered sufficiently for short walks, so when the telegram arrived, she insisted that they all return to Russia. The Yusupovs agreed and the coach was made ready and attached to the Nord Express, the fastest cross European train. The duc could not accompany them because of family financial transactions. He would join them in Russia in July. At the train station he presented Tamara with a splendid diamond bracelet. Tears filled her eyes and he kissed her, parting with words of love.

Returning to St. Petersburg Tamara sensed that the atmosphere of the city had changed. A feeling of anxiety permeated the newspapers and conversations. The "word" war was spoken everywhere; many believed the Kaiser, a cousin of the tsar, would never attack Russia; others felt the military build up in Austria and Germany could only lead to war; still many did not have a sense of urgency and continued living their daily routines. It had been the same in France, but Tamara had not noticed; she had been too preoccupied with entertainments, fittings and meetings with the duc.

The Dashkovs greeted the return of the princess with great aplomb. While Lidia was disappointed that her match-making between the princess and Count Perovsky had failed, she was delighted that Tamara would change her great family name for another of high rank. The Princess Dashkov had made inquiries and already knew details about the duc's family history: his mother, his finances; and his reputation. All seemed in order save for the last. Tamara calmed her nerves by telling about the incident at the chateau. The Princess Dashkov felt his actions showed strength of character and conceded; besides, she had important news for the princess. Since her eighteenth birthday was on the 15th of March, her presentation to the Empress Alexander was scheduled for March 20th at the Alexander Palace in Tsarskoe Selo. The Princess Dashkov would accompany her since her own mother was deceased.

The marriage of Princess Irina and Prince Felix took place in the Anichkov Palace on February 22, 1914. The tsar himself escorted Irina into the baroque palace chapel, but even His Majesty had to wait for the bridegroom. Felix had taken the elevator, but it had stopped half-way between floors. Grand Dukes, princes and counts galore worked feverishly to extricate the forlorn prisoner. The tsar found it amusing, but Felix, who loved perfection in all things, was dismayed.

Princess Irina wore a magnificent white satin dress embroidered in silver with a long train. Her lace veil had belonged to Marie Antoinette and was held by a diamond tiara. Tamara, also in white satin decorated with pink and lavender lace, followed carrying a bouquet of white calla lilies. The Russian orthodox ceremony dated from ancient times and the gold crowns held over the heads of the bridal couple glistened in the candlelight. A carpet of pink silk was placed before the bride and groom, an old Russian custom. By tradition, the first one of the couple to step on the silk would rule the household. Irina had planned to outdistance her husband, but her sore, weak ankle hindered her. Felix took advantage and quickly stepped first on the carpet. The happy couple looked at each other and laughed. Afterwards a grand reception was held at the Moika Palace and another at the Grand Duke Alexander's palace. Finally, worn out from the activities of the day, Felix and Irina departed on their honeymoon to Egypt. The marriage had been a splendid affair attended by the elite of Russia.

March was the end of the social season in St. Petersburg and Tamara was quickly engaged in dances, teas and theater. Word about her alliance with the Duc de Chevreuse spread through upper class salons and she was greeted everywhere as the duchesse. It often made her blush, but she always smiled kindly. After her birthday, which in Russia was not considered as important as one's names-day on the church calendar, preparations for the presentation to the Empress kept the Dashkov household busy. The jewels of Tamara's mother were brought from the bank: a diamond tiara, a pearl choker and a diamond and ruby ring. The dress arrived from Paris and Lidia was not only astounded, but somewhat envious. When Tamara was practicing her curtsy, Lidia said, "I should have known that Zenaida would have those Parisians create something extraordinary."

On the day of the presentation to the Empress, the Princess Dashkov and Tamara, ostentatiously dressed in white satin and jewels, boarded the tsar's special train coach which was used for debutantes. Only one other young lady, the daughter of a titled diplomat, and her mother accompanied them on the short ride to Tsarskoe Selo. A surprise awaited Tamara at the Alexander Palace which reflected extreme simplicity compared to the palaces of the Yusupovs and the grand dukes. The pages on duty that day were the Princes Vladimir and Pavel. Lidia knew her son would be there and was delighted at Tamara's amazement. Vladimir instructed the ladies about the proper deportment when in the tsarina's presence: they must not speak unless spoken to and answer all questions briefly.

By believing in Rasputin's power to sustain the health of her hemophiliac son, the Tsarevich Alexis, and by isolating the royal family in the Alexander Palace twenty five miles outside St. Petersburg, the Empress Alexandra had alienated most of the nobility and the royal family, including the Dowager Empress Maria Fedorovna. Reared in Great Britain by her grandmother, Queen Victoria, Alexandra retained the restraint associated with the English upper classes. The Russian "madness" or "joie de \illegible text\ to her nature and she never adapted to her adopted country's mores. Preferring to speak English, she lived only for her family and did court duties only when necessary.

Tamara and the Princess Dashkov were the first to enter the tsarina's study. Felix Yusupov had described Alexandra's style of decorating "as the worst possible taste," and Tamara understood when she saw how badly the tables and mahogany chairs were arranged. The wall paintings appeared of good quality, but they were hanging indiscriminately: a large war painting next to a portrait of the tsarina; a bouquet of flowers near a family group; and photographs filled spaces between the pictures.. The room seemed stifled with an unpleasant atmosphere. The Empress Alexandra was standing in the middle of the chamber and both ladies curtsied before her. When Tamara looked into her eyes, she sensed a tormented soul. The Empress looked at her dress and said, "Your dress is very fine." Tamara explained that the Princess Yusupov created it in Paris. At the mentioning of Zenaida's name, Alexandra winced and turned to the Princess Dashkov. "I understand your ward has accepted the proposal of the Duc de Chevreuse." Lidia nodded and confirmed the news. Alexandra looked at Tamara and said, "I congratulate you and wish you every happiness." Tamara thanked her. Alexandra nodded to Prince Vladimir who was standing in a corner. He came and handed the Empress a medal on a light blue ribbon. She stated in a hollow, strangely accented Russian that she welcomed Tamara as a Maid of Honor and gave the award back to her page who placed it around the princess's neck and shoulder. At that moment the Empress looked at the doorman and he opened the portal. The interview was over and the

Maid of Honor and Princess Dashkov curtsied before leaving the room.

Since 1914 was also the debutante year of the tsar's two eldest daughters, Olga and Tatiana, a grand ball was held in the Anichkov Palace. The Empress did not attend, using the tsarevich's health as an excuse; yet most believed that it was because the palace was the residence of the Dowager Empress Maria who loved mirth and entertainments. She had been reared in a Danish royal family noted for its liberal attitude and erratic behavior. Her father, King Christian VI, had taught her acrobatics and the family was so boisterous that Queen Victoria called the children "barbarians!" Maria grew up with cosmopolitan ideals. She was the only member of the royal family who had Ethiopians in her service. The tall black footmen wore Oriental costumes and tall turbans, reminding Tamara of the Baskt stage design for the ballet "Scheherazade." When the guests were assembled in the large reception room of the glittering palace, the Master of Ceremony, dressed in a gold-embroidered tunic, black silk breeches and black patent leather shoes, announced in a great basso voice: "His Majesty, Emperor Nicholas II."

It was a thrilling moment. Tamara almost held her breath. She had never met the tsar, and He, the monarch given power, as Russians believed, by God Almighty was entering the hall. Yet it was anticlimactic. A short, timid man dressed in the uniform of a colonel of the infantry strolled in while stroking his beard.

He seemed in awe of his subjects and nodded his head to one and another almost mechanically. When he was in front of Tamara, she curtsied, but when she rose, he was still looking at her. She could not speak, but he didn't either. It was an awkward moment. Finally the two tall grand duchesses, who were in the cortege following him, came up behind and he moved on. After receiving the guests, the tsar opened the ball, dancing the ceremonial polonaise march with the Grand Duchess Olga.

The senior pages of the tsar attended and were allowed to dance when free of duties. Prince Pavel Voroshilov finally managed a dance with Tamara. He knew about her involvement with the duc and congratulated her, but his words did not seem sincere. She realized that she had hurt him, but she preferred to avoid the issue. He did not. While he was cordial through most of the dance, at the end he whispered, "I still love you and will love you always." Tamara thought of her words to Shota and felt very disheartened. Tears came to her eyes and Pavel noticed her grief. Thinking that she was depressed because of him, he added, "Is there still a chance you care for me?" Tamara turned her head. She couldn't answer. Fortunately the music stopped and he led her off the floor.

When Tamara was informed the next morning that she had a telegram, she assumed it was from the duc and hurried to the orangeries where the Princess Dashkov was having tea. She opened the envelope and read aloud, "Arriving April 1. Vadim transferred to St. Petersburg. Aunt Zita." Tamara's face showed such disappointment, Lidia could not control a laugh, but quickly expressed her view of the situation. Tamara would stay with the Dashkovs. She was eighteen now and there was no reason for her to be chaperoned by the countess. Tamara thanked her kindly and felt great relief.

During the week the Trushinsky's stayed at the Dashkovs, Zita was unable to regain control over her niece. Tamara had excuses whenever she was invited for a visit with Rasputin, or for a shopping excursion or for a tea with countess "this" or princess "that." She did accompany her aunt to church and was appalled at the great reverence the countess pretended. Tamara had been away from her relatives for some time and now viewed them through different perspectives. Her aunt now seemed a most superficial and decadent woman. Her uncle, Count Vadim, was just the opposite. She had loved him before, but now she adored him. He talked with her seriously about the marriage with the duc and gave her interesting insights into possible difficulties. He assured her that he would always be her protector should she need one. He also answered Tamara's questions about the political crisis spreading over Europe. He believed, as did many others, that it was only a matter of time before a conflict occurred and he expressed his regret that many high officials were confident in Russia's power and saw no reason for alarm. Tamara enjoyed her talks with her uncle and was glad he had returned to the capital city. At the end of a week, the Trushinsky's possessions arrived and they moved into a large apartment near the Alexandovskaia Lavra.

Free of her aunt's unwanted supervision, Tamara joined the activities at the end of the social season. Since she was now unofficially engaged, she went to parties and theater with Prince Vladimir and his fiance Princess Olga. The latter continued to be supercilious and condescending, but Tamara always pretended that she didn't notice. She was too happy for such snobbery. Her daily routine became filled with waiting for a dispatch from the French Embassy. The duc had become involved in some diplomatic activity and had access to the wireless in the Department of Internal Affairs. He sent messages quite often to the French delegation in St. Petersburg and Tamara thrived on them. However, instead of announcing the date of his arrival in Russia, he was continually postponing it because of his new duties. His repeated apology was deemed sincere by the Princess Dashkov because gifts of great value arrived: a diamond broach from Cartier, which made Faberge settings look passe a malachite bracelet set in gold and an excellent diamond necklace with a large emerald centerpiece. The latter so impressed Lidia that she began telling her friends that she was responsible for the liaison between Tamara and the duc.

In the beginning of May Prince Dashkov announced that he had business on his estate in the Ukraine, Kholmka, and invited Tamara to accompany him and the princess. He outlined several reasons why she would enjoy the trip. Since they would stop in Kiev, the duc could send his messages to her through the French legation in that large southern metropolis. Also, they would visit with the Grand Duchess Elizabeth whom Tamara had met at Tsarskoe Selo. And thirdly, her brother Valery would join them there after his graduation in Tiflis. That news thrilled the young princess, but Lidia had yet another reason why Tamara should join them and said it most expressively: "You must go because it's May!"

taking it for granted that her ward knew Gogol's descriptions of starry May nights in that land of cossacks and boundless borders.

Kiev, located on high bluffs along the Dniepr River, proved a fascinating experience for Tamara. She had passed through the city before on trains, but she had never visited the famous Pechersky Monastery with its subterranean halls filled with the corpses of saintly priests from the 11th and 12th centuries. Spring had already come to the area and flowers of all colors were blooming profusely. Compared to cold St. Petersburg, it was like being in another world. The Grand Duchess Elizabeth was dressed in her nun's habit when the Dashkovs visited her at the monastery. She remembered Tamara and blessed her future marriage. The Dashkovs knew her when her husband was Governor of Moscow and supported her charitable works. Two very pleasant days were spent in Kiev before leaving for Kholmka.

While the Dashkov's lands in the Ukraine were larger than their estate outside Moscow, the large wooden manor house at Kholmka was not nearly as ostentatious as the columned mansion at Radnoe and the atmosphere was different. There was no gold-gilt panelling and the servants did not wear uniforms. The simplicity of the house created a restful feeling and Tamara felt relaxed from the beginning of their stay; especially after viewing one of the great starry nights over those far-reaching expanses. If one looked at a single star, it would grow larger and seem to be falling toward you. Yet concentration on one star was not easy because the sky was filled with large, blinking, shining lights.

Prince Dashkov had come for the spring sell of yearlings from his stables. It was an engaging time as neighbors, merchants and peasants from around the countryside would visit, picnic and purchase. Occasionally a race would be held for the presentation of a particular horse or breed. Tamara and the Princess Dashkov occupied themselves with charity work in the villages on the estate with social calls on nearby landowners. One day after lunch on a terrace, the prince told Tamara that an interesting race would be held in the afternoon and invited her. Since she loved horses and used to ride at her grandmother's estate, she accepted with pleasure.

Entering one of the large stables, Tamara noticed a young dark-haired Cossack tightening a saddle on a large roan horse. Something about his build and moustache reminded her of Shota and she caught herself staring at him. He noticed and before she could turn away, he smiled at her. Tamara pretended as if she had not noticed and felt guilty for having stared. She followed the prince toward the back of the building, but as they walked the handsome cossack passed by them leading his horse. "What a fine animal," the Prince commented, stopping the passerby and examining the horse more closely. As he walked around it, the cossack looked at Tamara and smiled. She looked away, upset by the young man's impertinence and ashamed that she had caused such an effrontery. The prince patted the horse's head and walked away. Tamara followed without looking back.

Cossack villages were scattered all over the Ukraine. In olden times there was a cossack culture with its capital, Cherkassk, on one of the islands of the Don River. Peter the Great had incorporated the roving, looting brigands into the Russian army and pacified their turbulent and rampageous way of life. Yet much of their tempestuous character could still be seen in their dare-devil horse riding competitions and enthusiastic folk dances. Tamara was reminded of Shota when she watched a race because the Cossack behavior was often careless and daring.

Prince Valery Zharzhadze arrived at Kholmka during the second week of the Dashkovs visit. Tamara was thrilled that they were together again but she soon felt that he had changed. He did not seem pleased with her attachment to the duc and asked little about him. Instead he was continually talking about his own career in regards to the oncoming war. For Tamara, now deep in the expanses of the Ukraine, the war seemed a remote possibility and she was disappointed that her dear brother had turned into another of those officers who thought only of heroism in battle. However, after a few days of showing off his knowledge of military history and European political entanglements, Valery lost himself in horse riding. He had excelled in equestrian activities in the Cadet Corps and enjoyed showing off his ability to his sister and the Dashkovs. His prowess brought on the attention of the Cossacks working on the farm and he developed a friendship with one named Oleg Dunatov. When they rode together, they exchanged riding techniques; when they drank together, they exchanged Georgian tales for Cossack yarns. Valery mentioned Oleg so often during dinner conversations with the Dashkovs that they began looking forward to his retelling of Oleg's adventures.

One day Tamara went riding alone in the large park that surrounded the manor house. As she was going up a hillock she was suddenly surprised by a rustle and gallop in the woods beside her. In seconds Valery and his friend came riding out of the forest and stopped in front of her. She recognized the Cossack she had seen that first day and quickly looked away. Valery laughed, thinking they had startled her. He could not present his friend in a formal way because of their class differences, but Valery was libertarian enough to say, "Tamara, this is my friend Oleg." The princess nodded, but did not meet Oleg's eyes. Valery shouted, "We're off!" and nudged his horse. Tamara looked up and saw Oleg smiling at her as he rode past.

Riding on alone Tamara thought of the handsome Cossack. He was another Shota, but there were worlds between them. Shota represented centuries of nobility; Oleg was a peasant. "How strange it is," she thought. "I cannot even think of him because of our blood; and it isn't even our fault. Course, I don't think of him that way, he just reminds me of Shota." Confident in her conclusion, she rode on; but the thought kept returning. Oleg was a fascinating man and she was sure he was taken by her. She wondered what the duc would think if he could read her thoughts. He was so refined and polished, a perfect gentleman. So what was Oleg's special allure? Suddenly she said aloud, "His eyes!" She realized that Oleg, like Shota, said everything through his eyes. Her judgement proved to be true. Every time she saw him, he would smile, but his eyes said much more. Tamara sometimes shuddered thinking of the message from his gaze.

May turned into June and the Dashkovs began planning their return to St. Petersburg. Tamara could hardly believe that a month had passed so quickly. She had received a few messages from the duc via the French legation in Kiev, but he still had not mentioned his date of departure for Russia. When Prince Dashkov was informed by the Interior Ministry that his presence was needed when French President Poincare visited Russia in July, the prince told Tamara that the duc might be in the suite of the French leader. She was delighted by the possibility and did not regret their leaving Kholmka.

During their weeks in the country, Tamara and Valery had restored their previous closeness. Little by little he had dropped his obsession with military triumphs and had lost himself in the joys of summer life: boating on the Dniepr, riding with either his sister or his friend, and flirting with peasant girls. Tamara admired him very much. He represented young manhood in its full flower: possessed with ability, aimed for achievement and conquering everyone with his charm. During their last ride in the park, Oleg appeared in a hollow. Valery greeted him, told him of their departure the next day and expressed his appreciation for his friendship. Oleg kept looking at Tamara who was forced to avoid his eyes. After a handshake, the two friends parted.

Since it was the last night in the Ukraine, Tamara walked out on the balcony of her room and gazed at the starry skies. She stretched her arms out into the warm summer air and remembered Gogol's monster "Viy," that could see through any charmed circle drawn by a priest on a church floor for protection against evil. Suddenly she heard a sound below and looked down into the moonlit face of Oleg. "Oh!" she gasped and moved back from the railing. She trembled. How could he dare! Generations of master and slave stood between them; but he was like a panther on a prowl. She became petrified; then she heard a rustle in the ivy trellis below her. In seconds he was on the balcony. He, the great masculine Cossack peasant, stood his ground, daring not to move forward toward a princess of ancient royal blood. Tamara felt a strong urge to fall into his arms and be devoured as Shota once tried, yet her upbringing, her faith and her ancestral pride overcame the urge. "No!" she whispered and backed into her bedroom. After a few seconds the rustle in the ivy on the lattice was audible. Tamara felt numb and wondered what she should do. If she told on Oleg, he would be seriously punished. She could not allow that because, as she admitted to herself, she might have led him on. How many times she allowed their eyes to meet, she could not recall; but it did happen and he could not be blamed. The next morning she said nothing, but as the Dashkov carriage left for the train station, she again saw that look in Oleg's eyes as he stood among the country folk waving goodbye.

On June 28, 1914, the heir apparent to the Austrian throne, Archduke Francis Ferdinand and his wife, the Duchess of Hohenberg were assassinated in Sarajevo, Bosnia. Earlier in the day the royal couple had escaped injury when a bomb was thrown into their automobile on the way to the town hall. The pre-arranged program was not changed and they sat through several hours of speeches. On the way back to their hotel, riding in an open carriage, a student-terrorist fired two shots point-blank and mortally wounded the archduke and duchess. It was proven that the assassin was connected to a Serbian nationalist-terrorist organization and therefore Serbia was blamed even though the government had not been involved. The dreadful incident in the Balkans caused diplomatic ripples throughout Europe and they soon turned into gigantic waves.

Dining at the Trushinskys the evening of the news from Bosnia, Valery and the count discussed, speculated and prophesied about possible future events. Count Trushinsky was sure that Austria would punish Serbia but he could not decide the degree of the vengeance. He rationalized that it all depended on how much help Germany would give its ally. If it led to war, which seemed unlikely under the circumstances, it could be disastrous. He was now in charge of the St. Petersburg Cadets and he would lose his senior class immediately if there was a general mobilization. It was not expected, but he felt that being prepared was very important. Valery was awaiting assignment after his graduation in Tiflis. His cadet training and background gave him the privilege of choosing his regiment, and he was considering the cavalry. Countess Trushinsky became displeased with Tamara because she didn't answer fully all her questions about the duc; she was also bored by the gentlemen's conversation, so she interrupted them with an account of a recent psychic phenomenon she had witnessed. When the gentlemen only listened and then continued discussing the political situation, she left the table, saying that she was expected at another seance. No one said anything because the men were in a heated argument over the Sarajevo incident. Tamara sat and day dreamed of France.

Life in the Dashkov mansion suddenly changed, not because of the news from Europe, but because of fateful circumstances in the family. A telegram arrived from Shota informing Tamara and Valery that their Grandmother Zhorzhadze had passed away; and, as an unpleasant coincidence can sometimes intrude into human lives, Princess Dashkov became ill the day of the bad news from Georgia. Doctors were summoned, but all gave contradicting diagnoses. She had been suffering pains in her abdominal area, but considered the problem simple indigestion. Suddenly on the morning of the telegram, the princess was in dire distress. By afternoon the pain was so agonizing, opium was administered. The princess herself asked that Father Gregory be brought to her bedside. Prince Dashkov would not leave his wife and with Prince Vladimir at the Corps des Pages and Valery at the Cadet headquarters, the only person available was Tamara. With tears in his eyes, the old prince stroked his white moustache and asked Tamara if she would be so kind. How could she refuse?

Father Gregory was at tea with a group of ladies when Tamara arrived at the apartment on Gorohovaia street. She was thankful that the countess was not among them. When the holy man saw the princess, he left the ladies, to their annoyance, and led Tamara into his study. She explained her mission and he agreed. However, saying how sorry he was at the news, he put his huge hands on her shoulders and tried pressing her to his chest as if to comfort her. She squirmed out of his grasp and backed off. He laughed, showing his darkened teeth and a mouth full of saliva. She backed farther away and he laughed again. "Some day my beauty, you'll find redemption in me!" Tamara winced as he continued laughing. When he opened the door, several ladies rushed in and grabbed hold of him, begging for prayers and help for salvation. The brusque spiritual leader brushed them aside with one stroke from his powerful right arm and led Tamara out of the room. Ladies followed them down the stairs, but he waved them away. Tamara's face showed her distress from the women's unbelievable display of indelicacy and, in her opinion, indecency. Rasputin only laughed and waved as they rode away.

Before when Father Gregory visited the Dashkovs, the old prince had merely tolerated him for his wife's sake; this time he was so desperate that he welcomed the holy man most kindly. He wanted any help possible for his ailing wife, especially God's. Rasputin sensed the change of attitude and knew how to take advantage of it. Once inside the bedroom, he asked for solitude, implying that everyone leave. The Princess Dashkov, holding her side in pain, uttered her thanks for his coming. The sight of the bearded peasant bending over the frail little princess in a gold gilt boudoir made Tamara feel nauseous. She gladly left.

The news of Grandmother Zhorzhadze's demise was a great sorrow for Tamara. Since the telegram was sent by Shota, it meant that he was now head of the clan. Her grandmother had suggested he would be and now it was true. Tamara thought of the Zhorzhadze clan and envisioned Somi and Shota at the estate.

The Princess Dashkov's illness helped divert Tamara's mind from the event in Georgia, but it often haunted her, bringing back many wonderful memories from her youth. "If I had married Shota as he wanted," she pined, "I would now be his Nestan and he would be my Terial."

Three days later, in spite of the prayers of the holy man and the counsel of the many doctors, the Princess Dashkov died. Since she was a Lady-in-Waiting to Her Majesty, Empress Alexandra, there was speculation about the location for the funeral. A question running through high society was, "Would the tsarina abandon her isolation and attend?" She did not, but she did ask that the funeral be held in the Cathedral of Kazan, the religious edifice used for funerals and weddings of the tsars. Prince Dashkov knew that his wife preferred the Alexandrovskaya Lavra more than any other church; besides, the Dashkov tomb was in the mausoleum on the cathedral grounds, so, in spite of the Empress's request, the funeral was held there. Two full choirs sang and Russian Orthodox chants rang out from each end of the large basilica. Princess Dashkov's ancestors dated back to the time of Alexander Nevsky and it seemed fitting that she lay on a bier near his large silver sarcophagus. Dressed in her finery and jewels, the princess appeared minuscule in the large domed expanse. Tamara prayed for the soul of her beloved benefactor and for her Grandmother Zhorzhadze. Prince Vladimir, Prince Valery and Grand Duke Alexander, representing the royal family, helped carry the coffin from the resplendant place of worship into the mausoleum. The tomb of the Dashkovs was open, waiting for the princess's noble soul.

On July 23, 1914 Austria sent Serbia an ultimatum deliberately framed so as to be unacceptable. The contents and tenor of the note created a chill all over Europe in the heat of a balmy summer. The Russian foreign minister, S.D. Sazonov, said, "C'est la guerre europeenne!" He urged extreme moderation, but the dreaded specter of war increased by the hour. Serbia accepted all the terms of the ultimatum except one: they refused the presence of Austrian officials during the judicial inquiry into the assassination of the archduke. Using the refusal of the one demand as an excuse, Austria declared war and bombed Belgrade on

July 29. Despite urgent, friendly telegrams between the German Emperor William and his Russian cousin, Emperor Nicholas, mobilization of armed forces was begun and war erupted on August 1st between the two great powers.

St. Petersburg was engulfed in a violent tide of Russian nationalism. A riotous mob stormed the German Embassy and broke up furniture, destroyed china and ruined oil paintings. German merchants closed their stores and went into hiding. The music of great German composers was banned from orchestra concerts. The Russian church banned Christmas trees, a German custom. The tsar even changed the name of the city to Petrograd, a more Slavic sounding designation.

Life in the Dashkov mansion was greatly changed during the furor of the oncoming war and its final foreboding presence. Princess Lidia was greatly missed and the old prince asked Tamara if she would mind helping the Major-Domo of the palace with the management of the large household since he would often be travelling on diplomatic duties. While she had no experience in running such a complex establishment, she accepted the responsibility without even realizing what would be expected. She was not greatly concerned because she felt that she could rely on the Major-Domo since he was used to taking care of everything; however, he abruptly joined the army and Tamara was left facing responsibilities for which she had no training. It was a shock.

Prince Vladimir was relieved from duties at court and given the rank of lieutenant in the army. Thanks to Prince Dashkov's intercession, he was stationed in a regiment at Gatchina, not far from the capital. Prince Valery also became a lieutenant, but his cavalry unit was sent immediately to the front. His departure for battle thrilled him and he was all smiles and tears as he said goodbye to his sister and the old prince. Tamara, finding herself alone in a palatial dwelling, sensed a grave foreboding about the future.

Managing the Dashkov mansion brought Tamara satisfaction and despair. She could answer some of the servants' questions quite easily, others she could not. Should the drapes be opened in the study every morning? Yes. Should the coachman continue locking up at night? Yes. Should the chef pay the butcher or should he

sign for it? She would find out. Tamara had never been concerned
with financial matters. She had always had an allowance which
was increased whenever needed, but she did not know who paid
for all the things that she had always taken for granted. Prince
Dashkov often laughed when she asked him various domestic
questions, but he always understood and kindly informed her about
the intricacies of servant relationships and banking arrangements.
Tamara tried not to show her lack of experience to the maids,
grooms, coachmen and other menials, but they realized her
inadequacies and made jokes behind her back. Conscription soon
took most of the male servants, so Tamara's task became easier. She
also relied on Prince Vladimir who was not stationed far from the
capital and helped her when the old prince was away.

   Since the war had caused an immediate cessation of grand
fetes and elegant formal dinners in private mansions, Tamara was
suddenly no longer the "belle of the ball." Managing the household
was boring and sometimes embarrassing. Her French duc had waited
too long in Paris and could not come to Russia. His messages
brought by the embassy staff were repetitious and forever full of
apologies. Her ennui was finally dissipated by the return of the
Yusupovs from their honeymoon.

   Princess Irina sent a car for Tamara the day after her arrival
from Germany. She and Felix had been in Paris on their way to
Egypt and had a gift for Tamara from the duc. The invitation was
readily accepted and the two young ladies fell into each others
arms, each giving the other the traditional three kisses on the cheeks.
At tea Irina related incidences from the honeymoon travels through
Egypt. Suddenly, while she was laughing about her ride on a camel,
a young handsome Abyssinian Negro ran into the room, grabbed
a book and bowed as he ran out. Irina looked at Tamara and raised
her eyes. She explained that while they were in Cairo this young
man named Tesphe threw a letter into their car which stated that
he was available for hire. Irina paid no attention, but when he
appeared at their hotel that evening, Felix engaged him and he was
with them the rest of the honeymoon. Tamara wondered about

the incident at Rasputin's, but said nothing. She could sense that Irina was not pleased with the situation, but felt helpless. In London, she added, Tesphe caused quite a ruckus. He sometimes slept on the floor outside their door and one morning he simply would not let the Queen Mother of

England and her sister, the Dowager Empress of Russia, into their suite. He was merely carrying out Felix's orders that the Yusupovs were not to be disturbed. Tamara laughed with her hostess. However, the more Irina related, the princess could tell that she was annoyed by the intrusions of the young servant into the Yusupovs private life.

Princess Irina tried allaying any of Tamara's fears about the Duc de Chevreuse. She assured her friend that the duc was still sincere and recounted how soulfully sorry he was that he had not come to Russia earlier. Irina had also visited the duc's mother and the Marquise could not have been more enthusiastic about the alliance between her son and the Georgian beauty. Tamara was comforted by her friend's narration and was surprised to learn that the duc had entered the French Military Intelligence Corps because his knowledge of European languages was needed. Irina was sure the duc had not told Tamara because he knew it would worry her. Felix interrupted the ladies and gave them both kisses and greetings. He handed Tamara a small box which she opened. It contained a ring with a beautiful tearshaped ruby surrounded by large diamonds. Tears filled her eyes and she looked away from her hosts. They comforted her by saying that the war would not last long and that the duc would be coming very soon. Also, since their apartment in the Moika Palace was not yet completed, they invited Tamara to join them for a week at Peterhoff, the pinkish-golden palace overlooking the Baltic Sea which Catherine the Great preferred over all palaces in the summer time. Since Prince Dashkov was on diplomatic duty in Finland, and Petrograd had turned into a city full of marching soldiers and military equipment, Tamara welcomed a rest in the country and readily accepted their generosity.

Peter the Great loved the sea and built a small palace at

Peterhoff. His daughter Empress Elizabeth enlarged it and Catherine the Great had the famous architect Rastrelli turn it into an Eighteenth-century architectural gem. Tamara was surprised that Irina was by herself when her driver brought her to the Dashkov mansion. It was arranged that Felix and Tespe would come the next day. Irina seemed unconcerned about the arrangement and expressed her pleasure that Tamara could join her. She loved the history of her ancestors and, as they drove to the palace, told Tamara about an incident during Catherine's reign. Two elderly spinsters among Her Majesty's ladies-in-waiting arranged to meet at a large statue of Adam in the park of the palace. They were late for lunch because they could not tell the difference between Adam and Eve: one had waited at the first and the other at the second. "I'll show you the statues," Irina added, "sometime when we take a walk."

Standing on a hillock Peterhoff offered a commanding view of the Baltic Sea. A large statue of Hercules fighting a lion stood in the front fountain which Catherine the Great had created in an effort to surpass the splendid fountains of Versailles. After the bustle of wartime Petrograd, the beauty and serenity of the surroundings seemed like another world. Since the palace was used only for receptions, the Yusupovs and their guest stayed in a small country house near the sea which the tsar's family occupied when attending court functions in the historic palace. When Tamara and Irina went for walks, they often strolled through the park in front of the stately mansion or visited some of its fascinating rooms. Tamara greatly admired the Amber Chamber where the large panels of carved amber given by William I to Peter the Great were displayed so artfully. Breakfast tea was usually served on a terrace overlooking the sea. One morning Irina revealed her secret. She was pregnant. Tamara's first thought was, "Can Felix do that, too?" but she controlled her amazement and wished Irina much happiness as a mother.

In Russia at the time there was a law stating that a family with only one son could have him exempted from military service. It had been created to protect peasant families who needed their son on their farm. Since Felix's older brother had been killed in a duel, he too was an only son. He used the law to stay out of military service and subjected himself to considerable criticism. The Grand Duchess Olga, Irina's cousin, visited Peterhoff while Tamara was there and wrote to her father, Nicholas II, that she was appalled that Felix was an idling civilian during such times of duress. She found Tesphe rather obnoxious because he was always staring and listening when uninvited. She also told Irina and Tamara that her mother, The Empress, was planning a hospital for the wounded and that she and her sister Tatiana were studying nursing. The idea appealed to Tamara and she asked for information, suggesting that she too would be interested. Olga was delighted and invited her to join her and Marie in their studies when she returned to St. Petersburg. Irina corrected her and said, "Petrograd." They all laughed. When the Grand Duchess left she told Tamara that she would be in touch about nurse's training. They parted as friends.

After a week of carefree hours in the magnificent park and the luxurious palace, the Yusupovs were scheduled for a visit with the Dowager Empress Marie in the Elaguine Palace, an Imperial residence located on one of the islands in the estuary of the Neva River. The Dashkov mansion was in the vicinity of Dowager Empress's residence, so they were able to drive Tamara home on their way. She refused an invitation to continue on with them to the palace, saying in jest for their amusement, that she had better check whether the chef had paid the butcher!

While the Russian army's invasion of East Prussia on August 17th had gone well at first, it soon faced major defeats because of its ineptness, unpreparedness, mismanagement and lack of coordination. On August 30th two army corps of the noted General Samsonov were entrapped by the Germans in a wooded region named Tannenberg. Over 300,000 men and 650 were lost. The general shot himself rather than face humiliation. The catastrophe greatly demoralized the Russians and confirmed the belief in the invincibility of the German military machine.

News that her brother Valery had been wounded during the

East Prussia campaign reached Tamara on her return from
Peterhoff. Prince Dashkov, through his diplomatic prestige,
located Valery in the "Their Imperial Highnesses Grand Duchesses Maria Nikolayevna and Tatiana Nikolayevna Hospital for
Wounded Soldiers" which was attached to the Church of Our Lady
of Feodorovo in Tsarskoe Selo. The reality of war came quickly to
Tamara. When she with the countess and the old prince arrived at
the hospital, they were informed that Valery's condition was very
serious and he could not be visited. After much pleading, they
were allowed to view him from a distance. A nurse led them through
several rooms of beds full of wounded soldiers. Finally they came
to a closed door. Through the windows they saw two bandaged
men lying very still in their beds. With tears in her eyes, Tamara
asked, "Which is my brother?" The nurse pointed to the right.
Valery lay like a mummy. An artillery shell had exploded near his
horse, hitting him with shrapnel and knocking him to the ground.
"Will he live?" Tamara faintly asked. The nurse didn't answer. The
old prince placed an arm on Tamara's shoulder and she leaned
against him, crying softly. He patted her and she looked back
through the window. Where was all that enthusiasm? that youth?
that "joie de vivre?" Prince Dashkov led her away, followed by the
woeful countess.

When the Yusupovs were informed about Valery, they did everything in their power to help Tamara. Felix arranged for her to
stay in his bachelor apartment on the third floor of the white baroque palace where she had visited in Tsarskoe Selo. Irina contacted her cousin, Grand Duchess Olga, who scheduled medical
nurse's training for Tamara. She had Anna Viroubova, a close friend
and confident of her mother, the Empress, enroll Tamara in the
intensive two month course that she directed in the hospital. In
short order the princess was near her brother and studying techniques that might help him later. Daily, when free from her lessons, she watched through the window of his room and prayed for
his recovery.

During her training Tamara became better acquainted with

the Grand Duchess Olga who introduced her to her sister Tatiana. Both the young ladies were tall, thin and attractive. Their modesty and sincerity impressed Tamara and she appreciated their help with her brother. Olga kept Tamara informed about his condition when the princess would not have free time during her training. One day when Tamara was tying a bandage on a wounded man's arm, Olga came in with Anna Vrubova; both had very serious expressions on their faces. Olga came directly to Tamara while Anna talked with the nurse in charge. Valery was asking for his sister and they had come for her. Another student took over Tamara's patient and she left with the grand duchess. Valery had never talked with her before and she was fearful of what it meant. She didn't ask Olga questions because of her fear. They hurried to the ward and Tamara was admitted by herself.

Approaching close to Valery, she understood the severity of his wounds. His body seemed encased in bandages and only the right side of his face was uncovered. The doctor stopped her and whispered that Valery was dying. Tears filled Tamara's eyes. She stepped by his side and looked into his eye. He recognized her and tried to smile, but his strength gave out. "Don't talk, Valery," she said. "I'm here and I love you."

The right side of his mouth opened and he uttered. "Tamarochka, bury me at grandmother's, please."

Tamara choked a cry. "Yes, Valery, but don't think—"

His eye closed and she realized he was dead. Her cry rent the hearts of the nurse and doctor, experienced though they were.

Since Valery was a veteran and a noble, Prince Dashkov was able to arrange passage on a military train for the countess and Tamara. The latter dreaded the long trip to Tiflis with the former, but it could not be helped. During the five day journey Tamara noticed the change taking place in Russia. Cities seemed filled with marching columns of men, railroad stations were crowded with military personnel, and in the countryside the fields had women and children laborers. While the two ladies had a first class compartment, going to the dining car was difficult. Tamara thought the countess enjoyed the comments and teasing of the soldiers when they walked through their coaches, but she dreaded going for each meal. There was no room service and the food on the train was for soldiers, not first class passengers. When Tamara remembered the private coach of the Yusupovs, she realized how fortunate she had been before.

During the trip the countess rarely mentioned her husband and Tamara was sorry that her uncle's administrative duties at the Cadet Corps kept him from joining them. The countess did press Tamara for information about the Duc de Chevreuse, but there was little she could give. She still heard from him through the French Embassy, but he told her very little aside from repeating over and over his love and devotion for her. His gifts had been resplendent, but his overdoing the emotional factor had caused a feeling of triteness. They actually knew very little about each other and Tamara wondered at times if they really were in love. What is it anyway, she asked herself, what I felt for Shota or for the duc? Must one just be a jewel in their milieu?

At the train station in Tiflis, Count Bagrov, now a colonel in the army, met the visitors. The countess had not informed Tamara that she had wired him about their coming, but actually he became an asset. In spite of her resentment of him, Tamara appreciated his making the arrangements for transporting Valery's body to Mtsety for the funeral. He also had Luda open up part of the Trushinsky's mansion for the ladies. When they arrived there, the old cook opened the door and Tamara fell into her arms, crying. Luda caressed her beloved child and said, "How's my tsarina." Through her tears, Tamara gave a short laugh and hugged the old friend again.

Count Bagrov drove the countess and Tamara to Mtsety for the funeral at the Samtavriskaia Cathedral, the location of the Zhorzhadze tombs. When the car passed the ruins of Dvzhari Church on the precipice overlooking Mtsety, Tamara cried, remembering how she and Valery usually stopped there and prayed for the souls of their ancestors. They drove to her grandmother's estate and were greeted in the courtyard by Somi. Tamara fell into her arms and cried, as her cousin led her into the old wing of the house. Somi now ruled in that area so long occupied by their grandmother. When they reached the courtyard, Somi asked, "My dearest Tamarochka have you ever forgiven me for marrying Shota?" Tamara looked up at her friend and smiled, wiping the tears from her eyes. "It had to be," she replied and they embraced. "Where is Shota?"

When the war started a regiment of Georgian soldiers had formed and was now training at Piatiagorsk. Shota would not be at the funeral. Tamara concluded that fate had decided for the best. If she saw her beloved, it would only make it harder for her, and she had enough to endure at the moment. Walking around the large old mansion, memories of her youth with grandmother and her cousins returned. When she looked up at the room that Shota had climbed in, she recalled his tempestuousness and shuddered thinking of his burning kisses. Several times she asked herself, "Oh, why did I ever leave?"

The Zhorzhadze clan collected for the burial of one of their warriors. They marched in a group through the ancient town as if they were going to the racing ground except this time they were all in black and silent. At the cathedral guests stood on the large stone engraved blocks in the floor which commemorated fallen heroes and famous writers: Bagration, who fell at the Battle of Borodino; Cholakashvili, the famous lyric and dramatist; and Chavchavadze, whose songs were still sung in Georgia. The priests performed the funeral service and Valery's unopened coffin was carried into the catacombs below the church to the Zhorzhadze sanctuary. He would lie by his beloved grandmother for eternity.

After the ceremony the clan feasted at the family mansion. Somi took Tamara aside for a chat because she wanted to share her secret. She was pregnant. Tamara, eyes tearing, gasped and embraced her cousin. "Oh, I'm so happy for you," she whispered, thrilled that Shota would have a son and sure that a child of Shota's

could only be of masculine gender. She asked if Shota knew and
Somi shook her head. She would tell him when he returned from
training. "How happy he will be," Tamara said, smiling and envi-
sioning her Terial holding up his son. Somi changed the subject
because, she was curious about Tamara's engagement to a French
duc. Did it mean that her cousin would live in France and not
come back to the Caucasus? Tamara assured her that they would
always be close and that she would visit. She also shared her secret:
she was not sure she would marry the duc. The war had made
everything so confusing and the past seemed to be slipping away
as if it never happened. So she told Somi that nothing was settled,
but that if she did marry the duc, she would never forget her
homeland. They walked back to the family arm in arm.

Back in Tiflis the countess decided that she would prefer spending a few days of rest before making the long journey back to
Petrograd. Tamara knew the reason was the count, but she too did
not mind. Most of her time was spent with Luda, hearing about
the old woman's grandchildren and ailments. The princess did call
on her old friend Nina Cherkessky, but found out, to her amazement, that Nina had married an officer and was living in Kiev.
Tamara had not been invited to the wedding because it had taken
place so quickly. Nina's husband was being transferred and he
wanted her with him. A simple civil marriage was arranged and
they left for his station. Tamara could hardly believe that there had
not been a church ceremony, but as the Countess Cherkessky said,
"It's these times!" Tamara nodded knowingly and took Nina's address. When she saw Nina's new name, Plotnik, she knew her friend
had married a peasant. Rather than embarrass Nina's mother,
Tamara did not ask questions and departed.

Returning to Petrograd required nine days of travel due to
heavy military transportation that continually took preference over
regular passenger trains. Tamara and the countess were forced to
share a compartment with two other women who were bourgeois.
Tamara was polite when they asked questions, but the countess
answered condescendingly and they soon left her alone. The cool

atmosphere that developed in the cabin was heightened by the countess's speaking only French with her niece. The two ladies would eye each other and make faces indicating that they considered the countess a snob. Fortunately they left the train in Kiev and no one took their place. The countess and Tamara arrived at their destination exhausted.

Tamara could not return to the place where Valery had died. She knew that the Yusupovs had opened a hospital named "The Saviors of Russia," in a palace they rarely used on the Fontanka in Petrograd. Since she had finished a few weeks of nurse's training before departing for Tiflis, she was sure she could qualify as a nurse's aid. She contacted Princess Irina and found out that she was suffering from measles. Being pregnant it was a serious affair. Princess Zenaida, who was watching after her daughter-in-law, made arrangements for Tamara to work at their medical facility and informed her that Felix would escort her. WheneFelix came for Tamara in his open-air Damlier, she could hardly believe her eyes because he was dressed in the military uniform of the Cadet Corps. He explained that he was taking military training at the institution. Tamara congratulated him, not knowing that he was purposely flunking every exam so that he would not qualify for a commission at the front. As he drove to the hospital, he told her about Irina's condition and asked her to pray for his wife. Tamara turned her head so that he wouldn't see her smile. She loved Irina, but the thought of Felix asking prayers for her somehow seemed absurd. He introduced her to the hospital staff and left, saying that Irina would like her company at any time.

Fall turned into winter early in 1914. Snow fell at the beginning of November, a bad month for the Allied Forces. On November 18th, Turkey declared war on the side of the Entente which meant that the Dardanelles were blocked to Russian shipping. News from the fronts was varied, success in Galicia, failure in Prussia. With the cold weather came an uneasiness among Russians. The malaise was caused by the realization that the war would not end as quickly as assumed and that it might even be disastrous.

Tamara lost herself in her duties at the Dashkov mansion and at the "Saviors of Russia." She rolled bandages, delivered drink and food to bedsides, wrote up reports for doctors. Occasionally she would visit Irina or the countess. The former had isolated herself because of her visible pregnancy and was therefore delighted for her friend's visits. The latter was still attending seances where prophecies were the rule of the day. For Tamara, both Irina and the countess seemed in different worlds from hers. She had the wearisome tasks of bedpans and paying the butcher. There was no time for a new generation or ridiculous predictions.

One day the princess went home from the hospital and found the French Ambassador waiting in the salon. She could hardly believe her ears when told that the ambassador himself had come. Always before a clerk in some department would deliver messages from the duc, so she knew that something important had occurred. Her first thought was that the duc was coming via Finland and she rushed into the salon. The ambassador, a tall , thin man elegantly dressed, stood up and bowed. Tamara greeted him with a look of surprise. He asked her to be seated and she sat in a Louis XV chair next to him. The furniture and paintings in the room had attracted his attention and he commented on the Fragonard hanging over the fireplace. Tamara wished he would tell her his purpose in coming, but answered his questions kindly. Finally he said it, "Ma chere, I have brought terrible news. I must most sadly inform you that the Duc de Chevreuse was killed in a bomb blast near the front."

Tamara only stared. No tears came to her eyes. She knew at that moment that she had never loved the duc and had only been deceiving herself. She expressed her remorse to the ambassador, but even he noticed that she did not seem overwrought. He continued by saying that the duc had provided for Tamara in his will and that she would be informed by his lawyers the extent of the provisions. Tamara did not hear him, but nodded when he finished talking. He departed after saying, "I know you have just had a terrible shock, so I shall not detain you."

Tamara walked around the salon, looking in the great goldgilt mirrors, lost in thought. The news seemed strange. Who was that man whom I thought I loved? Did I really meet a French duc and promise to be his wife? Was I really going to live in France? And what am I to do now? She glanced at herself again and said aloud, "Au revoir Duchesse de Chevreuse!"

CHAPTER 4

1915

Layers of ice on deep snow covered Petrograd during January of 1915. Few vehicles could manage the deep ruts on many streets and horses strained pulling carriages or sleighs. Prince Dashkov and Tamara usually ate dinner together by a fireplace in a small study of the Dashkov palace. The edifice was not well heated because of the conservation of firewood. Keeping warm was difficult, so they sometimes ate in coats and scarfs as they discussed the war. The news from the front was frightening and a sad foreboding was developing through out the city.

Prince Dashkov often talked about his family's duty to the tsar. The old prince still believed in the traditional concept of the ruler as God's representative on earth. The tsar was the spiritual father of his people, guided by God. The prince did feel that Nicholas II was too greatly influenced by the Empress, but he blamed the bureaucracy for the problems in the country. When he heard people speak contemptuously about Nicholas II's weakness and vacillation, he would defend the tsar. He felt, as many conservative Russians did, that Nicholas could triumph if the wall of bureaucracy keeping him from his people and duties could be broken down. Then the tsar could chart a clear course between despotism and republicanism in Russia's encounter with modernity. The prince retained the mystical reverence for the tsar as God's mediator with mankind.

At the "Saviors of Russia," Tamara, because of her education and knowledge of French and Georgian, was used more and more in the administrative office of the hospital rather than in the wards. She filled out forms for patients who were illiterate and wrote up diagnoses for doctors. She often had trouble deciphering the handwriting of a Dr. Sergey Frolov whom she would contact about a particular phrase or word. He was a stout, brown haired man with a pleasant face, but he was always very serious. She attributed his attitude to his terrible work load and to the ghastly operations he performed almost daily. Consequently, she was very surprised one day when he suddenly asked her during one of their conferences if she would accompany him to a literary society meeting after work the next day. She asked, "What society is it?"

"The Acmeists," he replied.

A puzzled look came on Tamara's face.

"It's the new literature. I'll tell you about it."

Tamara remembered being asked about Merezhkovsky in Paris and how embarrassed she had been for not knowing current Russian literature. She thought it would be interesting and there seemed no reason for refusal. In such times the stigma of class differences was ridiculous and the countess could hardly complain. Just look at the life she was leading! Tamara accepted and noticed the first smile she had seen on the doctor's face.

Dr. Frolov was from a merchant's family of moderate means. He had become a doctor through great difficulties and was devoted to his work. He had observed Tamara for some time and was entranced by her beauty. While he never commented about her appearance, he sometimes messed up his penmanship so that she would be forced to talk with him. He knew that she was an aristocrat, but he was not aware of her close relationship with the Yusupovs, the benefactors of the hospital. Since he had a close working relationship with Tamara, he felt that the class barrier was no longer a problem and chanced an invitation. Her acceptance greatly pleased him.

After finishing her reports for the day, Tamara waited in the hospital office for Dr. Frolov. She had told the old prince that she would be late, implying that her work at the hospital would detain her. So, she was having an adventure on her own and nobody knew. She had brought some pastries and prepared tea. Dr. Frolov came and they shared a small repast before leaving. While they drank, the doctor explained the new literary movement called Acmeism.

The "Acmeists" were a group of diverse literary talents who were unified only by their distaste for the abstractness in the Symbolist movement of Russian literature. They berated poets who sought hidden meanings in every word or phrase. They wanted concreteness. They wanted to admire a rose because of its beauty, not as a symbol of mystical purity. The Symbolists, who had dominated Russian literature since the turn of the century, were becoming unpopular because of the realities of the war. The psychological change in peoples' attitudes determined a new aesthetics. Acmeism stood for classical purity; something intellectuals could readily understand.

"What does Merezhkovsky say about Acmeism," she asked.

"It's making him passe and he knows it. Have you met him?"

Tamara shook her head.

"Would you like to meet him?"

"You know him?'"

The doctor mentioned that he had met the noted writer and that they have a mutual friend. "He might be at the meeting this evening."

Tamara and the doctor went to a working class section of Petrograd in a landau and entered a four-storied run down building. A large meeting hall on the second floor had about thirty-five adults waiting for the speaker. Just as Tamara and the doctor sat down in the back, the president of the society, "The Poet's Guild," N.S. Gumilev, a short, stout baldish man entered and went up to the podium. He greeted the audience and started the meeting with announcements. With a grin on his face, he stated that at their next monthly meeting they would have a poet who had survived Symbolism and was now definitely in the Acmeist camp: Michael

Kuzmin. Several in the audience laughed and several applauded. Mr. Gumilev shook his finger at one man who was laughing and said, "Our colleague has made a true contribution to Russian letters, let's not forget that."

Tamara whispered to the doctor, "Whom are they talking about?"

"Later," he whispered back and they listened as Gumilev discussed the necessity of formal perfection in poetry. Vagueness was unrealistic and the mystical a metaphysical artifice. He read some of his own poems based on his extensive travels in Africa and Europe. Romantic scenes and exotic landscapes were presented in well-controlled, precise lines. His themes were a fullness of being, struggle, fulfillment and a restraint of emotion. He believed that poets should be men of action and therefore they should use more verbs than adjectives in their poetic endeavors.

Tamara had never heard such an intellectual discussion of literature. Her tutor in Russian letters had concentrated on the masters of the 19th century. She knew Pushkin, Gogol, Tolstoy and Chekhov, but she was oblivious to contemporary trends. The speech fascinated her. The war, Irina's pregnancy, the old prince, the hospital—everything was forgotten during the lecture and subsequent questions.

After the meeting the doctor introduced Tamara by her first name only to several people who had been seated near them. He mentioned whether the person he was introducing was a writer or a journalist. Her beauty caused many to stare and a few asked who she was. The doctor only mentioned that she was an assistant in his hospital. He wanted to present Tamara to the speaker, but it was already eight o'clock. As they left, Tamara asked, "What makes you so interested in literature?"

As they left, he explained that as a doctor he often had life or death in his hands. The religious meaning of life did not satisfy him and he was looking for meaning in philosophy. Poets were known for their sensitivity and clairvoyance and he found their ideas challenging. His yearning for understanding impressed Tamara and she felt as if something new and fine had come into her life. She thanked him kindly for inviting her and asked to be taken back to the hospital. He offered to take her home, but the thought of driving into the courtyard of the Dashkov mansion with him bothered her. They parted at the medical facility. She was delighted that the doctor had no ulterior motive in his invitation. It was the first unchaperoned outing in her life and there had been no problems. It made her feel quite mature. The hospital doorman hailed her a coach.

The next Sunday Tamara was invited to the Moika Palace for an afternoon with Princess Irina. The physicians had assured her of an uncomplicated birth and she seemed radiant. The two ladies chatted away the afternoon. When Felix joined them for tea Tamara told them about the "Guild of Poets."

"They're all decadent!" Felix commented with a wry smile. "The stuff they write is tasteless and absurd."

"They're trying to say something new," Tamara protested.

Felix laughed sarcastically. "Remember how the son of the famous historian Solovyev wandered around the desert in Egypt all dressed in black looking for the Goddess of Wisdom, Sophia? Bedouins almost killed him, thinking he was the devil.

Tamara shook her head.

"Well, he's just a typical malheure among them."

Tamara put forth a rebuttal, trying to remember Gumilev's theories on perfection in art: that it must have classical purity in form and meaning.

"Oh, that's neo-Classicism. Nothing new."

Tamara surrendered. She realized she could not make a point with Felix and was sorry she had tried. He always knew it all and usually he was right. She greatly respected his knowledge of the arts, but this time, she thought, he was being unfair in not letting her give her understanding of the new trend.

Felix noticed her submission. "Tell you what, Tamara, he said, "There's a new exhibition of avant garde art. Would you really like to see what's happening in the creative world?"

Irina interrupted. "Yes, Tamara, do go with us. I'm going to wrap up in fur so that no one will see."

Tamara smiled, then nodded.

"Lovely," Irina commented and added, "Now, let's play cards!" They agreed. A servant brought in an inlaid Italian marble table and set chairs around it. Tamara could hardly concentrate on the cards as the hospital and the poets' guild crowded her mind. How odd it seemed to be flitting away time playing cards in a palace when bombs were bursting at the front and the hospital was full of wounded men. Suddenly she laughed. Irina and Felix looked at her and she said, "I'm sorry, but I just realized how ridiculous the world is. Poets are seeking perfection while destruction is raging all around them. Is that not peculiar."

"Oh, they're all decadent," Felix said, repeating his assessment and shrugging his shoulders.

Tamara almost laughed, but controlled herself. 'He should call THEM decadent!' she thought and trumped his ace.

During the Spring of 1915 the "Saviors of Russia" filled up with wounded. Dr. Frolov's written reports became brief and short; there wasn't time for thorough diagnoses. With less paper work, Tamara spent more time in the wards helping nurses attend the wounded. One day on the casualty list in the "St. Petersburg Times" she noticed Prince Pavel Voroshilov; the next day, Count Igor Perovsky. The flower of Russian youth was being wasted away. She remembered Peter's declaration of eternal love and the haughty temperament of Igor. No more would Peter ask if he still had a chance; no more would Igor brag about his ancestors. At least her uncle Vadim was not on the list. Reading the casualties every day, she sensed fears and anxieties that she had never known before. It was as if a new and empty world was developing around her, and it did not have Acmeist perfection.

Count Trushinsky returned to Petrograd on leave and the countess asked Tamara for his homecoming dinner. She was thrilled that her dear uncle was safe. The count related horrible stories about his experiences. Tears even came into his eyes as he talked about the lack of supplies and materials. Over half of his cadet corps seniors was now deceased and a third wounded. Tamara mentioned Voroshilov and Perovsky. The count only shook his head and said, "A page of the tsar and another cadet. Russia is losing a generation."

Countess Trushinsky had waited patiently for the count to unburden himself from the horrors he had seen and encountered. When Tamara and her husband quit talking about the war, she said, "Father Gregory has a wonderful idea for me." The count and the princess looked at her, waiting for the revelation. "He thinks that I could serve my country very well by following in my niece's example. I want to become a nurse." While the count congratulated his wife, Tamara realized why the countess had invited her for dinner: Aunt Zita wanted something. "Since you know the Yusupovs so well, ma chere, I know you won't mind asking them to help me."

"What could they do? You can easily take nurse's training at any hospital."

"But I would like to work with you and its their hospital."

"They rarely come there. Besides, you don't need them to sponsor you. We are so short of help, your efforts will be most welcome, I'm sure."

"Why thank you; chere! I shall tell Father Gregory that I'm taking his advice."

Tamara wondered what the scheme was. She knew that Felix had ceased visiting the so-called holy man. Was Father Gregory trying some sort of intrigue through her aunt? Tamara could not believe that her aunt was sincerely interested in helping others since her whole life had been spent in self-gratification. It all seemed peculiar, but the princess said nothing. The next day the countess appeared at the "Saviors of Russia" and Tamara introduced her to the nurse in charge of training. If there was a scheme, it was starting.

On Sunday afternoon Irina, Felix and Grand Duke Dmitry came for Tamara at the Dashkovs. Tamara wore Princess Dashkov's "breitschwanz" ensemble, made of unborn Persian lambs, smooth as silk. It could not match Irina's sable wrap or Felix's bear coat, but it looked distinguished, especially contrasted with Dmitry's military uniform. When they entered the Dobychin Gallery a few blocks from the Winter Palace, guests looked more at the foursome than at the exhibition which was called, "The Last Futurists Exhibition of Paintings: 0–10."

Felix shook his head as they walked around the gallery. He and Dmitry exchanged snide remarks in French. The walls were covered with canvases painted with colored cubes and strange geometrical structures of metal and wood. Through the gallery windows one could see the intricate fencing of the Summer Garden of the tsars and the columns of palaces from the time of Catherine the Great. The contrast between the fine art of the past and the new creations was immense, certainly not for the taste of an aesthete like Felix. He could only smirk and whisper trite phrases to Dmitry.

To be companionable, Tamara smiled at Felix's remarks and traded comments with Irina, but she was also curious about the true nature of the exhibition. Were the artists represented in the show the same as the poet she had heard? Were they, too, seeking something new, apart from emotional nuances or the mystical? She knew she could not ask Felix because he would only scoff; she decided she would ask Dr. Frolov.

Tamara's delving into the intellectual currents of the time was suddenly set aside by the illness of Prince Dashkov. When the Yusupovs took her home after a repast in "The Bear," she learned from a servant that the old prince had retired early because he was not feeling well. She did not wish to disturb him and retired herself. The next morning the prince did not appear for tea in the heated study, and when his valet informed her that Prince Dashkov had a severe fever, Tamara invaded his sanctuary. When she saw the prince, she was immediately alarmed. Anyone whose face was so flushed in the hospital would be taken to a special ward. She knew something drastic was ailing him and that a doctor must be called in spite of the old prince's objections. When the physician came, he was the same old man who had aided the late Princess Dashkov and Tamara was concerned, especially when the diagnosis was a slight chill. She decided on bringing in Dr. Frolov for a second opinion.

At the hospital the doctor was in surgery. Tamara worked on his papers until he finished. She told him about her relative's plight, but he had several operations yet that day. When he noticed how distraught she was, he said that he would go home with her in the late afternoon. At that moment the countess came in, apparently quite upset, and interrupted the conversation. "Ma chere, you didn't tell me what an impossible woman that head nurse is!"

Tamara was embarrassed, but asked what was wrong. The doctor, to Tamara's relief, left without waiting for an introduction.

"She always finds fault with what I do, no matter what it is! I won't be criticized all the time in front of those creatures."

Tamara almost laughed. Vanity in times like these! She assured her aunt that the head nurse was competent and that she herself made many errors while in training. She recommended that Zita remember the war and not pay any attention to criticism. "Besides," she added, knowing how to calm her aunt, "You go home everyday a countess, your colleagues are just nurses."

The comment worked and Zita walked back into the training area with her head high and condescension in tact.

Dr. Frolov and Tamara arrived at the Dashkov mansion in the late afternoon. "You live here?" he commented when their carriage drove into the courtyard. Tamara only confirmed his observation and led him into the great hall. As they went up the stairs, the doctor looked in every direction, amazed at the wealth around him. The old prince seemed asleep when they entered the room, but the doctor took one look at the deep red face and hands of the patient and whispered, "I fear it's diphtheria" The servant attendant moved away from the bed, saying that the old prince had been asleep for some time. The doctor's fears were certain. The old prince's jaw had locked and his fever was extremely high. "Tamara Borisovna," he whispered, slightly shaking his head, "he is dying."

"Is there nothing you can do?"

"It's too late."

The doctor was correct. In minutes the old prince expired. Tears glistened in Tamara's eyes and she covered her face with hands. As she walked away from the bed, Dr. Frolov put his arm around her and led her out of the room. At the base of the large curved stairway, Tamara turned and put her head on his shoulder. He patted her and expressed his regret. When she looked up into his eyes, he could not control himself and started to kiss her. She quickly turned her head and whispered, "Not now." He held her tightly until a servant came.

At the headquarters of the general staff, Count Trushinsky arranged the return of Prince Vladimir Dashkov from the front. The Department of Foreign Affairs prepared the arrangements for the funeral and once again a prince of ancient heritage who had served his God, tsar and country was laid to rest in the mausoleum at the Aleksandrovskia Lavra. Because of the war, the ceremony was simple, but decorous. The old prince had served his country as a distinguished diplomat for many years. In spite of his age and ailing health, his tact, sophistication and knowledge had been relied upon in many extreme situations. He would be missed.

While Prince Vladimir was home for only a few days, Tamara sensed a change in him. Aside from his fatigue, she noticed that he was not arrogant or demanding; he was even kind. In conversations, he did not always uphold his haughty fiancé, Princess Olga Vorontsova; in his dealings with the servants, he was straightforward and respectful; and in making plans for the future, he was considerate and generous. When, after the funeral, Tamara sat down with him and his fiancé for a discussion of family matters, the prince asked Tamara if she would please continue living in the mansion. She would not be alone. He had already asked the Count and Countess Trushinsky to move in and they had agreed. Much of the house would be closed, but he wanted a continuation of her supervision over the main part of the huge building. He thanked her kindly for the help she had given his parents, especially his father after the death of the princess. Tamara found it strange that nothing was said about the marriage between him and Olga. Since the latter did not object to her staying on in the mansion, Tamara decided that their wedding had been postponed. Since Vladimir had been so kind, she agreed to stay, even though the thought of living with the countess in the huge edifice was worrisome.

On March 8th a car from the Yusupovs arrived at the "Saviors of Russia." The chauffeur brought in a note and the head administrator told Tamara that she was wanted at the Moika Palace. When she arrived, Felix met her on the stairway and burst out with joy, "It's a girl!" Irina had given birth that morning and wanted Tamara to see the child. She was led into a boudoir and found Irina sitting in bed holding the baby. Tamara smiled and congratulated the princess as she leaned over her and kissed her forehead. She looked down at the baby and asked, "What have you named her?"

"Irina, after me"

Tamara smiled and patted the head of the new heiress to the greatest fortune in Russia.

When Felix drove Tamara back to the hospital, he told her that the birth had been normal, but that they probably would not have more children. Tamara wondered what his comment implied, but could not ask. He also implored Tamara to visit more often. He stated that since the tsar had made his father Governor of Moscow, his parents would be taking up residence in their old palace there. Consequently, he and Irina would be much alone on the Moika. "Irina will need you," he concluded.

By the summer of 1915 shortages of materials and foodstuffs on the home front and on the battlefields were severe and special councils were established for national defense. The councils supervised the mobilization of industry, transportation, fuel and produce. In the beginning the ministers and administrators of these governmental units were honest and forthright because of their patriotism. As conditions worsened, those same upright citizens lost faith and were susceptible to intrigue, corruption and bribery.

The great bureaucracy that was created in establishing the councils became unwieldy due to incompetence and lack of unity.

At the hospital Tamara first ran into the bureaucratic morass when she ordered new mattresses for various wards. There were priorities for such materials and a private hospital could obtain them only by applying to the industry council. That application needed approval by the overall governing council of the councils. That council could accept only military orders. It soon became obvious that there was no way the hospital could receive the merchandise. Tamara turned the matter over to Felix and for the first time in his life, he was not able to buy what he wanted. However, money, as always, spoke loudly and he was able to procure the mattresses via the black market.

Dr. Frolov had shied away from Tamara after visiting the old prince at the Dashkov mansion. She sensed a change in his attitude toward her immediately after continuing her duties in the hospital. He was cordial and polite, but he did not talk much with her. When she did look into his eyes, he looked away. Their class variance had made a difference. She regretted his attitude and felt it was absurd in a world that seemed doomed for chaos. Besides, who cared? Her friend Nina had even married a peasant. Yet she did not know what she should do. It was not in her nature to be forward, but one day she simply asked, "Does the 'Guild of Poets' still meet?"

"It hasn't since Gumilev went into the army. Others might continue the meetings. Are you interested?"

"Very much."

His weary face smiled.

"At the last meeting they mentioned another poet. You told me you'd tell me about him later."

To Tamara's surprise, Dr. Frolov laughed. "Oh, Kuzmin. I doubt that he'll read. Gumilev was just being kind in allowing him an audience."

"Why?"

"He's a pure aesthete. His poetry is considered decadent, but he's a good writer. His novel "Travelers by Land and Sea" has just been published.

"Have you read it?"

"No, and I won't. It's not for you or me." He looked away and then added, "I'll let you know if there's another meeting."

Tamara thanked him and wondered if she had done the right thing. Two days later he mentioned that the "Guild of Poets" was having a meeting the next evening. They would go.

The next morning when Tamara told the countess that she would be late that evening, Zita asked why. Tamara did not commit herself fully and aroused the suspicions of her aunt. When Tamara met Dr. Frolov at the office that morning, she realized that she was looking forward to being with him that evening. During the day when he would enter and leave some papers or come for reports on patients, she would observe every move he made: scratching the back of his neck as he read something, pursing his lips when something did not seem correct, and shrugging his shoulders when something seemed beyond his control. Tamara knew that she was falling in love. She had not experienced such feelings since she parted with Shota.

After work the two friends hailed a coachman, not knowing that the countess was watching from a landau across the street. Riding to the meeting in the brisk April air, Tamara suggested to the doctor that he not use her title if he introduced her to anyone; he agreed, and asked if she would call him Sergey; she agreed, smiling and placing her arm inside his. They sat close and quiet the rest of the trip. As they entered the hall of the "Guild of Poets," a short, red-haired woman in a lavender dress with green make-up around her greenish eyes came up to Dr. Frolov and said in a voice Tamara found very affected, "Sergey, we haven't seen you in ages."

"Tamara, allow me to present the distinguished poet Zinaida Hippius."

The princess extended her greetings, noticing that the woman before her was observing her face most steadily. "Where did you find such a marvelous specimen?" the poet asked. Dr. Frolov grinned and said to Tamara, "Don't mind Zinaida, she has a way with words."

"No, really. Since we are leaving for the Caucasus, I was enchanted to see such a Georgian beauty among us."

"You're leaving?" the doctor asked.

Zinaida nodded and explained that she and her husband, D.S. Merezhkovsky, were disgusted with everything that was going on in Russia and had decided on settling away from all the horrors and disorder that were taking place. The doctor asked if her husband was present and she shook her head. "Headaches. Another reason we must get away." Zinaida suddenly excused herself and went to another man coming into the hall. The doctor led Tamara to a seat and whispered, "Don't mind her, she's always like that."

Since Gumilev was serving at the front, his wife, Anna Gorenko, who wrote poetry under the name Anna Akhmatova, conducted the meeting. The short, dark-haired woman ascended the podium and announced that there had been a change in the program. That evening the young Futurist poet Evgeny Essenin would talk. A very handsome, well-built blonde-headed young man stood up and began his talk by reading one of his poems. His language showed that he was a peasant, but as a village bard he was charming and his lyricism flowed out in poetic lines full of melancholy and nostalgia. One could not help but be entranced by such a vibrant figure. Tamara thought of Oleg Dunatov at the Dashkov estate in the Ukraine. He did not resemble the poet, but the naturalness and simplicity of his manner seemed the same. The audience applauded the young poet enthusiastically.

When their carriage arrived at the Dashkov mansion, Dr. Frolov thanked Tamara for going with him. He took her hand and pressed it, causing her to shiver. She expected an embrace, but it did not come. After an awkward moment, he stepped out of the carriage and helped her down. He led her to the door and they parted: she, wondering why he hesitated; he, knowing that he had no right for what he wanted.

As Tamara went up the grand staircase to her boudoir, she saw the countess on the upper landing. She did not speak until Tamara neared her and then invited the princess into her suite.

The niece followed her aunt and faced the outpouring of contempt that she expected. The countess was appalled that Tamara had forsaken everything that her name stood for.

"And how have I desecrated my honor?"

"As an aristocrat of royal blood you, of all people, should ask such a question. With your name you inherited the highest principles mankind has ever imposed."

"You, too, are an aristocrat. Are you upholding those principles when you cower before that so-called holy man!"

The countess's eyes flashed and she sat down on a boudoir stool. "How could you judge Father Gregory's teachings. He has the sanction of God Almighty. I am thrilled in his presence."

Tamara laughed and looked away.

"I will not have you making fun of that holy man!"

"Nor will I have you judge me for going out with Dr. Frolov!"

"And where did you go, may I ask? And what did you do?"

Tamara related the activities of the evening. As she spoke, the countess gradually calmed, picked up a brush and began stroking her hair. When Tamara finished, the countess asked, "Has he taken liberties with you?"

"No, he hasn't, but I wish he would."

The countess's jaw fell, showing her disbelief. "What are you saying?"

"I'm saying that I want to marry Dr. Frolov."

The countess dropped her hairbrush and put her right hand on her forehead. "You wouldn't. Surely you wouldn't. You, who were to be the Duchesse de Crevreuse? Oh, you couldn't!"

Tamara began speaking slowly as if forming her thoughts as she spoke. "Aunt Zita, you are living in a world that no longer exits. The duc is dead, Valery is dead, Shota is married, Pavel Veroshilov and Igor Perovsky are dead. Everyone's dead. Why shouldn't I enjoy the man I love while we are still alive. For all I know, we'll all be dead soon. Does it matter whether I am a princess or a wife in these times." She paused and walked over by the door. "Don't worry, my faith and my virtue are still in tact, but with the world falling apart, I'm wondering how much longer I can believe in them."

The countess stood up. "You've upset me very much. Let's continue another time. There's still so much you don't understand."

"You're right. I do not understand how you could deceive my dearest uncle and pretend to be so religious and forthright."

The countess's jaw dropped again, but before she could speak, Tamara left the room.

In June, 1915 anti-German riots spread all over Moscow. German merchants were stoned and their businesses badly damaged. The Grand Duchess Elizabeth, Danish by birth and the sister of the Dowager Empress, was in the "Convent of Mary and Martha" when a mob threw stones yelling for her arrest as a German agent. Since she had been a nun since her husband Grand Duke Sergey was blown up by a terrorist bomb in 1909, the accusations were even more ridiculous, but showed the unthinking hatred developing in the country. A large mob outside the Moscow Kremlin demanded the execution of Rasputin and the arrest of the Empress Alexandra as a German spy. Shouts and placards saying, "Away with the German Woman!" and "Arrest the German Whore!" were heard and seen among the angry protestors. When the Empress Alexandra heard what had occurred, she demanded that Prince Yusupov be fired for his inability to control crowds. The tsar carried out her wishes and invited the prince for a conference. Realizing the tsar's intentions, Prince Yusupov used the opportunity for a severe criticism of Rasputin, showing his disgust that the royal family was under the control of such an unscrupulous, corrupt fiend. In spite of Yusupov's earnest and well-meaning intentions and forgetting the fine work he had done in Moscow, the tsar fired him on the spot!

Irina and Felix received a letter from Zenaide with all the details about the meeting with the tsar. When Tamara came for her

usual Sunday visit, the conversation concentrated on the events in
Moscow. The senior Yusupovs were planning to retire to their estates in the Crimea. They saw no way of helping their country
under the circumstances. They asked Felix and Irina to join them
at their estate outside Moscow, Arkhangelskoie, for a week before
they moved south. The younger Yusupovs invited Tamara to join
them. Irina practically pleaded, and Felix added, "Ma chere, I have
long wanted to show you that beautiful place. Will you not go?
It's so beautiful down there in the late summer and it would make
us so happy."

Tamara was torn by her loyalties. She sympathized with Irina
because she felt she was lonely and in need of her companionship.
Since "Bebe" came, Felix was spending more time with Grand
Duke Dmitry than with her. Yet there were her duties and responsibilities at the hospital; she was needed, and, a fact that pressed
her more than any, she was in love. Dr. Frolov was not responding
as he once did and she could not understand his distancing himself from her. She decided that maybe a short vacation would be
beneficial; maybe he would miss her and see how he needed her.
After settling things at the Dashkov mansion with the countess,
who was delighted Tamara was going with the Yusupovs, she called
on Dr. Frolov in the hospital office. He was busy with some papers
as she entered, but put them down when he saw her. She explained
that some friends had invited her for a week in the country. She
would like to accept their invitation and had come for his permission. Dr. Frolov was very cordial and thought she deserved some
time off. His business-like attitude seemed cold to Tamara, but
she heartened when he said, "We shall miss you."

Looking into his eyes, she replied, "I'll miss you, too."

Arkhangelskoie was one of the most magnificent country estates
in Russia. The manor house was started in the 18th century by a
Prince Galitzin. When he suffered financial loses and could not
finish the chateau, it was sold to Prince Nicolas Yusupov, Felix's
great, great grandfather, who finished it in superb taste and beauty.
The park around the estate was enormous and full of exquisite

Italian marble statues. A metal plaque in one marble column had a poem about the estate written by A.S. Pushkin in commemoration of his visit there. Another column with an eagle on top indicated that Tsar Alexander II had once been a guest. The Moscow River was visible from the front terraces and from the great columned entrance hall. Two rooms were reserved for the paintings of Tiepolo and Robert and a library contained over 40,000 volumes, many of them ancient, rare books such as a Bible dated 1462. In spite of the imposing proportions of the great rooms, there was an atmosphere of intimacy. The furniture was comfortable and there was a profusion of plants and flowers. Arriving from Moscow, one approached the chateau from the rear through a large circular colonnade surrounding the courtyard.

Tamara had seen many palaces, but she soon agreed with Felix, Arkhangelskoie had a special quality and a special charm. From her bedroom window on the second floor of the left wing, she could see a long wisteria arbor in bloom and from somewhere the aroma of honeysuckle flowed through the air. She spent many free minutes looking out over the statues of the park toward the Moscow River in the distance. Felix told her that Napoleon's soldiers broke the noses off the statues when the Emperor confiscated the estate in 1812 and all underwent extensive repairs. In the afternoon of the day they arrived, Irina and Tamara walked along a flowered alley way and had tea served in a gazebo overlooking the forest and river at the bottom of the long slopping hill.

"Irina, may I ask your opinion about a matter very important to me."

The princess looked surprised. "Why Tamara, I thought we discussed everything quite openly."

"Yes, I've appreciated your sincerely, but I have a delicate problem. I'm in love with a doctor."

Princess Irina's eyes opened wide. "Really? How charming! Is he in the "Saviors of Russia?"

Tamara nodded.

"Tell me about him."

"I don't know where to begin. I haven't felt this way since I was in love with my cousin Shota whom I mentioned to you."

"Yes, I was so sorry for you."

"I know, but this is different. He's … he's …"

"I understand. He's a Philistine."

"Not really. He's not petty bourgeois."

Irina laughed not scornfully, but showing her amusement. "Don't tell me he's a peasant?"

Tamara shook her head and smiled. "Oh, he's just…well, he's not an aristocrat."

"Gentry?"

Tamara shook her head again. "Oh, Irina, I admire him so very much. You should see the operations he does. He's saved so many lives one can't help but respect him. Imagine how wonderful it would be to have such ability … such training … such devotion to one's work. He performs miracles every day."

When Irina saw tears in her friend's eyes, she looked away and wondered what she should say and how she could say it. She started with herself. "Ma chere, I shall tell you a secret that no one knows. I, too, was once in your situation."

"Really, Irina?"

"Yes, my darling. Yes. He was a colonel in the army and instructed Olga and me in fencing at the Winter Palace. His name was Fedor Kacharovsky and he was so handsome I almost swooned the first time I saw him."

"What happened?"

"You know how impossible it is to keep a secret in a palace. Servants always pass on anything untoward, thinking they will obtain some reward."

"But how did they find out?"

"Olga became ill once and was absent for three weeks. I continued my lessons and one day when he was holding my arms to show me the correct position, I turned and accidently kissed him."

Tamara's mouth opened in disbelief. She finally uttered, "Really?"

Irina nodded. "But it was a hopeless situation. I'm sure he cared for me and expressed it beautifully, but what could we do? Besides, negotiations were going on for me to marry a baron of Hesse. When my parents learned of my tryst, they were appalled and my dear teacher was transferred away. I never heard from him or about him."

"I'm so sorry," Tamara sympathized, shaking her head, then continued, "But Irina, your experience was different."

"How?"

"You see, that was peace time and you were a niece of the tsar. It would have been unthinkable. But now it's war. Russians are dying and everything seems on the brink of chaos. My brother's been killed and so many friends are dead, does anything matter anymore?"

"You're still a princess from a family of royal blood."

"Oh, we were royal so many centuries ago, and what does a title mean today when there's no need for it? Will it save a life? Will it help the war? What is it for?"

Irina could only slightly shake her head. There were no answers for her friend's dilemma, there were only questions.

The elder Yusupovs arrived at the estate in the late afternoon. They immediately went to their suite in the right wing and appeared for the evening repast. When Princess Zenaide came into the orangeries for the first course, Felix stood up and complimented his mother on her lovely yellow silk evening dress. She thanked him and kissed his right cheek. Turning to Tamara, Zenaide mentioned how pleased she was that the princess could join them for a week of relaxation. "We really need it," she added, sitting down on a lounge covered in a lavender-colored material. Her beauty was heightened by the yellow and lavender combination.

Prince Felix Yusupov the elder entered and bowed to the ladies. He was born Elston-Sumarokov, but because Zenaide was the last of the Yusupovs, he was permitted by the tsar to accept her family name. He took a small tumbler of vodka, made a toast to God and country and drank it all in one swallow. He sat down and

began immediately to talk about his being fired as Governor of
Moscow. Both Zenaide and Felix were livid with indignation that
they had been treated so badly. The prince told about all the evidence he had presented to the tsar about the orgies and bribery
being perpetrated by Rasputin. He stated that he had given names
of sworn witnesses to the madman's dissipation, corruption and
perversion. Still the tsar was unmovable. "So, I realized that I would
have to attack the Empress herself." When I mentioned Alexandra,
the tsar cowered and wouldn't look at me in the face. When I
suggested undue influence on government matters by Rasputin
through the Empress's position as wife of the tsar, he finally objected. He gave no excuses, he offered no evidence to the contrary,
nor did he defend her. He merely stated that I was no longer Governor of Moscow and asked me to leave without further explanation. "I was so furious, I left. If I had stayed one minute more, I
hesitate to think what I would have done."

"It's all too disgusting for words. When I think of how the tsar
and Alexandra came so often to our fetes and musical performances,
I could just cry. Nicholas himself sang with me in one of our musical productions. And now, look, a Siberian peasant of despicable
character has them in his filthy hands. Oh, God, how can they
stand Rasputin?"

"Someone ought to kill him," Felix the younger stated and his
comment lodged in Tamara's memory.

During the week at Arkhangelskoie friends from neighboring
estates visited. Discussions always centered on the war and
Rasputin. Tamara decided that the whole world knew about the
holy man's hold on the royal family. Princess Irina told her in
private that the Empress was so devoted to Father Gregory because
in her opinion he was the only one who could help the Tsarevich
Alexis, who was a hemophiliac. Several times the boy's bleeding
had ceased after the holy man had visited. Tamara suggested that
Father Gregory was using hypnotism, adding, "You've seen his
eyes, haven't you?"

"I only met him once and it was most unpleasant."

"Did he look at you here," Tamara quickly pointed to her breast and dropped her hand.

Irina nodded and they both laughed.

In the middle of the week Felix suggested a drive and Tamara asked how far the Dashkov estate Radnoe was from their location.

"Only about an hour. Let's go!" The threesome drove off into the countryside wearing goggles and light dust jackets. Horse trading was going on at the Dashkov property when they arrived and Felix bought several stallions merely because he found them beautiful and never refused himself anything that appealed to him. While he examined horses, Tamara and Irina walked through the manor house. It seemed forlorn without Lidia and the old prince. Tamara told

Irina about them and tears came to her eyes as she remembered their kind hearts and munificence. When they went back to the stables, Tamara could hardly believe her eyes. Felix was talking with Oleg Dunatov. The latter immediately smiled when he saw Tamara. She looked away, but could not help smiling herself and he noticed.

Oleg bowed and said, "Princess, your brother's death saddened me. I greatly admired him."

"Thank you, Oleg," she replied and asked him what he was doing at Radnoe. He had delivered horses from the Dashkov estate Kholmka in the Ukraine. Tamara inquired further about Kholmka; she was curious about the management of the estate since the Dashkovs had passed away. Oleg informed her that Prince Vladimir had appointed him overseer because he was an only son and would not be drafted. "I'm glad you're still there," she replied and walked off with the Yusupovs. When they were seated in their car, she saw Oleg watching her. They both smiled. Driving back to Arkhangelskoie Felix questioned Tamara about Oleg. She related details of her stay with her brother at the estate and told them about the companionship that developed between Valery and Oleg. "They both acted like Cossacks. It was beautiful to watch them ride like daredevils." She fell quiet, thinking of Valery. Felix, sensing her grief, ceased his inquiry.

The next day after the visit to Radnoe, Felix and Irina had some business in Moscow and asked Tamara to accompany them. The ancient capital was only about forty-five minutes away and they would have lunch at their city mansion which was built by Ivan the Terrible in 1551. It had been the tsar's hunting lodge, but he used it for elaborate entertainments. After his death the edifice was not used for over a century; then in 1729 Peter the Great gave it to Prince Gregory Yusupov for his service to the state. Tamara was amazed at the large collection of gold and silver plate that decorated a dining room. The rooms were vaulted and decorated with ancient frescoes and armor. It was like stepping into Russia's medieval past. Felix claimed that skeletons were found in niches of an underground passage when his parents had the mansion renovated. "We never live in this part of the house; it's used only for fetes and receptions," he explained as they walked through the large, dark rooms. "There's too many ghosts in these passages and niches. Don't you feel it's a bit creepy here?"

Tamara and Irina agreed as they followed him into a wing connected to the mansion by a winter garden. Servants served a light lunch and Felix told of his father's predilection for curious Moscow oddities. "When they lived here, he was interested in dog-clubs, bird-fanciers' associations and bee-keeping." The ladies laughed and Felix related facts about the "Skoptzis," a strange sect of castrates whose voices were soprano and their faces were feminine. Once when he was a boy, his father took him for a visit to an apiary run by a group of Skoptzis. They served them lunch and a choir of old wrinkled women's faces sang folk songs while they ate. It was sad and funny.

Driving back to Arkhangelskoie they passed through an enormous wooded area called "The Silver Forest." Felix related what he considered the strangest incident in his life. Once while he and his deceased brother were passing through the forest which stretched for miles without a single dwelling, they suddenly saw a train pass silently through the trees. The coaches were brightly lit and one could see people seated in them. The two valets who were with them also saw it and crossed themselves. One said, "The powers of evil!" Felix and his brother were stupefied because no railway existed there. He also had never found any explanation for the occurrence.

Tamara mentioned her aunt's interest in spiritualism and Felix snickered, "That's all gaff!"

"We don't know for sure," Irina protested, giving the standard argument in support, "They laughed at electricity in the old days and look, today we cannot live without it."

"There's no mystery in electricity," Felix said in rebuttal.

Irina added, "There's much mystery in life."

Tamara, to her own surprise, commented. "Mysticism seems to be losing its importance now during the ravages of war. Look at Symbolist poetry, they now criticize it for being vague." No one responded immediately and Tamara, thinking she had made an intellectual observation, felt proud of herself.

Felix drolly exclaimed, "Tamara's becoming a literary critic! Heaven help us!"

All three laughed.

On the train back to Petrograd Tamara reminisced about the week that had passed so quickly at beautiful Arkhangelskoie. She understood why the painter Francois Flameng, after staying a week at the estate, told Zenaide, "Princess, Promise me that when my career is over you will allow me to become the honorary pig of Arkhangelskoie!" It was such a magnificent place and run so superbly that anyone would want to stay forever. Recalling the pleasant days there, Tamara could hardly believe she was returning to a world of disorder and horror. The hospital would be full of new casualties and the paper work would be tremendous. There was also Dr. Frolov. She had thought of him often during the week and meditated on the conversation with Irina about the doctor. She still was not sure of her feelings. She knew she loved him, but was not sure it was proper. At least the week at Arkhangelskoie had given her needed rest and she felt invigorated and ready for the tasks ahead.

Count Trushinsky had left for the front when Tamara returned to the Dashkovs. The countess had finished her training and was working two afternoons a week as a nurse's aid at the "Saviors of Russia." Other afternoons were either spent assuring her salvation at Rasputin's or attending seances which had turned into sessions of prophesying about the outcome of oncoming battles and the fate of Russia in the future. Because of the war time shortages of everything, the rest of her time was spent trying to find the basic essentials of her life: her special face cream, her favorite perfumes and a seamstress who could sew the patterns of the latest mode. She and Tamara began living separate lives, While the countess wanted to resume the serious conversation she had with her niece about Dr. Frolov, the two accepted anunspoken truce and avoided questioning each other

Dr. Frolov greeted Tamara most kindly when she returned. There was not much time for talk because he was scheduled for many operations that day, however, he took a few moments for a short chat about her week in the country. Having been away for a week, she noticed how weary he looked and told him that he must have rest. That was impossible. As she assumed on the train, the hospital was overflowing with wounded and more came daily. She invited him for dinner at the Dashkovs after work, but, to her regret and apprehension, he refused. There still seemed no way to develop a close relationship with him.

In September, 1915 two incidents occurred which convinced government leaders and social lions that the tsar and Empress were definitely under the control of Rasputin. A great debate took place in the Duma, the Russian legislative body. The majority of the members were alarmed by Russian military defeats and wanted the Emperor to adopt a political line of national unity. A Progressive Bloc formed of parties ranging from Cadets to Progressive Nationalists who demanded a united government and the end of religious and ethnic discrimination and persecution. Russian Prime

Minister Goremykin did not approve of the plan and visited the Empress and Rasputin. Two days later the Russian Duma itself was prorogued. A second affair which had disastrous consequences for Russia happened at Mogilev, the headquarters of the Russian army at the front. Tsar Nicholas II discharged his uncle, Grand Duke Nicholas Nikolayevich, as head of Russian military forces. The tsar. unprepared and not capable in military matters, made himself head of Russia's army. It became known that Father Gregory had advised the Empress of the necessity of the tsar's leading Holy Russia to victory over the German Hun. Rumors became rampant about the Empress and the holy man and society and governmental officials became divided over the scandal. There was no moderate position; one either believed that Rasputin ran the government or one retained a belief in the tsar's omnipotence and leadership.

While great society balls were no longer held after the beginning of the war, less ostentatious dances became so popular that many hostesses were criticized for such entertainments during wartime. Anna Vrubova, the Empress's confidante, often expressed her indignation that such merriment should be taking place in such desperate times. If she made such caustic remarks, it was taken for granted that she was only giving the Empress's opinion. Society did not agree. Night clubs were filled with merrymakers. There was a desire by many to forget the horrors that filled the papers daily or the rumors that spread constantly throughout the city. Tamara was not surprised when she received an invitation from Betsie Shuvalov for a dance at her palace. While she was not interested, she felt obligated because of a note written on the side of the invitation by the hostess which said, "Please come, it's for the servicemen and your beauty would be so pleasant and beneficial for our heroes." Before the war Betsie, as a leading social lioness, had welcomed Tamara into society most courteously, so she now felt that she should help the hostess in turn.

When Tamara entered the resplendent Shuvalov mansion on the Fontanka the evening of the dance, she noticed immediately a great difference from the previous party there. The sense of elegance and luxury was missing. There were no bouquets of splendid flowers or thousands of burning candles. It was not dazzling as before. Now the great entrance way seemed bleak and the ballroom just another hall. Instead of the colorful apparel of grand dukes and pages of the tsar, the place was filled with khaki uniforms. Ladies were well dressed, but there wasn't the grand display of jewels that always added sparkle to a ball. Tamara herself had worn only a black garnet necklace because a general feeling prevailed for not parading one's finery. Since there were more servicemen than ladies, she was immediately swamped with offers for a dance. Dance cards were not used, so she was surrounded each time the orchestra started a new melody. Late in the evening she asked one officer if he would mind sitting out a dance as she needed a short reprieve. He escorted her to the alcove where Pavel Voroshilov had confessed his dying love. Tamara started to ask her escort if he would mind going a little farther down the hall, but he had already moved a chair for her and motioned that she be seated. She sat down and he took a chair opposite her.

"I'm Foma Dunevich" her curly blonde escort said, smiling snd waving to a waiter.

"I'm Tamara Borisovna," she replied, leaving off her title and not mentioning her family name.

"You're very beautiful."

She thanked him and accepted a glass of wine.

It was Foma's first leave since the war started and he was enjoying Petrograd. He told her about his uncle's farm and how he had been drafted. She knew from his background and speech that he was a peasant and found it ironic that she was now in the alcove under such different circumstances. He questioned her about herself, but she avoided anything about her background so he would feel at ease. She related that she was a nurse's aid and worked in the "Saviors of Russia." The young man was so happy to be seated with the "belle of the ball," as he expressed it, that he begged her to sit out the next dance, too. Tamara agreed readily because she was quite fatigued. She also liked his openness and lack of pretense. However, everything was suddenly shattered when the hostess came by on the arm of a general and said, "Oh, here's the Princess Zhorzhadze. I want you to meet her."

Foma's eyes opened wide in surprise. Tamara was sorry she had been revealed, but was obligated to acknowledge the hostess's entreaty. She nodded to the general and started to introduce the private, but Foma excused himself quickly and left. Tamara was very disappointed because she had tried so hard to avoid giving the young man any feeling of condescension. Yet it had happened. She talked briefly with the general and Betsie and then looked for Foma. She could not find him and, since it was after midnight, excused herself and had the doorman call the Dashkov coachman in the courtyard. Riding home she hoped that she had not offended Foma. He was fighting for his country and deserved what happiness he could have. He had seemed so pleased to be with her and she was sorry it ended as it did. Yet again she marveled at how things were changing in society. Before the war she could have never had such an experience, now a princess and a peasant could meet socially at a ball. Her world was truly changing.

Countess Trushinsky arrived at the hospital one afternoon on the arm of a very well-dressed, manicured gentlemen. When they entered the office, she walked over to her niece and said, "Tamara, I want you to meet Prince Michael Andronnikov." The princess looked up and saw a man obviously wearing make-up. He bowed and expressed in French his pleasure in meeting her. The princess was perplexed because her aunt had not mentioned the gentleman before and she did not know what was expected of her. The countess told Tamara that they would return for her later and have dinner at "The Bear." When the princess reminded her aunt that she was supposed to help in the hospital that afternoon, the countess said, "Didn't you receive the note I sent around? I have to be excused today. I'm so sorry." Tamara did not argue, but the countess could see that she was aggravated. Not paying any attention, she left with her new friend.

During the afternoon Irina and Felix paid a surprise visit.

Tamara escorted them, showing the new mattresses and bedsteads that Felix had purchased though the manufacturing council. In various wards they talked with servicemen. In some halls Felix described social events that had taken place in the palace when he was a boy. The Yusupovs had used the edifice only for receptions and banquets. Irina asked about Dr. Frolov, but he was, as usual, in surgery. When they returned to the office Tamara asked them about Prince Andronnikov. Felix's eyes showed surprise. "How did you ever meet that miscreant?"

"You know him?"

"Everyone knows him. He's a notorious Narcissus, if you know what I mean?"

Tamara looked puzzled, but assumed the name was used in the classical sense. "His clothes were elegant and I think . . . oh, I must be wrong."

"What?" Irina asked.

"I think he had on make-up."

"I'm sure he did," Felix commented. "You see, not a military cadet in the corps is allowed to visit his apartment."

Tamara thought of Felix and Rasputin. Again he was condemning someone for actions he himself performed. She explained that her aunt had introduced him.

"He's now one of the Rasputin crowd. Just avoid him. A bigger scoundrel doesn't exist. He acts as an intermediary for channeling bribes to Rasputin. He's not accepted by any decent family."

Tamara thanked Felix and escorted them out of their hospital.

When the countess and the prince returned, Tamara tried unsuccessfully to avoid going with them. Reservations at the most expensive restaurant in the city had already been made and the countess insisted that her niece accompany them. Tamara knew that Zita invited her only because she did not want to be alone with her escort in public. It seemed strange that her aunt still cared about public opinion.

At "The Bear" the threesome was led to one of the private dining rooms on the second floor of the restaurant. Before they had removed their wraps, Rasputin entered and embraced the countess and the prince. When he turned to Tamara, she nodded and slipped behind a chair. The holy man laughed and pointed a finger at her, "She's still afraid of me!"

The countess gave Tamara a look of disapproval as they seated themselves at a small round table. The princess managed to sit across from Father Gregory between her aunt and the prince. Zubrovka vodka and caviar were ordered, followed by pirozhki and borscht. After several toasts of the smoothest vodka ever made, the gentlemen became very jovial and began telling rather unseemly anecdotes. Guffaws and giggles filled the room. Tamara disheartened as she watched her aunt laugh and tease. Finally, during the soup course, the princess found out the reason for the meeting. Since the Yusupovs owned and supported the "Saviors of Russia," and since Tamara was a close friend of the benefactors, would she arrange a meeting between them and Father Gregory.

"But you already know Felix," she said to Rasputin. "I saw him at your apartment."

"Yes, I did know the dear boy, but since he married, he has quit coming and won't see me."

"But that's his affair. How could I intrude?"

"It would be advantageous for you to help me."

"How?"

"Your hospital needs medical provisions that I can supply."

Tamara had heard how the holy man had control of practically every department of the government. Through his relationship with the Empress, he could have ministers fired and generals transferred. The hospital was having difficulty purchasing materials and any help that could be given was needed. Yet Tamara was disgusted that her aunt had brought her into such a scheme. She decided that she would tell Felix about the proposal and let him discern what should be done. To the countess's delight, Tamara reluctantly agreed to the scheme.

The next day the princess called Irina on the hospital phone and received permission to drop by in the afternoon. When she arrived at the Moika Palace, she was led to the new apartment that Felix had created in the left wing. Princess Irina and Felix welcomed her cheerfully. Tamara did not know where to begin. She apologized for having dined with the very man they had warned her against, Prince Andronnikov. She went into detail about the reason for the dinner and apologized again for even considering the plan. Yet she explained her motives. She knew that the hospital was having trouble procuring various products and the plan gave assurance that they would be made available.

Felix suddenly smiled most happily. "Tamara, ma chere, you have helped me more than you can ever imagine."

The princess looked at her friend in astonishment.

"Because we know we can trust you with a secret, I shall tell you just how much you have aided us. Irina and I have been discussing for some time just what should be done about Rasputin. To carry out any plan, it would be necessary to restore relations with him and I have been wondering how I could manage it. You've just presented the perfect way. I had planned on simply dropping by his apartment, but he is extremely suspicious and would have doubted my motives. Now you've come forward with an invitation from him. It's perfect. How can we ever thank you."

Tamara sighed and told them she was very relieved. She had been greatly distressed and had shed tears over whether she should approach them with such a ridiculous scheme. She valued their friendship over all others and would not harm them in any way. "Enough, Tamara," Irina interrupted. "We love you and know your feelings. You've done the right thing."

Felix agreed to meet Rasputin and Prince Andronnikov at "The Bear" for dinner. What transpired at the meeting, Tamara did not know for some time, but the "Saviors of Russia" soon had all the supplies it needed. Anything that was ordered was delivered. The next time the princess was with Irina and Felix, they disclosed that a plan was being carefully worked out and that they would inform her about particulars in due time. There might even be a role for her. When she questioned what they meant, they begged her patience and thanked her again for her help.

The first Zeppelin attack on London in October, 1915 caused apprehension in all the large cities of the Allied Countries. The prospect of bombs dropping indiscriminately from the air added new dangers at the home front and the staff of the "Saviors of Russia" held a meeting about a plan of action in case there should be such an attack. Dr. Frolov gave a short talk in which he encouraged all his doctor colleagues to sign an appeal that would be sent to the transportation council asking that the most seriously wounded be sent by hospital trains to the interior of Russia. It seemed the most logical course of action and there was general agreement. After the meeting, Tamara asked the doctor if he could join her for dinner at the Dashkovs. She added, smiling kindly, "My aunt will be there, so all is in order."

He looked distraught. After a short pause, he said, "I would like to join you more than anything in the world, but I must not."

"Sergey," she said, using his first name for the first time.

"Please tell me why?"

He hesitated and then asked, "Could you go with me for tea right after my last operation today?"

"Of course," Tamara replied. "I'll be here waiting."

The afternoon passed slowly. Tamara was glad that Zita was not there that day and she sat thinking of the doctor as she looked at the paperwork in front of her. Could he possibly be refusing her company because of her title? Surely that cannot matter now. Or was it the Dashkov mansion? Perhaps he knows I have an inheritance and is embarrassed because he is poor? All of that seemed superficial and Tamara decided she would dispel any anxieties he might have on those accounts. Suddenly some military officials entered carrying a stack of papers. Tamara knew immediately that a wagon full of wounded had unexpectedly arrived. When the troops were carried into the various wards, one soldier needed an immediate operation. Dr. Frolov was the only surgeon still at the hospital that day and went right into surgery. He stopped by the office on the way and told Tamara that he would come to dinner at the Dashkov mansion when he finished. She walked with him toward the operating room and said that her coachman would be waiting for him whenever he was ready.

When Tamara arrived at the Dashkov palace, she found a note from Zita informing her that she would not be dining at home that evening. Prince Andronnikov was taking her to a party. Tamara was afraid that the doctor might think that she had arranged a scheme, but there was nothing she could do about it. She told the chef that dinner would be in the dining room and she went to her boudoir for a change of clothes.

When Dr. Frolov arrived, Tamara was waiting in the salon. He marveled at the furnishings and stated that he could not imagine anyone living in such luxury. Since Tamara had known no other life but indulgence and comfort, she had taken it for granted. Wanting to avoid talking about the mansion, Tamara said, "You must be very tired. Let's have dinner at once." She put her arm in his and led him into the dining room. Again he was taken aback by the opulence and she wished she had arranged dinner in the study. A servant brought vodka and wine with caviar and smoked sturgeon. The doctor ate heartily since he had been operating since morning. When the entre came, he ate two portions of stuffed chicken. They finished the dinner with tea and torte. During the meal their conversation centered on the hospital, but when they finished, Tamara led him in the study for a liquor.

"Why did you not want to come today?"

"I did not want to come because I knew I should not."

"Is it my title or wealth?"

"No, it is neither."

"Then you don't care for me."

He walked over to her by the fireplace and looked directly into her eyes. "I have never cared for anyone so much in my life. You are beautiful beyond description and I want so badly to enfold you into my arms."

"Then do!" she softly exclaimed and stepped up to him.

He turned away. "I mustn't."

Tears came to her eyes. "But why?"

"I have deceived you and I can hardly stand myself for it."

"What do you mean?"

"I mean that I should have never invited you out. I did not have the right."

"But I don't understand. Don't you love me?"

"I do love you. I've never loved as I love you. You're the kindest, most caring human being I've ever known."

"Then Sergey, surely—"

"Tamara, I'm married."

The words were like a knife into her heart. She was willing to forget her noble name and wealth to serve this servant of humanity all her life, but his words took away the chance forever. She burst into tears and fell toward him.

Dr. Frolov caught her and held her in his arms. She looked up at him pleading and he kissed her with all his heart. When he broke away, he went out of the room. Tamara collapsed on a leather chair and cried.

CHAPTER 5

1916

Only a few people gathered at the Moika Palace to welcome in the New Year, 1916. A large fete did not seem fitting with the country ravaged by war and disorder. Since the Countess Trushinsky had gone to Tiflis for the holidays, Tamara spent the season with the Yusupovs and noticed how everything had been scaled down. The custom of placing a large Christmas tree in the entrance way was not heeded and the palace was not filled with guests. Russian Christmas fell on the 8th of January that year and the princess, when not working in the hospital, helped Irina and Felix decorate a Christmas tree in the library and arrange festive wreaths in various windows. Most of their time was given to Bebe who was now crawling and the center of their universe.

On Christmas day Tamara was joined by Irina and Felix for a visit to the "Saviors of Russia." They took large bags of gifts that Felix had a store prepare and passed them out to the soldiers. Dr. Vlasov a punctilious type who had replaced Dr. Frolov in the surgical department when he suddenly transferred to a hospital at the front, helped them distribute the packages. Irina and Felix questioned Tamara when they heard about Dr. Frolov's departure and the princess related to her friends the details of what had happened. They were shocked, but Tamara only spoke well of the departed.

By 1916 the Russian military situation looked very bleak. Over 2,000,000 men had perished at the front in the previous year and the grievous losses continued. Bulgaria overran Russia's allies Serbia and Montenegro and the British abandoned the Dardanelles. The Russian fleet was bottled up in the Black Sea. The only good news came from General Brusilov's forces which had concentrated their power against Austria and had captured over half a million men; yet there had also been over 300,000 Russian casualties. Tamara no longer read the lists in the newspaper because it took too much time and she feared recognizing a familiar name. Dread and fear permeated the atmosphere of the capital. While night clubs were filled with party makers, their jovial merrymaking was a pretense hiding their frustration and despair.

Countess Trushinsky returned from her rendezvous with Colonel Bagrov in Tiflis and continued her previous routine of giving as little time as possible to the hospital and keeping company in diverse places with Prince Andronnikov. Occasionally Rasputin would let her visit for spiritual enlightenment, but he had become so popular the countess had difficulty continuing her liaison. She satisfied her needs through the debauched characters she met through the prince.

Life at the Dashkov mansion reflected the growing crisis in the nation. All the male servants had been drafted by the late spring of 1916 and most of the maids had returned to their native villages. The old coachman and the chef remained, but cleaning ladies and garden workers changed repeatedly. It was simply not possible to maintain such an edifice under war time conditions.

There had been no word from Prince Vladimir in some time, so Tamara took some measures on her own.. More rooms were closed off and part of the garden abandoned.

In May another incident occurred which raised the public's temper against Rasputin. Because of the German advance in Poland, the new prime minister, S.D. Sazonov proposed offering the Poles a two-house legislature after the war if they would continue fighting along with Russia against their invaders. Rasputin opposed such a plan and visited the Empress; she took a train to Mogilev and spoke with the tsar; two days later Nicholas dismissed Sazonov. Rumors spread throughout Petrograd, increasing the atmosphere of intrigue and suspicion. On the Duma floor a cadet even denounced the Empress and Rasputin, calling out, "Is this insanity or treason?" It was an episode unprecedented in the annals of a powerful country: a student calling his Empress a traitor in the seat of government.

As conditions worsened on the battlefields and on the home front, supplying basic needs became increasingly difficult. Tamara noticed that the hospital was able to procure many things not available in stores and she assumed that Rasputin had kept his word and was arranging distribution to the medical facility. At the Dashkov mansion, it was another situation. Fedor, the chef, began apologizing for the dinners he created and old Yakov the coachman complained about nothing being available in the stores when he went shopping. Yet the countess seemed to have a limitless supply of perfumes and cosmetics. One day before leaving for the hospital, Tamara knocked and entered Zita's room. Her aunt was still in bed, but had awakened. The princess walked over by a boudoir stool and explained that Yakov was having the carriage wheels adjusted that morning and might not be back at noon for the countess's trip to the hospital. Zita waved her hand as if it were unimportant and said, "I'm not sure I'm going today anyway."

Tamara's forehead wrinkled. "You're scheduled for today."

The countess wet her lips and muttered, "Can't a person be ill anymore?"

Tamara noticed several new fancy bottles of French perfume on the dressing table. She picked up one named "Heure de se couche," and asked, "Where did you ever find these?"

"Michael gave them to me."

"Prince Andronnikov?"

She nodded her head and rolled over, away from Tamara.

"Do you know what they say about him?"

She rolled back over toward her niece and asked, "No, what?"

"Felix says that he's a Narcissus?"

"Felix should know."

"What do you mean?"

The countess laughed. "Don't tell me you don't know that Felix is a well-known homosexual."

Tamara was stunned by the word. She remembered the scene with Felix and Rasputin in the latter's apartment. Still she had to object, "Felix is married and has a child."

The countess laughed again. "One thing that has always impressed me about you is your naiveté."

"Well, you'll soon have people talking about you if you continue your association with the prince."

A look of disbelief spread on the countess's face. "And what about you and Felix?"

"It's not the same."

"Oh, it is. He's just as flagrant as the prince. Besides, who today gives a darn. With everything going to the devil, who cares anymore."

Tamara was shocked by her aunt's language and attitude. A lady never curses and a noble lady certainly must care. The terrible change in the outside world had come into their home. Tamara felt weak and started out of the room.

"Ma chere," Zita called. "Please wait a moment. Forgive me for talking like that. I know it's improper, but I've been so worried about Vadim of late that I've just done anything to keep my mind busy."

Tamara knew it was a lie; she was sure the countess rarely thought of her husband, but the fact that she had apologized did make the princess feel better. As she left, the countess thanked her for letting her know about the coach and said she would see her at dinner.

At the hospital Tamara found a stack of forms on her desk. New casualties had arrived and she wondered where the nurses were able to find space for them. As she worked through the papers, she came upon the name Count Boris Sheremetiev and quickly looked at his ward number. She was relieved that he was not in isolation which would mean that he was mortally injured. Having finished her filing, she noticed the time and knew that the nurses would have completed their morning chores. She went to the designated ward and found Boris walking on crutches. He looked shorter than she remembered. When he caught sight of her, he exclaimed, "The beautiful princess!"

Tamara renewed their acquaintance and asked about his wound. "Just a broken leg. Nothing dramatic, I fell off my horse." He laughed and Tamara could not help but join him. "Yes, I wanted to be a hero and had no idea my horse would make me one." She laughed again. "What are you doing here?" She told him about her training and her work. He expressed his pride for her and asked about Vladimir Dashkov. She explained that she heard from him rarely, but that he was still at the front. "God help him," Boris uttered, shaking his head. "It's hell out there!" After a short talk, Tamara promised to return in the afternoon.

Going back to the office Tamara remembered how the pages of the tsar stood at the foot of the grand staircase in the Dashkov mansion waiting for her entrance. They were so marvelous in their beautiful dress uniforms covered with gold braid across the front. They represented some of the most famous families in Russian history and now Gagarin and Vorshilov were dead. She recalled that Perovsky was there, too, but she did not miss him. It all seemed so long ago and how everything had changed. In the late afternoon, her office door opened and Boris walked in slowly on his crutches. "What?" Tamara exclaimed. "Does your nurse know you did this?"

"I don't care what she says, I wanted to see you again." The stout young man hobbled in as best he could and Tamara gave him a chair. After a few humorous phrases, Boris told the princess how sorry he had been when he heard about Valery. He did not know him well, but heard many fine things about him. Tamara only nodded.

"Have the doctors told you how long you will be with us?" she asked for a change of subject.

"You want me to leave already?"

She smiled. "Of course not, but I know that everyone who

comes here is always anxious to leave."

"I was until you came back into my life."

She laughed kindly. "If I were your nurse, I'd paddle you for walking all this way."

"I'd let you."

Again she laughed and their banter continued for some minutes. Suddenly an old wrinkled nurse came in and said, "Oh, so this is where you are!" She looked at Tamara and shook her head. "I know why you're here and I don't blame you; but now you're going to walk slowly back to your bed."

"Must I?"

The nurse put her hand under his arm and helped lift him. "Promise me you'll come see me in the morning."

Tamara nodded and gave a sympathetic smile.

That evening when the princess arrived at the Dashkovs she noticed Prince Andronnikov's carriage parked in front. She dreaded the evening, but it was worse than she anticipated. As she went up the stairs, the countess came out of the salon. "Ma chere, we have guests for dinner. Please come down as soon as you're ready. We'll wait for you." The princess nodded and wondered how she could avoid the gathering, but she was hungry and decided at least to have dinner.

When Tamara entered the salon, she could hardly believe her eyes. Caviar, smoked sturgeon and roasted pheasant hors d'oeuvres were on a marble table by a tall silver ice bucket holding champagne. The prince stood up and bowed, inviting the princess to join them. The countess, looking a bit apologetic, waved her hand at the table of riches and told her niece to help herself. "Where did you find such things?" Tamara asked.

The prince laughed and said, "You don't find these anymore, they fall like manna from heaven." He enjoyed his own witticism and laughed again.

The countess tried making excuses. "They were given to the prince for his services, Tamara, and he has been kind enough to share them with us."

The princess wondered whether she should eat or not, but she was hungry and approached the table. It was obvious that the prince was dealing in the black market and she was benefiting from his corrupt dealings. It saddened her, but she took some caviar and accepted a glass of champagne from the host. She figured that there was an ulterior motive behind the feast and waited for them to reveal it. For a while the conversation was about the war, then the prince mentioned that in his service to help the country on the home front, he was having trouble finding places for storage. "You just cannot imagine how badly the products I deal with are needed by our soldiers."

Tamara could not understand what he was suggesting. There were military supply agencies that handled materials for the army; they would not want black market goods. The countess alluded to the enormous amount of space in the Dashkov mansion that was not being used and Tamara understood immediately. "No," she adamantly stated. "Prince Vladimir would never sanction such a thing!"

"But if it's for the war effort?" the countess said as if she were flabbergasted that her niece did not comprehend.

Tamara stood up and put down her glass. "But it's not for the war effort. I'm disgusted that you would play along with such a scheme. To store things in this palace would be the epitome of hypocrisy." Tamara started walking out of the salon, turned and said, "I'll write Vadim and Vladimir if you even dare."

The prince laughed and rushed to the princess. "Oh, you misunderstand, ma chere. Zita was just being helpful. Of course I didn't mean to imply that I wanted to store things here. I was just commenting about one of my greatest problems. Please come have some more to eat."

"Is this true?" Tamara asked her aunt.

"Of course, ma chere, you misunderstood. I merely suggested this palace as a joke. Of course we wouldn't do that."

Tamara knew her aunt was lying, but for the sake of propriety she accepted her explanation. However, when they went into dinner and she saw a choice piece of beef being carved by the chef, she again felt bitterness and, with a look of incredulity on her face, asked the prince, "Where do you possibly obtain such food?"

"It is all quite legitimate," he quickly replied, but the look on his face showed anxiety. "I help people make contacts; it's part of my effort to help my country."

The princess looked at him as his face muscles quivered and he sheepishly tried offering her a chair, "Contacts with Rasputin, I suppose."

"He helps, but…"

The countess interrupted and said, "Dima, you have some too when you take it in the kitchen."

Tamara looked at her aunt and said, "You're so egalitarian these days."

The countess pretended not to notice any sarcasm and led the conversation away from the exquisite food they were eating.

When the prince had left, Tamara went to her aunt's room and asked, "Aunt Zita, how can you associate with that man?"

"Let's not start that subject again. Prince Michael is very kind to me and I meet very interesting people through him."

"Yet you lecture me about our position in society and go around with him."

"He is a noble just as we are."

"To what has nobility fallen."

"What do you mean by that?"

"Just what I said. You know what his reputation is and don't mention Felix in the same breath."

"Is one decadent different from another?"

"Oh," Tamara exclaimed and left the room.

The first Zeppelin raid on Paris increased the fear and consternation in the large cities of the Allied countries. At the hospital it was decided that the lesser wounded should be moved into medical facilities in the interior of the country. A large hospital train was requisitioned from the government council of transportation and made ready for transfers to Moscow. The "Saviors of Russia" chief administrator asked Tamara if she would accompany the train personnel as a document clerk. She thought it was unusual that she should be asked, but assumed it was because of the shortage of workers and gladly accepted. She knew the countess would be delighted at her absence for two days and she informed Irina and Felix about her short trip. When she stopped by Boris Sheremetiev's ward for a good-bye, he happily announced that he would be on the train with her. A nice coincidence, she thought and knew that he would be amusing during the journey.

The railroad station was in chaos when Tamara arrived in a horse drawn ambulance with some wounded. Another military hospital train had just arrived and the wounded coming in had become mixed with the wounded going out; chaos reigned. After some hours of sorting and arranging, during which Tamara found out that she was in a coach with Boris, the Moscow train pulled slowly out of the station.

"While you're in Moscow, you must stay at Kuskovo," Boris stated soon after their departure.

"I'm sure I'll have a military assignment."

"To heck with that. I won't let you stay anywhere else but with us."

"We'll see." She half-way agreed, just to humor him.

In Moscow everything had been arranged and she understood why she had been asked for the first time to accompany the wounded on a train. Count Boris had used his family's influence and contrived her visit to their estate. She realized just how intent he was about their relationship. She knew he considered her very beautiful and that he liked her very much, but it was now obvious that he had greater intentions. She could not help but laugh to herself. Boris was short and she remembered how she stooped when she danced with him. Even talking with him on his crutches she would carefully, avoiding offense, bend slightly over to be on his level. She could not imagine going through life leaning over and thought of Princess Lidia's strange manner of walking. Besides, the idea of being in bed with the stout, little man was even more amusing.

At the station in Moscow Tamara turned over her packet of

documents to the authorities and found out that she was scheduled for a return trip on a military train in two days. She knew the delay had probably also been arranged by Boris, but did not make a fuss about it. He had been most pleasant on the train and helped entertain the other troops in their coach. His light teasing had been fun and the long trip went by faster than she had anticipated. A chauffeur was waiting for the count and he walked along side Boris in case one of the crutches slipped. The drive to Kuskova took about an hour

During their ride it became obvious to Tamara that Boris was trying to impress her with his family's illustrious history and wealth. He should have known that those things would not influence her. She was a princess and he was a count, which meant that his family received their title in the 18th century when Peter the Great started giving titles for services rendered to the state. Her title dated to the 10th century. Besides, she thought, can a title still mean anything today?

The park at Kuskova was famous for its large orangeries and fabulous gardens. The carriage drove by a small lake in front of the manor house and pulled into a Doric colonnade at the entrance to the mansion. Boris's mother, the widowed Countess Elena Sheremetiev met them at the large double door with a servant standing by holding the traditional bread and salt. Tamara curtsied and accepted the hospitality offered. The countess, a little, stout woman with bald spots in her hair, stepped forward and said, "Ma chere, I am delighted to have you here at Kuskova."

Tamara was impressed by the kindness and sincerity of the countess and felt that Boris had already told her that he was interested in marrying the guest he was bringing. She noticed that the hostess was looking her over from top to bottom and seemed very pleased with what she saw. Tamara was amused, but controlled herself as they led her into a beautiful 18th century salon. The French furniture was exquisite and the settees were covered in peach-colored silk, the same material of the draperies. The countess ordered tea and pleasantries were shared. After a short while, Tamara was escorted to her suite and she laid down for a rest.

While dressing for dinner, Tamara heard a knock on the door. The countess asked if she may enter. The princess agreed and the elderly lady walked in wearing a magnificent diamond and ruby necklace with matching earrings. She asked if she might have a brief talk with her guest. Never one for subterfuge, the countess admitted that Boris had asked her to talk with Tamara. He was in love as he had never been and wanted so much to make the princess the next Countess Sheremetiev. The little lady soon had tears in her eyes. "You see ma chere, I want only his happiness, and after what he has been through, I want it even more for him. You are very beautiful and you have a name that outshines even ours, but you would not be sacrificing to marry my Boris. The Sheremetiev fortune would be yours and I would be so proud for you to inherit our estates."

"Oh, madame!" Tamara exclaimed, falling before the countess. "I am so honored, but I cannot marry your son."

"And why not?"

"We don't know each other that well and besides, I am taller than he is."

The countess laughed. "It would be awkward, n'est-ce pas?"

Tamara nodded, standing up and thinking that the countess understood.

"But that doesn't matter my dear. The two of you look so fine together."

Tamara doubted that remark, but decided that it was better not to offend. She suggested that some time be given to the thought of marriage and begged the countess's patience. The little lady agreed and left after giving Tamara a kiss on each cheek, which, of course, she received by stooping over.

When Tamara joined the countess and Boris, she explained that she had only brought one dress with her and it was not very fancy. They both told her she looked just wonderful. Dinner was served in an enclosed terrace and fine limoges china in pinks and gold were used. Their conversation was mainly an exchange of episodes from their families' histories. When they finished dining, the countess suggested a walk through the gardens, saying that only a part of their park was being cared for as most of the gardeners were at the front. The threesome walked slowly out into the fresh air through paths of plants pruned into elaborate designs. The countess soon excused herself and left the couple alone. Tamara was sure her departure was preplanned.

Nearing the orangeries Boris, adjusted his crutches and asked, "Have you forgiven me for my intrigue?"

Tamara smiled kindly. "Of course, but Boris, why did you act so impulsively? We've known each other such a short time and with the war going on it's no time to think of marriage."

"It's the best time. One never knows if there's a tomorrow."

"But there is a tomorrow and if one acts too quickly today, one pays for it later."

He stopped and looked up into her eyes. "It's because I'm too short, isn't it?"

A look of distress came on her face. It was partly true, but what could one say. "Boris, short or tall, how could we marry when we simply don't know each other. You feel no passion for me and—"

"But I do. I want to embrace you and love you forever."

Tamara looked away. Again she heard that word "forever." "Boris, please!" Her voice showed her anguish and he understood that there was no chance at all for a union.

As a gentleman, he changed the subject and continued walking slowly on his crutches toward the door of the huge orangeries where his ancestors grew fresh fruit in the wintertime.

The next morning the countess told Tamara that she had arranged a luncheon at their Ostankino estate. "Don't worry, we'll have you at the station in time for your train." Tamara thanked her and was glad that she would have a chance to see the legendary summer palace of the Sheremetievs. The countess walked her into the Kuskova gallery and showed her a picture of a beautiful woman from the early 19th century. "She was a peasant girl in our private theater. She could dance and sing so exquisitely that Boris's great-grandfather married her. In those days it was called a mesalliance, but we Sheremetievs didn't care about that. So you see, my dear, a Georgian would fit into our family pattern too."

"Touche!" Tamara remarked and the countess laughed.

The Ostankino summer theater palace was built by Count Nicholas Sheremetiev at the end of the 18th century. Its theater had a stage 72 feet in depth and the floor of the auditorium could be raised to the level of the stage, making a huge ballroom. Walking through the many salons, the hosts and guest entered a gallery where European masterpieces were hanging. "Napoleon's men carried off a lot of our pictures and they were never returned," the countess mentioned and led Tamara into an oval sun room where Alexander II had signed the liberation of the serfs in 1861 while visiting the Sheremetievs. "It would be an honor to be a Sheremetiev," Tamara said at the end of the tour; and turning to Boris in front of the countess, she continued, "And I hope some day in the future, you and I will feel that we want to share this lovely place together."

"Bless you for those words," Boris kindly whispered and tears came to his eyes.

"God bless you, ma chere," the countess added as the chauffeur drove up into the courtyard for the drive to the railroad station and the afternoon military train.

After the long overnight train ride, Tamara was tired, but her reports were due at the hospital and she joined a coach of doctors going there. Again there was a stack of papers on her desk and she knew another trainload of wounded had arrived. The numbers of victims seemed endless and she wondered if anyone would survive the holocaust. Much of the work she put off until the next morning, but when she arrived back, there was another pile of forms and documents. "Where are they bedding them?" she asked herself and started on the filing. Toward noon a nurse came in and told Tamara that a young lady was asking for her. She thought of the countess, but knew the adjective was not apropos. Perhaps it was Irina, but she would come in. Tamara left her desk and went into the hall. Her former maid Louise was standing near the reception desk in a dress that looked unkept. The princess could hardly believe her eyes and walked over to her and said in French, "Louise, I'm so surprised to see you."

"Princess, may I speak with you privately? Please?"

The urgent look in the young girls face caused the princess to remember the last time the maid had asked for privacy. It had caused much impropriety. Tamara nodded and led her back into the office. No one else was in the room and she listened while Louise explained her problem. "I have dared come to you again because you were so kind the last time I asked for help."

"But I didn't help you."

"You tried."

"Was your friend released?

"No, Ivan was shot."

The princess winced.

"Don't worry, I didn't blame you. And now I've come about another friend."

Tamara looked puzzled and Louise stated that her friend Grisha needed a hiding place. The princess winced again and asked why. "Because he was in a student group that wanted a change of government."

"Against the tsar?"

"No, against the Empress and Rasputin. The tsarevich could be named tsar and his uncles would guide him."

Tamara was perplexed. The maid's friend was not a revolutionary and was actually wanting what many in society were proposing. She had heard that the legislator Purishkevich had even attacked Rasputin openly on the floor of the Duma. Schemes for a palace coup were rampant in society with little effort for secrecy. The princess would have liked to ask Felix about the matter, but he and Irina were at Rakitnoie. The thought that another student might be pointlessly shot also bothered her. "But why have you come to me?"

"Because the Dashkov mansion is so enormous and no one would suspect his being there."

"How can I take in a stranger?"

"Please trust me, he is very honest and could work for you. He can garden and clean. Surely you need help these days with everyone gone to the front."

"Why isn't your friend in the army?"

"He was, but was wounded. He can still work and would help you a lot in the big house."

The proposition, which had sounded so preposterous at first, now seemed worthwhile. There was a great need for help in the Dashkov edifice and no one would know that a gardener was hiding out. Aunt Zita would not pay any attention to a workman and would be glad to have another person she could order around. Even if she did question, the fact that Grisha was a veteran would suffice for his needing work. It was a difficult decision and Tamara hesitated. Finally she told Louise to bring her friend to the mansion that evening around eight o'clock. The countess would be at one of her silly seances until late and the princess could talk with the young man.

That evening after Prince Andronnikov and the countess left for a spiritualistic meeting, Tamara told Yakov that a young man would be coming for an interview. He would work in the garden and sleep in the carriage house. The old coachman said he would watch for him. About 8:30 Yakov came to the princess in the study and said that there were two visitors, a young woman and a man. Tamara went out with him and led the visitors into the study. Grisha reminded Tamara of the young soldier she had met at the Shuvalov dance. He was blonde and well-built. His language was not cultured, but he seemed quite intelligent. He and Louise related how their group was working for the removal of the tsar, considering such a change the salvation of the country. Tamara agreed, having been influenced by the Yusupovs. She explained that her aunt lived with her and that she was very suspicious. Grisha should avoid her whenever possible, however, if she did ask for something, he should do it. Should she ask a personal question, he should immediately emphasize that he was a veteran. In the morning Yakov would show him his duties.

Louise curtsied to Tamara when she thanked her and Tamara shook her head. "Tell me, Louise, how is it that you a young French lady should be so interested in Russian political affairs?

"I came here as a maid because I knew I would be able to attend classes and better myself. At the university I have met so many fine fellow students that I've lost myself in their cause."

"Your Russian has certainly improved," Tamara commented and added, "By the way, Louise, would you like to work as a maid again?"

The young lady was ecstatic and accepted readily. Tamara suddenly added, "I'm afraid you'll have to do cleaning, too."

The new maid agreed and thanked her mistress. The princess suggested that Louise show Grisha around the palace, told them Yakov would show them out and retired to the library.

Throughout the summer of 1916 Russian defeats and casualties on the Eastern front continued, causing a mass migration of civilians toward the interior of the country. The situation was creating havoc in the large cities where supplies were already limited. Tamara received word in September that Prince Vladimir Dashkov was ill with typhus in a hospital in Lutsk. She thought of traveling there, but the countess convinced her of the uselessness of such a trip. Not only would she have extreme difficulty reaching the city on the edge of the battle front, but she could not offer him any help because he would be in a quarantined ward. Still she felt she should make an effort and thought of Princess Olga Vorontsov. Surely the fiance of a hero would make every effort to help him. Tamara called at the Vorontsov mansion on the Fontanka and asked for Olga. She came after some time, condescending as ever. She had heard about Vladimir and was concerned, but she was at a loss about what should be done. Tamara suggested they both go at once to Lutsk even though it would be very difficult. They could receive railway passes through the transportation council. Olga was aghast. She would not even consider such a mission. Persuasion was wasted and Tamara left feeling miserable. "Oh, if only Vladimir will live to see through that woman!"

While the princess was saddened by Vladimir's situation, there was good news, she assumed, in regards to Shota. Russian troops on the Caucasian front had pushed into Turkish Armenia as far as the city of Trebizon. Tamara was sure that her beloved Terial was fighting in that arena of the war and that he was undoubtedly safe if the Russian advances had been so successful. She wrote a letter to Somi and asked if Shota was in the campaign in Armenia.

Irina and Felix returned at the end of September and invited Tamara to spend their first Sunday back with them. They had news.

Princess Zenaide was having an interview with the Empress that day and would report to them as soon as she came back from the Alexander Palace in Tsarskoe Selo. Irina and Tamara played with Bebe most of the morning until the wet-nurse came for the child. Walking into the great library, they chose seats under a large, ancient tapestry for their tete-a-tete. Tamara related her experience with Boris Sheremetiev and Irina could not control her laughter. She felt sorry for Boris, but she could envision Tamara bending over for a kiss. Felix entered and asked what was so funny. When told, he joined them in laughter, saying that the Sheremetievs had humor in their history also. "Imagine letting the tsar sign a declaration in your own house that would free all your serfs, the very basis of your wealth!"

A rustle was heard in the hall and Princess Zenaide burst into the room exclaiming, "Oh, it was awful!" Everyone stood up and rushed around the princess. They helped her take a seat and let her tell what happened. "When I entered Her Majesty's room, she was standing in the middle with her arms folded. I thought that was a rather hostile stance and it was. She knew why I was coming and evidently prepared what she was going to say. She didn't even motion for me to sit down. I curtsied and asked about her family. She was very cold and made a few remarks about their health. When I told her that I was resolved to make a last attempt at opening her eyes to what was going on in court circles, her eyes opened wide and a look of contempt spread over her face. It was terrible, yet I was determined and I continued.

I begged her, I actually begged her to understand that I was thinking of Her and Her family as well as Russia. She didn't say a word. I mentioned several of the disgusting and vile things that had been reported to me about Rasputin and how he was damaging the prestige of the royal family. I pointed out that even our Holy Russian Orthodox Church had condemned the monk. She became livid with anger. Still I felt it was my only and last chance and so I continued. I then turned to Rasputin's interference in the government, mentioning that Russia was rife with rumors about the so-called holy man's briberies and intrigues. Her Majesty still said nothing but looked as if she could explode. Finally I begged her again to understand the sincerity of my intentions and reminded her of the happy days we had when we were young. Nicholas had even performed with me in our theater at one of our fetes. Her Majesty's face showed sarcasm. I remember that I wiped some tears from my eyes when I finished. When I looked at her she said, "I hope never to see you again."

Everyone was speechless. Zenaide cried and Felix put his arm around her. "What are we going to do?" she exclaimed. "What will happen to us if this continues?"

The family was joined by Prince Felix the elder who listened while Zenaide related her experience again. Everyone listened a second time with as much interest as the first. It had been a shocking occurrence and seemed a foreboding sign of an oncoming disaster. After Zenaide finished her narration, she felt better and asked her husband what they should do? He comforted his wife and suggested that they ask Grand Duchess Elizabeth to come from the monastery in Moscow and talk with her sister, the Empress. "Surely her own sister can influence the mad woman," he stated and said he would contact the grand duchess. Zenaide liked the plan and the elder Yusupovs retired to their suite.

During a luncheon repast, Tamara had other news for Irina and Felix. She recounted the incident with her former maid Louise and told how splendidly the new workman Grisha was helping at the Dashkov residence. She related that he was a veteran who was hiding from the authorities because he had openly criticized the influence Rasputin had in the government. Felix was interested and said he would help the young man if he could in any way.

When Tamara asked about Felix's own relationship with Rasputin, he told her how he had renewed his acquaintance through Prince Andronnikov and though he loathed them both, he felt that he was convincing them of his sincerity and friendship. After his mother's experience with the Empress, Felix was sure that the time was coming when something drastic would have to be done. His association with Rasputin, in his opinion, was establishing a relationship that could be used for an advantage should the plan he was considering be necessary. He also repeated his wish that Tamara develop distant but friendly relations with Father Gregory. "We might need you," he concluded. The princess was very curious, but Felix had said earlier that he would divulge details at the appropriate time, so she remained silent.

In the middle of October the countess gave her niece an opportunity of furthering Felix's plan. Zita, after completing her morning chores at the "Saviors of Russia," a task she was doing more rarely than ever, left a note for Tamara at the office. The prince and the holy man would be their guests at dinner that evening and she would appreciate Tamara's being home by seven for the first course in the salon. The princess imagined that smoked salmon and caviar would be plentiful that evening!

Prince Andronnikov, dressed in a navy blue suit of exquisite material, arrived with Father Gregory, whose brow was sweaty and his long hair haggard and unkept. Their arms were filled with fancifully wrapped packages: Belgium chocolates and French perfumes were presented to the ladies. Tamara smiled at Rasputin for the first time but stepped back a little when he handed her a package. "Oh, she's not so afraid of me now," he exclaimed and his eyes, which had seemed dull and gloomy when he entered, took on a radiance as he stared at her. The countess was joyous over her gifts and asked the new servant Grisha to help the gentlemen with their coats. He did and carried them out to the entrance way. When he returned, he was carrying a tray holding crystal decanters of flavored vodka and a bottle of champagne. The guests asked about the servant and the countess raved about him, explaining that he was a wounded veteran whom they were helping. Prince Andronnikov was especially taken by the young blonde man and asked if he could borrow him sometimes. "You know how scarce servants are these days." The countess agreed and presented her guests with caviar and smoked salmon.

Tamara's smile had aroused Rasputin and he insisted on sitting by her. She remained aloof, and even though his breath reeked of garlic she listened closely as he expounded on spiritual matters. Watching the large so-called monk drinking sloppily and chewing fish with his mouth open, she could not imagine how any woman would let the creature near her. He was obnoxious and his glassy eyes seemed to undress her body as he carefully scrutinized her from head to toe. She wondered if Felix was planning for her to become intimate with the monster for some particular reason, like enticing him to a rendezvous. If that was what he wanted, how would she be able to tolerate Rasputin's disgusting physical presence. She hoped that Felix would not use her in his scheme, but she would help if needed.

Conversation at dinner was spiritual and banal. Rasputin bragged about his God-directed mission to save Russia from its enemies and he howled with glee about the efforts to disenchant the Empress about him. Prince Andronnikov, through his corrupt dealings, had access to police reports about the holy man and related an incident concerning the Empress. She was given proof that Rasputin kissed a young man and she replied, "Read the Apostles: they kissed as a sign of greeting!" Rasputin let out a roar and held his sides as he chuckled. The countess was also amused and said, "Chacun a son gout!" Again there was laughter. Tamara smiled but she was appalled at the monk's abominable hypocrisy, disgusting licentiousness and incredible unscrupulousness. She wondered if she had fallen into a den of thieves. How could her aunt associate with such people and why was she doing it? Surely perfume and candy could not replace the principals of her class? Had she become so wanton that she was amoral? Such questions rose in the princess's mind throughout the evening and she was heart sick when the party ended. Rasputin pressed her hand tightly and the prince bowed when they left.

"Aunt Zita, I have to ask. What would Vadim say if he saw you cavorting with the prince?"

"Cavorting? You would use such a word to me when you run after Felix all the time."

"Auntie, don't bring him into this. I'm speaking of my dearest uncle."

The countess sat down with a smirk on her face. "Well, I've had just enough champagne to settle something with you, young lady. It's none of your business, but I'm going to tell you. Your dear uncle whom you love and protect so well has not touched me in years. And do you know why?"

Tamara's face showed her despair

"Because he can't. That's right, he can't. You see, there was a freak accident and he was injured as no man should be. Now do you understand why he never objected to my relationship with Count Bagrov? And through the prince I meet other friends. Now do you understand?"

Tamara's eyes filled with tears. "Oh, Zita, I don't understand such things. It just seems wrong. If I've hurt you,

I'm sorry, but aside from the physical, which isn't my business, there's the moral aspect. Surely the prince's activities aren't proper and you should not be involved."

"I'm not involved. I'm really just a front for him and he pays me well for it."

"Oh, auntie, it seems as if the world is collapsing. The war is reaping such devastation, the hospital is so full of hopeless cases and our class is losing itself. I don't know what we stand for anymore. I don't know if I want to go on living."

The countess stood up and straightened her dress. Her face, which had been so full of anger and sarcasm, showed pity and she put her arm around her niece. "Ma chere, I have no answer. My own frustrations have led me astray and I know it. But you, you're young and you have a future. Your beauty will save you. I remember that Dostoevsky wrote that 'beauty will save the world.' I don't know if that applies, but I know you're too beautiful to be wasted. There has to be hope and values in the future or else everything is lost."

"Isn't it now?"

"I don't know." The countess squeezed her niece and led her up the stairs to their rooms.

In mid October a new government scandal permeated salons, clubs and governing institutions. A new prime minister had been designated, A.D. Protopopov, but it was soon evident that he suffered from severe mental deterioration, verging on insanity. Yet as unqualified as he was for the position, the more shocking news was that Rasputin had chosen him. The monk had nominated him above all the candidates presented to him through Anna Vrubova from the Empress. Rumors exaggerated the facts out of proportion and vile caricatures of the holy man sitting on Alexandra's lap spread through Petrograd. The government was in a crisis situation and nobody could foresee an expedient and practical solution to the dilemma.

Irina and Felix again invited Tamara for a Sunday in late October. After they had private mass in the Yusupovs' chapel, they ate a lunch in the dinning room right off the grand staircase. While the table was banquet size, five places were set at the end near the entrance. Zenaide wanted to be close at hand when the Grand Duchess Elizabeth returned from visiting her sister Alexandra. The Yusupovs and Tamara were eating sherbet when the nun, who rarely left her convent and even more rarely visited her sister, was seen through the windows that overlooked the staircase. Zenaide rushed out and enclosed the weeping Mother Superior into her arms. They walked slowly into the library on the other side of the staircase and the others quickly followed. The grand duchess was trembling and through her tears recounted her experience. "Alexandra greeted me with the sign of the cross, but she did not kiss or embrace me. I found that strange and recalled an incident in our youth when we were visiting Fredriksborg Castle. She interrupted me and would not let me finish. I had never known rudeness on her part and I must have shown fear in my eyes because she walked away from me. When I mentioned the name Rasputin, she stamped her foot and demanded that I not mention any details about that holy man. I know I cried, but she was unmoved. When I appealed to her to save Russia, she said that Father Gregory was doing that. I finally realized the hopelessness of my mission, but I tried once more. It was then that my own sister told me to 'Get out!' Never in my life had I been spoken to like that. She drove me away like a dog. Oh, our poor Russia!"

"Something has to be done!" Felix adamantly stated to Irina and everyone agreed. But what?

At the end of October Tamara received a telegram from Prince Vladimir stating that he would be released soon and would be given a long leave. In a few days he arrived at the Dashkov mansion where he was warmly received by the countess and the princess. His appearance was alarming. His hair had turned white as a consequence of the disease and he was extremely thin. It was obvious that his health was still in danger. He informed his relatives that he was going to Radnoe in hopes that the country air at the Dashkov estate outside Moscow would be beneficial. A military nurse had been assigned to him so he did not accept Tamara's offer of accompanying him. He knew she was needed at the hospital and felt every nobleman should do his part. He was surprised that his fiance Olga refused the trip by claiming that her mother was ill. When he visited them he did not find the Princess Vorontsov in any particular state of distress and rebuked Olga for not helping him. She only made excuses and

Tamara was delighted that Vladimir was seeing the real character of the woman. Vladimir approved of Grisha's service and after settling financial matters, took a military train south.

One day Tamara needed Grisha for an errand and could not find him. The Daskhov building was very large and much of it closed off. She went into the courtyard and assumed he was in the carriage house. When she entered the main hall her eyes could hardly believe what was before her. Stacks of boxes were lined up with labels such as sugar, flour, dried fruits, etc. and in another section the containers had French labels of unheard of luxuries for the time: Maron Glacé, Chocolate, Petits Fours, etc. Prince Andronnikov was using the Dashkov mansion for his supply house because it would be beyond suspicion. Tamara called out Grisha's name and he came running down a hall in the stable area. She demanded an explanation. It was simple. The prince had found out that the police were looking for him and had bribed him. The prince would not tell if Grisha, who had access to keys, would allow him storage space in the carriage house. Tamara sat down on a box and listened dumbfounded. "I had to do it. He was going to report me."

She nodded. The blame was elsewhere, but what could she do? If she disclosed the contraband to the police, the prince would reveal Grisha's hiding place. Since the prince had access to police papers, he might even be able to cover the whole thing up through Rasputin's influence. How rotten the world had become, she thought and realized that she was caught in a dishonest intrigue. Finally she stood up and said, "Alright, Grisha, I shall pretend I didn't see it."

That evening she accosted the countess. Yes, she knew the prince was using the carriage house and saw no problem with it.

"But what if Vladimir had seen it?"

"Fortunately, he didn't. So, go along with the flow of things. You've lost nothing by observing the status quo and besides, you've helped Grisha and the prince."

Tamara found her attitude so degrading and the situation so humiliating that she simply walked away to her room. She was tired from her day at the hospital and needed rest. She collapsed on her bed and felt as demoralized as the Russian army at the front.

Meanwhile Felix Yusupov was considering several schemes for a final solution of the Rasputin debacle. He first considered bribery. Since Rasputin spent freely and gave money little consideration, Felix thought that he might persuade the monk to leave Petrograd by promise of worldly riches. A second scheme was to entice the mad monk into a compromising situation of such proportions that even the Empress would be disillusioned. Felix was sure the police would help him and the exposure would be published in all the city newspapers. A third scheme and the one Felix dreaded was murder.

During one of his visits with Rasputin, Felix realized the pointlessness of the first plan he had given consideration. Anytime the subject of money would be mentioned, the monk would laugh and comment that he did not need it because people were always so generous. Women paid bills for him, they gave him jewels and they promised him everything. "Ah, what fools these women can be!" he exclaimed. "They are so naive and can be coaxed into even dropping their pantalettes!" Felix dropped the thought of bribery.

A compromising situation of scandalous nature was a problem. Rasputin had already committed many scandals and the Empress had never believed any of them even when evidence was produced. Felix knew that the monk was fascinated by the beauty of two women: Tamara and Irina. He had often expressed a desire to become better acquainted with them. Felix chose Tamara for his plot because she was single and not compromised. Irina was his own wife and if the scandal were revealed as a plot, a niece of the tsar would be involved. Besides, Irina was occupied with Bebe. Therefore Felix invited Tamara for another Sunday.

Not being sure of the details of his scheme, Felix explained to the princess that he was considering using her as a decoy to entice Rasputin into a scandalous situation. Tamara agreed that the monk had shown great interest in her and that she had lately, according to Felix's earlier suggestion, been friendly toward him. "Excellent," Felix commented. "Now I'd like for you to go with me to his apartment. It's merely to see if he shows the kind of interest in you that would be needed for my plan."

Arriving on Gorohovaia Street in the late afternoon, Felix led Tamara up the back staircase and into the kitchen. It was empty but strange noises were resounding from the other rooms. Felix opened a door and realized they had come at an importune time. A "radenyi" was in process, the ceremony performed to create a religious ecstasy that turns into an erotic frenzy. Rasputin was a devotee of the practice ever since the mystic in him was awakened in his homeland, Siberia. In those days he was drawn to a sect called "Khlystys," or Flagellants who attained communion with Christ though monstrous and bestial practices. Their ceremonies were a combination of Christianity and paganism. They believed that once a person attained spiritual ecstasy through invocations and chants, he was no longer responsible for his sins; they were now the burden of the spirit possessing him. The sect members spun themselves into dizziness until they fell, then they performed the most degrading perversions and orgies. In the brief moment that Felix looked through the door, he saw Rasputin naked in the middle of the dining room table holding a whip which he was using on several naked women and men writhing and spinning senselessly. Felix closed the door. The monk had not seen him and he quickly led Tamara out of the apartment.

Upsetting as the scene had been, it only convinced Felix that he must carry out his plan. Rasputin had to be destroyed. Tamara was invited back for the next Sunday and when she came a new scheme had been organized. Felix told her that he had arranged a meeting with Rasputin and was taking with them a friend from his childhood, Countess Elena Gravov, who believed in the monk. "She doesn't know our feelings and thinks we, too, are disciples. I invited her for authenticity. He might otherwise suspect just you and me."

Countess Elena was impressed that Tamara was a Maid of Honor to the Empress whom she admired greatly for believing in Rasputin. The countess was a persistent chatterbox who never ceased praising Father Gregory. "When I'm in his presence, I have such a feeling of divine comfort. All worries evaporate and the troubles of this wicked world just seem oblivious. He is truly a man of God. "Tamara and Felix listened and occasionally nodded or said "yes" at appropriate times. "Rasputin is the only consolation that Russia has. The Empress knows that her son is safe under the protection of that God-sent angel. Evil forces have tried to destroy him, but the power of God protects him and keeps him safe from his enemies." Her remark troubled Felix, but he was now determined no matter what.

Rasputin greeted his guests with open arms, kissing each of them three times on their cheeks. Tamara could hardly stand the smell of garlic that poured from his innards, but noticed his great look of satisfaction from finally kissing the face that attracted him so greatly. He led the threesome into his study where they sat down. Felix told the holy man that he felt he was ready for the cure the monk had promised him. The countess as thought Felix meant a spiritual awakening and Tamara wondered if he meant from perversion. Father Gregory clapped his hands once and said, "God be praised. We can start immediately." Felix suggested they start another day when the ladies were absent, but the monk was adamant. He led Felix into a bedroom and had him lie down on a cot. Staring into his victim's eyes, he ran his hands over Felix's body and whispered a chant. Then his head came very close to the prince's head and their eyes were only a few inches apart. Felix was sure the holy man was practicing hypnotism again and played along. Rasputin's shining eyes became like two phosphorescent beams of light that blended at times into a small circle and then at times enlarged. Felix felt a little dizzy and closed his eyes. The monk whispered another chant and then shook his victim. "You were asleep, my dear," Rasputin said and announced that the first treatment was over. Felix knew he had not been asleep, but agreed and thanked the practitioner, claiming that he felt much better. "Oh, with a few more treatments, you will be cured."

The countess had kept up a stream of praise for Rasputin while she and Tamara waited in the study. When Felix and the monk returned, another session was scheduled. The countess was simply ecstatic that Felix had found comfort from Father Gregory's treatment and said, "Another miracle to your credit, most holy one." Rasputin liked the compliment and embraced the countess, somewhat indecently. After her release, she straightened her dress and again babbled about God's revelation to man through a simple, holy monk. "It's wonderful what faith can do!" she concluded. Rasputin laughed as Felix escorted the ladies out of the apartment. He drove the countess home first and then Tamara, telling her that he felt the trip had been successful. It had been obvious that Rasputin was very interested in Tamara, and he himself had again established a close and trustworthy relationship with the monk. The scheme was working.

A few days later at the "Saviors of Russia," Tamara was surprised by an invitation in the mail from the Grand Duchesses Olga and Tatiana. She had liked them very much when they were so kind to her during her training at the hospital in Tsarskoe Selo. A tea for Maids of Honor was to be held at the Alexander Palace the next week. Tamara was glad she would see the tsar's daughters who had been her fellow debutantes, but she regretted that the Empress would undoubtedly attend. She returned her card of acceptance and wondered what she should wear.

The "Saviors of Russia" became Tamara's obsession. In work she found the distraction she needed from the events taking place in her life. Another shock came quit unexpectedly as always. Count Trushinsky came walking into her office using a cane. She ran into his arms and embraced him tightly. When she started talking, he shook his head and pointed at his ears. His hearing had been destroyed in a bomb blast. Tamara gave him a pencil and paper and he wrote out briefly what had happened. While riding in a convoy, two large artillery shells exploded on each side of his section.

Many were killed around him, He lost his hearing and received shrapnel in his right leg. Tamara read as he wrote and kept an arm around his shoulder. Since he was being released from military service, he was considering returning to their home in Tiflis. He had already asked the countess, but she was staying in

Petrograd for her war work. Tamara knew that was an excuse, but did not consider the countess a wife anyway. She told her uncle that she would join him in Tiflis as soon as she could. He thanked her and after a few days rest in the hospital, departed for Georgia on a military train.

An invitation from Irina for tea on a Wednesday was a departure from the Yusupovs' usual Sunday gatherings. Tamara figured that something was developing in Felix's plan and accepted without hesitation. Irina first showed her friend the baby's attempts at walking and then had a nurse take the child away. "We are leaving for the Crimea," Irina said, "and I do wish you would go with us."

"But what about Felix's plan?"

"That's what I invited you for. It has all changed. Felix has decided not to involve us in his scheme for our own protection. He thinks it would be too great a risk with such a madman. So, he's found help elsewhere. Grand Duke Dmitry and a member of the Duma, a Mr. Purishkevich, I believe, are going to be his partners in the solution. He is not going to tell you or me what is actually going to be done so that if we should be questioned, we won't be compromised. Knowing nothing, we could hardly be involved."

"But what are they going to do?"

"I fear for the worse."

"Murder?"

Irina nodded.

"But the Empress will have Felix shot!"

Irina winced and nodded. "What can I do? He's determined, and that's why he's sending me to Ai Tudor. I will be completely out of the plan and he would like for you to go with me, not just for your companionship, which I treasure, but for your own protection, too."

Tamara hesitated, wondering what she should do. She had promised her uncle that she would come to him in Tiflis and now Irina wanted her in the Crimea. Her real duty, in her opinion, was in continuing her work at the hospital. She postponed an answer and returned to the "Saviors of Russia."

Tamara boarded the special railway car for "Maids of Honor" at the station in Petrograd on the day of the Grand Duchesses' tea. There were seven others on board including Princess Olga Vorontsov whose dress was elegant, but the brim of her hat was so wide and so unsupported, it flopped over her face occasionally, amusing Tamara, but she said nothing. Olga had heard from Prince Vladimir whose health was improving. She was hoping he would return for the coming holiday season, but she was not sure. Tamara thought her attitude rather lackadaisical and wondered if perhaps there was a schism between the two.

At the Alexandra Palace the ladies were shown into a reception room near the entrance way. Grand Duchesses Olga and Tatiana greeted them all very cordially. The conversation dwelled on the tea cakes being served and the weather. It soon became obvious that everyone was avoiding the current events of the day: the disastrous war, the indecisive government and the rumors about Rasputin. Politeness and propriety were observed. After a while the Empress entered and everyone stood up for a curtsy. Alexandra, aloof and uninviting, walked among them exchanging tidbits of information about their families. When she reached Tamara, she studied the princess's face carefully and said, "I was very sorry about your brother."

"Thank you, your Majesty."

Looking into the Empress's eyes, Tamara felt a sincere sympathy for her. She was weary beyond words and nervous to the point of almost trembling. The princess sensed that Alexandra was desperately holding on to a belief that God was helping her save her son from hemophilia through the auspices of Rasputin. She thought of Felix and what he was planning and how distraught the woman before her would be if his scheme was carried out.

The Empress stayed only a few minutes. The grand duchesses carried on as hostesses by telling about their work in their hospital. Later they introduced a Lady-in-Waiting, Countess Gradekov, the wife of General Kalichevsky, who sang for the assembled Maids of Honor. The afternoon passed quickly and pleasantly.

The train bringing the Maids of Honor reached Petrograd just as a strike of the railroad workers' union was in progress. It was unheard of during a wartime crisis for there to be a disruption in transportation services planned by labor leaders, but the effrontery showed the frustrations developing in the country over the malfeasance of the government, which seemed in a chaotic state due to the continual change of ministers, and the terrible mismanagement of the armed forces, which had caused continual defeats at the front due to the tsar's lack of military prowess. When Tamara and the other young ladies started leaving the tsar's private coach, a group of workers shouted insults and made threats. It was unimaginable. The nobility was being attacked by the rabble. Olga Vorontsov was so indignant, she walked off from the others toward the station. A rotten squash hit her coat and splattered all over her. "Police!" she screamed as the other ladies ran and surrounded her, slowly walking her into the station without further mishap. Tamara suffered a dual reaction: she was actually amused that it should have been Olga who was hit, but she was horrified at the significance of the incident. What was happening in Russia?

Princess Irina left for the south with Bebe in the Yusupovs private coach. No one was told about her departure except Tamara who was sorry not to accompany her friend; but she felt her obligations at the hospital were more important and in the end Irina agreed. The work at the hospital continued in momentum and Tamara had little time for entertainments. Occasionally Prince Andronnikov was the countess's guest at dinner; one time he told the princess that Rasputin had been asking about her. He had mentioned that she had visited along with Felix Yusupov as one of his harem, as he expressed it; but that the beautiful Georgian girl had not returned. Tamara gave the impression that she had been too busy for visiting, but would eventually. The countess was pleased that her niece was at last being considerate of the monk.

In the afternoon of December 29, Tamara received an unsigned note by courier that had a hand printed message: "Do not try to contact me. I will be in touch when I can." She knew that only Felix could have sent such a missive and she contemplated what it meant. Was he really going through with his plan?

On the morning of December 30th, the countess came running into Tamara's room before her niece had arisen. "What do you know about it?" she screamed.

"What?" Tamara asked, sitting up in bed, surprised by her aunt's threatening tone.

"Rasputin! Did Felix murder him?"

"What do you mean?"

"You really don't know?"

Tamara shook her head.

The countess explained that ghastly rumors were spreading around the city that the holy father had been assassinated. Prince Andronnikov had learned at the police station that Father Gregory was missing and that gun shots were reported last night in the vicinity of the Yusupovs' Moika Palace.

"How horrible!" Tamara uttered, but noticed that her aunt was watching her face very closely for any indication of foreknowledge of the incident.

"We could all be investigated," the countess stated with dread in her voice. "It could be very serious."

Tamara dared ask, "How deeply involved are you in the prince's and Rasputin's black market dealings?"

"Not at all," she snapped, "It's just …" she broke off and walked heavily out of the room.

Alone, Tamara whispered to herself over and over, "He did it! My God, he did it!" She wondered what she should do. His note had forewarned her and she was glad she haddestroyed it. Yet how did he do it and who helped him? And where was it done? Surely not at the Moika Palace? Questions continually led to others until she remembered her work at the hospital. She realized that she must not change her routine and do everything in a normal fashion. She arose and started her day.

Petrograd almost erupted. Everyone grasped for information, any shred of detail. At the "Saviors of Russia" Tamara was asked about Felix, but she had not seen him for days. The story broke into the newspapers in headlines, "Rasputin Missing;" "Prince Yusupov Questioned:"

"Gun shots at the Moika Palace on the evening of December 29 were explained by Prince Felix Yusupov as the antics of a guest who was shooting at a watch dog in the courtyard."

On December 31, Prince Andronnikov learned at police headquarters that Felix had been directed by the strictest orders of Her Majesty the Empress not to leave the city and to stay at the palace of Grand Duke Dmitry until further notification. Again the countess asked her niece if she knew anything about Rasputin's disappearance? Tamara could honestly say no and thanked Felix for so arranging the ordeal. Since it was New Year's Eve, the countess and the prince asked Tamara if she would like to accompany them to a party. She refused, implying tiredness.

Tamara retired early. She was weary from the questioning and the unknown. What would happen? She could not surmise and suddenly whispered aloud, "Will the world ever be beautiful again?" She was sleeping when 1916 departed.

CHAPTER 6

1917

The headline of the evening newspaper, the "Petrograd News" for January 2, 1917 read, "Rasputin's Body Found" with a sub-line stating, "Prince Yusupov And Grand Duke Dmitry Held." The article revealed that the body had been found near the Petrovsky Bridge through a hole in the ice. It was taken to the Veterans' Home at Tchesma, near Petrograd. After a post-mortem, a nun named Akoulina who had been exorcised by Rasputin prepared the corpse for burial. The tsarina sent a crucifix to be placed on the holy man's breast.

Because of his contacts in the police department, only Prince Andronnikov could give Tamara any additional information. She regretted being dependent on him, whom she loathed, but he was her only source. From his spies in the police headquarters the prince learned that Felix was denying that he was involved, but a member of the Duma, Vladimir Mitrophanovich Purichkevich, had told a policeman who had gone to the Moika Palace after hearing the shots that Rasputin had just been murdered. The investigation was on going and the Empress had ordered Grand Duke Dmitry and Prince Yusupov confined to their palaces. She had at first ordered that the prince be shot immediately, but was persuaded otherwise by family members and the Prime Minister, Protopopov. Tsar Nicholas was returning to Petrograd from Mogilev and would investigate the affair personally.

Tamara was still in a quandary. She could not see Felix, but not helping him caused her anguish. There was also the possibility that the police might question her since she had visited Rasputin with Felix. The more she thought of the situation the more she regretted not having accompanied Irina. In the south at the beautiful Ai Tudor estate, they would both have been out of the fracas.

At the "Saviors of Russia" Tamara was busy with paper work when a mysterious, tall lovely woman entered. She was elegantly dressed in black with a black veil over her beautiful face. She approached Tamara and said, "Can we talk here?"

It was Felix! Tamara almost fainted, but grasped one of his hands and kissed it. He explained that while he was confined to his palace, it was very easy to enter and leave in such an outfit. He had come to their old palace for two reasons: to pick up some papers stored in the upper section of the building and to see Tamara. She was thrilled and had him sit with his back to the door in case anyone came in. "Although, really, no one would suspect that you are you. You look wonderful."

"I was always told that."

"What have you heard from Irina?"

"She and Bebe are fine. I was supposed to leave last night on the express, but the Empress's arrest warrant stopped me at the train station."

"Oh, Felix, you've done such a wonderful thing."

"Yes, and I hope Russia will appreciate it."

"It does. Everyone does."

Felix smiled at the word "everyone," and assured his friend that the Empress was capable of the worst. For Tamara's sake, since she was involved in one plot that was not carried out, Felix quickly recalled the major events of the murder.

His accomplices were Grand Duke Dmitry, Purichkevich from the Duma, Dr. Lazovert and Captain Sukhotin."

"The wounded captain who was in Ward #5 for a while?" Tamara interrupted.

"Yes, I became friendly with him while visiting and when I proposed his help, he was more than willing."

Two servants in the Moika Palace, Gregory and Ivan, were sworn to secrecy and helped set up the basement room that Felix had chosen for the deed. Since Rasputin would have been surprised to enter an unfurnished basement room, Felix had treasures from the Yusupov collections included in the furnishings. An oriental carpet was spread and rare Chinese vases were put in niches and on tables. A white polar bear rug was in front of a fireplace. When finished, it had the appearance of a gentleman's study.

The plot was as follows: Rasputin was invited in order to meet Princess Irina in whom he had always shown great curiosity. "Like in you," Felix added. The prince drove over for the monk and when they returned they entered through a basement door. Dmitry and the others were upstairs playing records and talking as if a party was going on. "I hate to admit it," Felix interrupted himself again, "but I was scared to death,"

Once inside the holy monk did not seem suspicious and Felix told him that Irina would join them when she could free herself from their guests. Rasputin believed him and accepted some poisoned wine and tea cakes. Dr. Lazovert had assured the conspirators that there was enough poison in one cake to kill anyone. Rasputin ate several, but found them too sweet and asked for Madeira. Felix tried changing his glass to one with cyanide, but the monk told him to use the same glass. Felix dropped it, supposedly accidentally. He filled a glass containing the poison and the holy man sipped it like a connoisseur. He drank off and on till two thirty and demanded that Felix sing while he enjoyed the wine.. "I was almost out of my mind from fear."

When Rasputin asked what the noise was upstairs, Felix told him that the guests were probably leaving, but he would check. Upstairs the conspirators were stunned when told that the poison was not working. The doctor said it was impossible. Felix borrowed Dmitry's revolver and descended the stairs. Rasputin began talking about God and the weakness of human flesh. When he saw Felix looking at a crucifix, he asked why. "I said, 'You'd better look at it, too.'" Rasputin's face showed fear for the first time and Felix shot him. He screamed wildly and crumpled on the floor.

The plan was that Dmitry and the doctor would drive away from the palace in an open car as if taking Rasputin home. Captain Sukhotin would be wearing the monk's coat. That guise was done in case the secret police had followed Felix and Dmitry to the palace. After they left, Felix began examining Rasputin.

Suddenly the monk's eyes began quivering and then opened. "They were like the greenish eyes of a viper and he stared at me with a look of diabolical hatred. My blood ceased flowing, I'm sure." With a violent effort, Rasputin leapt on his feet and gave a wild roar. Blood flowed from his mouth. He rushed at Felix and grabbed him tightly. The prince freed himself only after a ferocious struggle. "I swear he was raised from the dead by the powers of evil."

Felix ran up the stairs and into a hall, screaming for Purichkevich. A noise behind him frightened them both. The stairway landing was a little room made up of eight doors. Only one opened into the hall where Felix and the legislator were standing. When they opened the door, they found blood on several of the doors. The monster had crawled up a stairway that had a right angle in its middle and had tried to find an exit. He did not try the only door that opened. The creature from hell was crawling back down the stairs when Felix and Purichkevich entered the landing. A secret door that was always locked opened and the monster went out into the courtyard. Purichkevich ran after him and shot him twice, but only a third shot stopped him. They beat him with chains until he was motionless.

At that moment two servants and a policeman ran into the dark courtyard. Felix stood at an angle so that the policeman would not see the monk behind a snowdrift. He explained that a guest had been shooting wildly at a watch dog, nothing of any importance. The policeman left and the servants were sworn to secrecy.

"But Prince Andronnikov said that in the police reports, Purichkevich had confessed that Rasputin was killed."

"Unfortunately, the policeman came back and Purichkevich,

nervous and scatterbrained, did tell him that. I just hope they'll accept my story that he was drunk."

"Who put the body in the river?"

When the other conspirators returned, they carried the body out and took it to the Perovsky Bridge. "And would you believe it, they say Rasputin drowned! He survived all the poison and bullets."

"Oh, Felix, what you lived through."

The stately lady stood up and whispered, "Come to us in the Crimea as soon as you can."

Tamara nodded and watched Felix walk gracefully out of the office.

Nicholas II was already a disheartened man when he arrived in Petrograd for the investigation of Rasputin's murder. The callosal military defeats and millions of casualties of the Russian army under his inadequate command had convinced him that he could not struggle against destiny. He was nervous and crushed by anxiety. The Empress's furor over Rasputin's murder only added to the Emperor's fatigue and fears. His energy exhausted, he became a confirmed fatalist.

When news of the involvement of Grand Duke Dmitry and Prince Yusupov in the murder of Rasputin spread through the city, workers' unions offered protection to the conspirators, military regiments celebrated and crowds of people gathered in front of their palaces praying and presenting flowers. There was a feeling that Russia had been saved.

Rasputin's followers were as livid with rage as the public was thrilled with joy. Several of them tried entering Grand Duke Dmitry's palace by visiting sick patients in the ground floor hospital he had created at the beginning of the war. A sentry at the upstairs entrance stopped them.

Grand Duke Alexander Mikhailovich, who was Chief of Military Aviation in Kiev, arrived in Petrograd on the 3rd of January and went directly to his sovereign. The tsar listened to his cousin and, evidently because of his weakened condition, agreed with the duke about the sentences of the conspirators. Grand Duke Dmitry was given orders to leave immediately for Persia where he would be under the supervision of a General Baratov. Prince Yusupov was exiled to the family estate Rakitnoie.

Investigations of the Rasputin affair continued. Prince Andronnikov arrived at the Dashkov mansion early on the morning of the 3rd. His informant at the police station had let him know that Tamara was to be questioned. Servants at Rasputin's apartment had listed her as one of the people who visited with Felix. The countess was aghast. "Surely you didn't know about the plan?" Tamara assured her she did not and awaited the summons. A police detective came later in the morning to the Dashkovs' and interviewed the princess. She prayed as she lied and the officer left confident that the princess had not been involved. The countess was so pleased with the outcome, she shared with her niece a beauty secret she had just recently learned: a particular curve of a small brush around the eyes made them stand out. When she started doing it on Tamara, she abruptly stopped and said, "Oh, those big eyes hardly need it!"

Tsar Nicholas II left Petrograd after the investigation. The pressure the Empress had placed on him during the upheaval had diminished his energy even farther. While the city was quiet when he left, at the beginning of March bread riots broke out in several sections of the enormous metropolis. Shortages of food and fuel at both the war and home fronts were causing a demoralization of the military and the populace. Workers' unions again began strikes and the centers of the city filled with crowds of protesting people. The city was soon in chaos. Fires were set in many places and shooting was heard. The revolution had started.

At military headquarters in Mogilev, the tsar was informed about the disturbances in Petrograd. He ordered the crowds dispersed and order restored, but the Ruler of All the Russias no longer had the power for his commands. Petrograd was an uncontrollable disaster, a debacle. The tsar left by train for the city, but he was met at Pskov by members of the Duma who asked for his resignation. A disillusioned and dispirited man abdicated to his cousin, Grand Duke Michael. The latter refused the crown and over 300 years of Romanov rule ended forever.

Circumstances in Petrograd changed at once. There was great confusion in the streets. Many political parties placed parades on the streets claiming control of the government; soldiers feeling that discipline no longer mattered wandered aimlessly along the avenues; and citizens hurried to and fro trying to make sense of the chaos, seeking news anywhere they could. Rumors were the information of the day.

With the death of Rasputin, Prince Andronnikov had lost his patron and his contacts in the black market. His stores in the Dashkov mansion were quickly dispersed and he was suddenly without a great influx of funds. Not being able to afford the lifestyle he had become accustomed to, he dropped the countess as quickly as he had taken her on. Since he no longer needed a front for his perverse and illegal activities, she was a liability he did not need. The countess was livid with anger that he could be so indifferent after the way she had helped him. She lectured Tamara on men for hours, pointing out that not one could be trusted and that they were all scoundrels, hypocrites and heartless creatures. Disgusted with her life, She announced that she was joining her husband in Tiflis and wanted Tamara to accompany her. The princess did not feel she could leave the hospital since Irina and Felix were depending on her and there was also the Dashkov mansion; Vladimir depended on her, too. The countess did not insist and left Petrograd, which she called "a city no longer with soul," for Tiflis, which she acclaimed as "a city still with heart."

Different from the American and French revolutions, during the upheaval in Russia in February, 1917, a call for a democratic government was proclaimed immediately. The monarchists who supported a theory of royal absolutism yielded power without a struggle. The major question of the day became what sort of democracy the country could develop? The two strongest political parties were the Duma and the Petrograd Soviet of Workers' Deputies. The former became the Provisional Government but was subservient to the latter which renamed itself the Petrograd Soviet of Workers' Deputies. The dual power of the two strongest parties turned the Duma's meetings in the Taurida Palace into shouting matches.

The Bolsheviks, which had been a small, obscure party that few gave any attention, suddenly burst forth during the chaos of establishing a government. In April the Germans allowed Lenin passage through their country from Switzerland where for years he had been writing pamphlets urging a communist revolution. He was met at the train station in Petrograd by some followers and the Bolsheviks gradually worked for the seizure of power.

Prince Vladimir Dashkov returned from the Dashkov estate Radnoe with shocking news. While his health had improved, the conditions he described in the countryside were catastrophic for the land owning class of the former Imperial Russia. The disorder among the peasants was alarming. They sent their cattle for pasture on gentry meadows without permission; they cut wood in the landowners' forest without payment; they took supplies from warehouses as if they were not stealing and they claimed a right of habitation in their cottages without paying rent. Worse still was the outright confiscation of land. The old patriarchal relationship between lord and serf was gone and there was only contempt for the property rights of the landlords. The rule became that any serf whose family lived on land before 1861, the year the serfs were freed, had the right of possession. Land was seized and landowners forced from their own property. In cases where they refused, their manor house might be burned or they might be shot

Tamara could hardly believe Vladimir's accounts. The Dashkovs had always been kind to their serfs and a very pleasant relationship had existed between them. No longer. Vladimir was told that the manor house was needed for a barn and that he no longer owned Radnoe.

"What about Kholmka?" Tamara asked.

"I haven't heard yet from Oleg Dunatov, but I suppose it's the same situation down there."

"What are we to do?" Tamara asked.

Vladimir shook his head, disarranging his long white hair.

A great deal of their wealth was being confiscated and they were helpless. The prince himself, because of his military record and education, had been asked to join the new Ministry of Foreign Affairs of the Provisional Government. Because he spoke German, he was being sent to the royal court in Denmark via

Finland. "I regret leaving you when things are so bad in the city, but I will need a profession in the future and this opportunity might not be offered again if I refuse. Yet I worry about you."

"Oh, you must go." Tamara insisted. "Don't worry about me. I'm so busy at the hospital I never worry about anything."

Before departing, Prince Vladimir settled accounts in his bank, arranging for the upkeep of the family mansion. Another problem was his fiance, Princess Olga Vorontsov. She was now indicating that she had changed her mind and would like to marry as soon as possible. While in the country restoring his health, Vladimir had changed his mind about her. He now figured that she was merely wanting to consummate their relationship because he was going to be a diplomat and she could go abroad with him. He made excuses, claiming that his situation in the new government was too precarious to be assured of a definite career and his financial situation was also unclear because of the peasant uprisings. When he refused, she was indignant and berated him for taking a position with a government so alien to their noble rights. He found it amusing that she had not been so upset before he postponed their marriage. Yet he himself wondered if he should work for the Provisional Government since his own family had served the tsars for centuries. Still he realized that incredible changes had taken place and a new order had begun. It was a matter of survival in the present in spite of the past.

The "Saviors of Russia" was having financial problems. The Yusupovs' enormous wealth still carried the burden of the medical institution, but government subsidies were difficult to obtain and that forced economical measures. The staff of physicians and nurses finally placed a limit on the number of casualties they could accept.

It was not a great problem for the military because the number of wounded had diminished since the army was in disorder. Reports of soldiers shooting their own tsarist officers were commonplace as was the ravaging of the countryside by hungry troops. In the cities slogans stating "All Power to the Soviets" were appearing and rumors about the Bolsheviks' determination to seize power spread. The Provisional Government therefore took strict measures to combat the growing menace of the small revolutionary group.

Tamara was at home one afternoon when Yakov came running to her in the study. "Princess, the police are searching us!" She quickly went into the entrance way and saw a large number of police going into the salon and up the grand stair case. She was speechless. An officer approached her with a paper in his hand and said, "By order of the Provisional Government, we are commanded to search your property." He handed the paper to Tamara and she stared at it, baffled by the suddenness of the operation and confused about its purpose.

"Why?" she asked.

"It's been reported that revolutionaries are hiding in this palace and we must check it out."

"But that's impossible!" the princess exclaimed, her face showing complete amazement.

"I am sorry to bother you, but we must carry out our orders."

Tamara nodded and sat down on a French Louis XV chair by a large golden girondole. She could not help but be amused by the spectacle before her. There she was sitting in a magnificent 18th century palace while police were searching for revolutionaries. It seemed like a comedy on the stage. Suddenly the humor of the situation paled. The police led Louise and Grisha through the front entrance way. An officer shouted, "We caught them trying to escape!" Tamara was horrified and could only stare.

At the same time another policeman entered from the back courtyard and called out, "We found the printing press." Again Tamara could hardly believe her ears. She looked at her former servants, but they would not face her. The police captain who had served the right of search, asked Tamara about her relationship with the accused. She was nervous and on the verge of tears. "I cannot believe they are who you say they are. He's a veteran; he was wounded. And she's French. How could they be revolutionaries?"

"Look," the captain said, pointing with a finger at a box of pamphlets that had just been brought in. "Power to the People" was printed in large letters on the covers. "And their printing press is in your carriage house."

Again Tamara looked at the servants, but they kept downcast eyes.

The captain told Tamara to wait where she was while he questioned the guilty. He led Grisha into the study and closed the door. Louise was given a chair near Tamara and looked at her for the first time. The princess only saw hate in her eyes.

Softly, hardly able to speak, Tamara said, "Louise, did you deceive me a second time?"

With a smug look of contempt on her face, Louise said, "Yes, I did. You were so naive I couldn't help but take advantage of you." But Louise, such…"

"Don't 'Louise' me. Your kind has had its day and now you'll pay for it."

Oh, Louise, you hated me all along and I didn't realize it."

"No, I didn't hate you. You were too kind to me, but you're an exception. The countess can burn in hell and I'll be happy."

"Oh, Louise, don't talk like that. She was kind to you."

"I've never known such condescension, but don't worry, we'll take care of her!"

Tamara winced.

"She treated you badly too. Do you know about the men she had in her suite?"

"Stop, Louise, I don't want to hear such things."

"Yeah, avoid the issue no matter what. That was the trouble with you aristocrats, you never saw what was going on around you." Tamara nodded. "I truly didn't."

"I mean how the majority of you treated people. You lived in riches while we lived in hell. Well, it's over for you now and we'll make you pay for it."

"Oh, Louise. I trusted you so."

"Lenin has taught us that the best way to overcome you is to take advantage of your weaknesses. Your trust did you in."

"Who is Lenin?"

"You'll find out. Oh, how you'll find out."

The police captain came out of the room behind Grisha who looked sullen. The captain waved Louise into the study and Grisha sat down where she had been sitting. He did not look at Tamara and kept his eyes cast downward.

After a short silence, the princess asked, "Grisha, is it all true?"

He nodded.

She paused. "Grisha, you deceived me, but you also helped me very much with the upkeep here. I thank you for that in case we never see each other again."

"You paid me," he uttered, not looking at her.

Looking at the young man, she wondered for what cause a person could sacrifice morality and life itself. He would probably be shot and there was nothing she could do. She was not sure she should sympathize since he hated everything that had made up her life, yet she could not help but wish that she could save him some way.

The captain escorted Louise out of the salon. Two policemen led her over by Grisha while the officer went to Tamara. "They both maintain that you are innocent. I assume that is true because of your name. Do you wish to press any charges against them?"

"What do you mean?"

"Property damage or false papers of identification?"

Tamara shook her head. "Where will you take them?

"To headquarters."

"What will happen?"

"They'll be booked and questioned. We've been after them for a long time. How clever of them to use you."

Tamara slightly nodded and looked at the prisoners. It had all been too sudden and too painful. Tears came to her eyes and she asked the captain, "Is there anything I can do?"

He looked at her in astonishment, shook his head and waved a hand at the guards who then led Louise and Grisha out of the palace. After all the police had left, Tamara called Yakov and Dima together. The detective had questioned them, but they knew nothing nor had they suspected anything. They were more interested in who would be taking over the work that Louise and Grisha had been doing? Tamara assigned Dima household duties, much to his chagrin because, as he explained, "I'm a chef, not a scrubwoman!" Tamara consoled him by reminding him that most of the palace was closed. Yakov would take care of the stable as before and help Dima when necessary. The princess apologized for asking such chores of them, but the times required sacrifices.

The noble world the servants had served was disappearing and what lay ahead, no one could foresee.

Tsar Nicholas II and Tsarina Alexandra were confined in the Alexandra Palace in Tsarskoe Selo after the February Revolution. Noble families, assuming that their rights would be respected under the Provisional Government, did not worry about their property in the cities. It was in the countryside that the revolution was having an effect on their way of life. Moderate attention was paid to the Bolsheviks and their socialist slogans; they were a nuisance but it was taken for granted that the Provisional Government would prevail. When the tsar and his family were transferred by rail to Tobolsk, Siberia at the end of July, 1917, members of aristocratic families began wondering what they should do. Most ladies took their jewels to their banks to wait out the change of government. Tamara took her valuables to the National Bank and placed them in the Dashkov strong box with her mother's and the Princess Dashkov's jewels.

After the takeover, the new government granted reprieves for political prisoners and exiles. Irina and Felix, who had been living comfortably at Rakitnoie where peasant uprisings had not yet occurred on the estate, could not return by their private railway car and suffered a crowded coach with some workers. When the train pulled into Petrograd, they were amazed at the disorder before them. Services that their noble families had long taken for granted no longer existed. Leaving the coach and entering the station, they literally pushed themselves through the crowds and had difficulty arranging for their baggage. At the Moika Palace their old dependable servants greeted them with joy because they did not understand the disorderly world that had enveloped them. It took a few days for the return of some normalcy. They drove by the "Saviors of Russia" and, after looking over the hospital, invited Tamara for one of their special Sundays together.

A Sunday away from the lonely Dashkov mansion was a treat for the princess and she went with great delight. The friends exchanged much news. Tamara related the incident with the police and her servants and the Yusupovs told about their experiences on the train. They all agreed that Petrograd had become a madhouse. The Yusupovs had tried establishing order in their household, but the confusion in the city was not conducive to a life with any semblance of their former existence. For that reason, they were moving to the Crimea where Felix's parents were living at their Ai Tudor estate. "This madness doesn't exist down there and it will be safer until all of it blows over."

"Will it?" Tamara asked.

"Surely someday, but until then, we think it would be best to be out of harm's way. Won't you come with us?"

Again Tamara refused. How could she leave the Dashkov mansion when Vladimir was depending on her. There was no way of avoiding the responsibility. Also, her work at the hospital was her salvation. How could she desert it? They understood and admired her; however, they made her promise that she would come as soon as possible.

News from Tiflis supported Felix's remark that the madness had not spread to the South. The countess wrote that life was normal and that a new science called "magnetism" was popular.

There were a few seances, but she considered them rather silly under the circumstances. Tamara was amused at her aunt's change of attitude about spiritualism. The countess revealed that her husband's hearing had not improved and that he spent a great deal of time playing solitaire. The thought saddened Tamara and she wished she could help him. There was no news about the Zhorzhadze relations. Tamara had read the letter quickly in hopes of finding out something about Shota. There was nothing, so she reread it slowly, thinking, "How typical of Zita, not mentioning what she knows I want to hear!"

In spite of the troubling conditions in Petrograd, hostesses continued giving evening parties. It was as if they were trying to hold on to the past in the best way they could. The affairs were not spectacular in the least, materials were not available for a luxurious fete. Yet each hostess did as well as she could just to keep life continuing, as if any effort might help restore some of the joy of the old days. Tamara was invited quite often, but did not attend many evenings. Her experience at Betsie Shuvalov's with the charming soldier Foma had disillusioned her about the blending of the classes. She felt that such a social change could not take place at once, but she had no solution.

At a party for the wounded at Madame Brianchaninov's, the princess had another experience that disappointed her. An officer asked her for a dance and she accepted. When they went on the dance floor, he tried holding her very close. She broke away and shook her head. She smiled and raised her arms as if she would continue the dance on her terms, but he grabbed her again and held her very tightly. She squirmed out of his grasp and walked away. He followed, seized her arm and said, "Not good enough for you, princess?"

"Please, not here."

"Where then, my bed?"

Tamara walked away. Never in her life had she been so accosted. No one helped her and she walked off the floor embarrassed. On hearing of the incident the hostess rushed to Tamara and apologized. "Ma chere, I don't know what is happening in our world. Knighthood is no longer in flower and we are left with the rabble." Tamara smiled, kissed her cheeks and left, knowing she would not attend another such party and would never try to be so egalitarian again.

Irina wrote from the Crimea that conditions there were changing very fast. Her father, Grand Duke Alexander and the Dowager Empress Marie were awakened one morning at 5:00 o'clock by armed sailors sent from the Sebastopol authorities with a search warrant. They demanded door keys and any private weapons. They searched the entire morning and found nothing but some old Winchester rifles that had been on her father's yacht. The Empress was forced from her bed by sailors who wanted to search it. She stood behind a screen in her housecoat while they stole her private papers and a Bible she had brought with her from Denmark as a girl of seventeen. Because of the sailors' insulting behavior, the royal personages were utterly shocked. For this reason, she and Felix were returning to Petrograd in order to discuss their rights with the head of the Provisional Government, Alexander Kerensky. They wanted him to intervene in the activities of the Sebastopol municipal commission. Tamara was glad they were coming home.

Princess Irina waited a month for an interview with the head of the government. Finally it was arranged and Felix drove her to the Winter Palace which Kerensky had made his headquarters. Old servants who knew Irina welcomed her with curtsies and bows when she entered. They ushered her into the former tsar's study and she sat down in a leather chair which she remembered was her uncle's favorite. Kerensky entered and made a most negative impression on her. He seemed embarrassed that he, a former Cadet, was being addressed by a member of the royal family. She explained the situation in Sebastopol and he claimed no responsibility. "Who then, but you, the head of the government, could have such responsibility?" He did not answer, so she badgered him until he promised that he would do what he could. She left knowing that her mission had been pointless. After saying goodbye to the servants, she left the Winter Palace of her ancestors forever.

Disillusioned, the Yusupovs decided on a return trip almost immediately. They visited with Tamara at the Dashkov mansion and suggested that she start hiding some of the treasures in the Dashkov collection. They had hidden some valuables at the Moika Palace. A secret room was built in the basement and much silver and gold placed inside. Also, Felix had cut two Rembrandts out of their frames in the gallery at the Moika Palace and they were taking them with them to the Crimea. Looking around the Dashkov salon, he said, "Those paintings by Boucher and Fragonard are of great value, I'd hide them some place."

Before the Yusupovs left Petrograd, the Bolsheviks made an attempt to seize power. Horrors were committed throughout the metropolis. Trucks full of soldiers drove around shooting indiscriminately; cars with soldiers on their running-boards raced through pedestrian areas and shot civilians who had not hurriedly taken cover. Streets were strewn with debris and bodies. Chaos reigned for several hours until the army and the police calmed the situation. It was, however, only the beginning of the Bolshevik terror.

Tamara was horrified by the ghastly murders she witnessed from her hospital window. When Yakov came for her, he had instructions from the Yusupovs to bring her to their Moika Palace. Once safely there, they begged her to go with them to the Crimea. "It isn't safe for you here and they'll soon be breaking into the Dashkov's." Felix told what had happened to them. A detachment of soldiers came and demanded occupancy of their home. He showed them around and told them it was more conducive to being a museum than a barracks. They left, but the next morning when he came out of their room, he found three soldiers sleeping on the marble floor. They said they had been sent to guard the property. "You see, Tamara," he continued, "It is only a matter of time before the city is in a state of anarchy. They will break into homes, pillage and murder. The city will be in the hands of a frenzied, bloodthirsty mob. You must come with us to the Crimea."

For the first time Tamara agreed. "Yes, you're right," she slowly said, thinking of the hospital and the Dashkovs. "I'll go with you."

Irina and Felix were ecstatic. They felt as if they had saved their friend from perishing.

Before Tamara left, final plans were made for their departure. She would spend her last night at the Dashkov mansion and hide what valuables she could. The next morning she would go to the hospital and explain her departure to the doctors who had become colleagues and friends. Then she would meet them at the railroad station at 3:00 P.M.

There had been no news from Prince Vladimir since he left for Denmark. Since war time communications were difficult, Tamara had not worried about him. She regretted leaving her responsibilities with the mansion, but she was sure Vladimir would understand. Her only recourse was Yakov. The old coachman had devoted his life to the Dashkovs and could be depended on, but what irony to leave such a palace under the care of a coachman!

Tamara questioned him about the edifice. Were there any secret rooms where things could be hidden? Yakov led her to a stairwell that had large panels along its sides. The third panel opened and exposed a small room already partially filled with silver urns and candelabra. She patted the old man on his cheek and thanked him. With his help they carried pictures and vases into the hiding place. Tamara informed Yakov that in the morning they would go to the bank and she would draw out sufficient money for any routine expenses he would have until she or Vladimir returned. Then she started packing her own clothes, falling exhausted on her bed when she finished.

The next morning Yakov drove the princess to the bank and she entered the vaults. In the Dashkov strong box she sorted out valuables that she was taking with her. Her mothers' jewels and the gifts from the Duc de Crevreuse were placed in a small sack which she tied inside her dress. She left the Princess Dashkov's jewels, assuming they were safe in the bank. Then she withdrew a large sum of money part of which she would leave in the hospital safe. She would arrange for Yakov to draw on the funds should money be needed for upkeep at the palace. Then they drove to the hospital.

Tamara entered the "Saviors of Russia" and went directly to the office of the chief administrator. He was not there and a nurse told her that he was in the ward of amputees. She walked through the halls past bed after bed until she reached a rotunda. As she was crossing it heading for the room of amputees, she by chance looked through a door where the shell shocked patients were lying. Instantaneously she stopped, looked again and shouted, "Shota!"

The princess ran into the ward up to the bed of her beloved and threw her arms around him. "Shota! Shota! Shota!" she cried as tears rolled down her cheeks. When she came to and stopped hugging him, she looked into his eyes and found only a blank stare. He did not know her. His expression showed puzzlement and he began pushing her away. "Nurse," he called and Tamara backed away. Oh, Shota, don't you recognize your Nestan?" she pleaded, still crying.

When she said the name, his face twisted into a grimace. He was not himself. He hid his face in his hands and shook his head. When he lowered his hands, he closed his eyes and did not move.

A nurse came and explained that the patient had come in that morning and they needed information about him. Would Tamara help them in anyway she could?

Tamara knew where her heart and duty lay. Yes, she would help them and she would stay with him. She told Yakov what had happened and he took her to the crowded train station. When the Yusupovs came, she related the experience even though talking was difficult on the noisy train platform. Irina understood, but Felix shouted over the mob that she should travel with them because Shota might never recover. Tamara would not listen and said goodbye. They parted in tears, promising to communicate as soon and as often as possible.

While at the train station, Tamara decided to wire Somi immediately about Shota. She pushed her way through the large crowd in the enormous waiting room and found the communications center. The lines to the three windows were long. She realized that she had never stood in such a line before. It was her first real comprehension of how her world had changed. She had always been waited on. A servant always did any errand she wanted. Now she must live as a menial. She entered the middle line in the back and waited in silence, thinking of the new order of things and feeling somewhat fearful. She noticed people staring at her, but she was accustomed to that, assuming it was her face. While her beauty played a role in their interest, it was her clothes that made her stand out all the more. She was not dressed in average apparel. Her hat alone was too fine. It suddenly dawned on her that even her clothes set her apart.

When she reached the telegraph window, she filled out the form as a clerk watched her closely. She wrote Somi that Shota was in the "Saviors of Russia" hospital and that she was watching after him. He was in shock from a bomb blast and would recover. When she handed the telegram to the curious clerk, he snapped, "Too many words. Restrictions allow only two lines." Tamara quickly marked out several phrases, leaving only the pertinent information about Shota.

Yakov was waiting in the carriage outside the station even though he had been forced away several times by police. Tamara let out a sigh of relief as they drove away from the crowds. At the Dashkov palace, Yakov helped the princess open the panel in the staircase and she placed her bag of jewels inside. She was ready for the new tasks ahead. At the hospital Tamara found Shota's documents in a pile of papers that had come with the new casualties. He had served in the army of the Caucasus, but because of his heroism, he had been chosen for officers' training and sent to Kiev. There he finished his course and became a lieutenant in the infantry. In a battle near Vilna a bomb blast blew him into the air, knocking him unconscious. Upon reviving, he was suffering shell shock and led away from the front line.

Tamara informed the doctors and nurses that Shota was a cousin and that she wanted to participate in helping him recover. Because of her work for the hospital and her relationship with the Yusupovs, a desk was arranged near his bed so that she could continue her secretarial duties and help watch after the patient. A routine developed: Tamara would walk with him in the mornings when he had his exercise, she would oversee his eating when his tray was delivered and she would talk with him whenever she could about the past and their homeland. At times it seemed to her that he was on the verge of recognizing her and was about to grab her as a lost relative would, but other times he would not respond and seemed farther away than ever. No matter what mood he was in, Tamara was thrilled to be near her beloved.

The princess's life in the hospital became her salvation and delight. Feeling greatly alone with her close friends away, Tamara rejoiced that she had such a meaningful mission in her life. What more could she want than to be helping her beloved Shota? The doctors and nurses were sympathetic and kind and helped her in any way they could. One day she asked the head physician if she could speak privately with him. They stepped out into the rotunda off the ward and she asked, "Do you see any improvement?"

"Yes, certainly. It's obvious that he's used to you and has accepted you as a nurse or helper. He really depends on you and will for some time."

"Will he get better?"

The doctor smiled and scratched his head. "That's the question for which everyone wants an answer."

"Is there hope?"

"There's always hope, you know that."

"But what can I expect?"

"I'm sorry to tell you that we don't know. Sometimes they come right out of such a condition and sometimes it takes a very long time. Sometimes years." Tamara looked downhearted and the physician added, "I'm sorry I can't be specific. You see we know so little about how the brain works. Somewhere in his confusion he is trying to make sense of everything. It just takes time. The brain heals itself."

"He couldn't die?"

"That's only in very rare cases. Usually when there's been damage to the brain itself. He's just in a bad case of shock."

"So I should just have patience."

"Yes, and keep up your normal routine. He's in a quiet stage now because he's adapted to your routine. Moving him would probably set him back where he was. So, you're doing the right thing and I wish you luck."

Tamara thanked her coworker physician and went back to her desk near Shota's bed.

While conditions in the hospital were cordial and the princess enjoyed being there, life in Petrograd was becoming worse by the day. The Bolsheviks were no longer shooting in the streets, but more such ambushes were expected at anytime and that kept an atmosphere of fear and apprehension prevalent in the city. When Yakov came by for her at the hospital, she would inquire whether Dima had been able to procure food for the evening repast. If he did not, then Yakov would drive the princess to a market where she would wait in line for whatever was available. One day the coachman informed her that Dima left. He had told Yakov that he was no longer going to serve the rich overlords. Tamara was stunned. So the Bolsheviks had reached even the chef! Evidently a sad expression came on her face because Yakov said in his peasant Russian, "Princess, Yakov not leave you!" Tamara smiled and thanked him.

The princess had never prepared food in her life. She thought of dear Luda and how wonderful it would be if her old friend could come to Petrograd, but the thought was ridiculous and impossible.

The princess would have to learn. She found in the kitchen the most famous Russian cookbook, "A Gift to Young Hostesses" by Elena Molokhovets. Paging through the three volume work,

Tamara almost cried. There were recipes for all the great dishes that had been served her all her life and she had always taken them for granted. In the lists of what to buy, she saw enumerated: smoked salmon, smoked sturgeon, caviar and so forth. Where would one find such delicacies now? She thought of Prince Andronnikov, but knew she would rather starve than ask help from him. So, she tried finding a recipe for the produce she had procured that day: eggs, rhubarb and chocolate. No such dish appeared and she could not recall ever eating such a dish. Yakov came into the kitchen and fried the eggs. Tamara sat down with the old coachman and ate readily, not even remembering that it was the first time in her life that she was dining with a peasant.

On November 6, 1917, the Bolsheviks took advantage of the turmoil in the government where numerous parties were fighting for control and launched a takeover of the capital. Shouting their slogans of "Peace, Land & Liberty!" and "All Power to the Soviets," they seemed to be everywhere at once. The crew of the cruiser "Aurora" sailed the ship up the Neva near the Winter Palace, signaling the seizure of Petrograd. The famous palace of the tsars was stormed and easily overrun. By the evening of November 8, most of the public buildings and other key points in the capital were under Bolshevik control. Communication, transportation and governmental facilities were suddenly under the Red banner. The incomprehensible and unbelievable had occurred. The Bolsheviks, a small political party compared to major political groups, had succeeded in overthrowing the Provisional Government and now ruled Russia. In seven months a three-hundred year old monarchy had fallen, replaced by a small group of slogan shouting idealists who had no set program for the future and no experience in running a government. Only chaos could possibly ensue.

Events of a colossal nature took place: a peace treaty with Germany was signed at Brest-Litovsk bringing home millions of men from the front; a police department called the Cheka was created with frightening powers to control the populace and a Socialist order was proclaimed in the government as the basis for a

new society. Citizens of Petrograd awoke to a new world in which
their money was valueless, their religion declared false and their
government communistic. Banks were closed indefinitely, former
governmental offices ceased operating and law and order disappeared.

Supplies at the "Saviors of Russia" were low and would last,
the doctors figured, only about two months. Tamara was fortunate
that she had taken her jewels and some money from the bank for
her departure to the south because all valuables in the state and
private banks were confiscated by the Soviets. She and Yakov had
sufficient funds for a limited time. While tsarist money was deval-
ued, in the beginning of the revolution it was still used for exchange. Barter, however, gradually became the standard means of
procurement. The Dashkov mansion contained thousands of objects that could be sold and while Tamara disliked selling the
Dashkov possessions, her needs forced the issue. Yakov became
very skillful at barter, but objects d'art did not procure their value's
worth. A Chinese vase given to the Dashkov's uncle by the Dowager Empress of China when he was Governor General of Siberia
brought only a half dozen eggs. It was a pathetic exchange, but
Tamara was helping to feed Shota as well as herself and Yakov.

Eventually the inevitable happened. One night when Tamara
had retired, she was suddenly awakened by a bang on her door. It
flew open and a group of uniformed hoodlums walked in carrying
torches. Flashes of light danced around the room as they looked it
over. When they surrounded her bed, Tamara sat up and pulled
her blankets over her. "Who are you?" a gruff voice asked.

"I am Princess Tamara Borisovna Zhorzhadze," she answered
automatically, forgetting that it would be wise not to use her title.

"Hey, one of the princely families!" another voice stated.

"Where are your jewels?" a third higher voice asked.

"In the bank," the princess answered, feeling it would sound
logical.

"Where's Vladimir Dashkov?"

"On diplomatic duty in Denmark!"

"For the provisional government?"

"Yes!"

Several of the men laughed. "Well, he ain't working for them no more."

"What do you mean?" Tamara asked, forgetting that the Provisional Government had been overthrown.

They laughed at her and one said, "She don't know there's a revolution!"

"What do you want?" Tamara asked.

"Ain't she pretty!" a voice from the dark commented.

"Where's your gold and silver?" another voice asked.

"The gold is in the bank," she lied, thinking they had believed her before, "and the silver is in the dining room."

"Come on, let's git!" still another voice growled.

A few men started out the door and others turned to follow. She heard a voice say, "I'd like to fuck her," and she cringed. The word was known in past society, but never used. Now it could be without shame? Tamara trembled, fearful and scared.

The robbers went from room to room picking up various things that they considered sellable and left after about two hours. Tamara put on her housecoat and ventured out on the stairway landing where a gas light was burning. She called, "Yakov? Yakov, are you there?" There was no answer. She went down the stairs and turned on a lamp in the great entrance hall. Near the front portals she saw Yakov lying on the floor. She rushed to him, but he was unconscious. He had tried stopping the looters, but they had knocked him out. Tamara brought some water and washed his forehead where a small wound was bleeding. Then she went into the study and found that the hoodlums had either not known how to open the liquor cabinet or else did not suspect that it had a lower compartment. She opened it with a key from a book on a nearby shelf and snatched a bottle of spirits. The robbers had taken the small vodka cups from a table in the room, so she simply poured some of the liquor onto Yakov's lips. He evidently sensed the smell and taste because his eyes twitched immediately and he began licking his lips. "Oh, thank God, you're alive," she whispered and wiped his wound again. Yakov slowly sat up. He had made the mistake of answering the door when the chimes rang. He promised he would never do that again. "At least we're safe," Tamara said and patted the old man on his shoulder, "but whom can we turn to?" At the hospital she learned that such robberies were commonplace and that it was even more dangerous to report the incident to the Cheka. One doctor said, "You would only bring yourself to their attention and that can be disastrous!"

A few days later an even worse event took place. Tamara was dressing for her day at the hospital when Yakov knocked on her boudoir door and called out, "Princess, people've come!" The princess quickly finished her toilette and went downstairs. A group of five women and men were examining the entrance way and salon. A middle-aged, frumpy woman whose uniform was not clean approached Tamara and said in an unpleasant voice, "Are you Princess Dashkov?"

"No, I am Princess Zhorzhadze," she replied, again carelessly, but automatically using her title.

"We are from the Soviet Committee for Property Distribution. I must ask you some questions."

Tamara asked if the woman would like to sit down. In a gruff voice she replied, "Never! I work for the good of the people and I will not slouch on my job!"

The princess first thought of asking how the woman had the right to invade her home and ask personal questions, but she decided otherwise. "Very well. What would you like to know?"

"How many rooms are in this mansion?"

"I believe there are 54!"

"Huh," the spokeswoman huffed, "she doesn't even know how many there are. She thinks there's 54."

Tamara said nothing and waited.

"How many people live here?"

"At the present, I am the only inhabitant. My coachman Yakov has a room in a servants' quarters next to the carriage house."

The woman turned to the others and shook her head. "One

person in a building with 54 rooms! It's incredible."

"Most of the house has been closed off," Tamara added and the woman looked at the others and laughed.

Walking over by her colleagues the leader began whispering. The princess could not overhear, but when the woman finished, the other members began walking into various areas of the mansion. Again Tamara had an urge to demand by what right these vile people had dared enter her home, but she refrained. So much ugliness had taken place under the new regime, she assumed their intrusion was in the natural order of the government.

Completing their assessments and measurements at their own pace took the so-called Soviet agents almost the entire morning. When they finished they gathered in the salon and seated themselves for a meeting. Tamara was amused at the contrast between their unkept uniforms and the beautiful French furniture which they sprawled over; yet she was also apprehensive about their reactions and plans. She heard phrases like, "You won't believe what's in that room," and "I've never seen such riches!" Again she realized how much she had taken for granted in her life.

When the agents finished, Tamara was called into the salon. The leader addressed their findings: the palace was capable of housing twenty families. "What do you mean?" the princess asked. The gruff woman explained that the Dashkov mansion was being confiscated by the Soviet government for housing the underprivileged. No longer would space be wasted on leeches, meaning of course the aristocrats. Realizing that a protest was pointless, Tamara asked, "But what am I to do?" A different agent, evidently one in charge of allotments, answered that the princess would be given her suite, that is, her bedroom and sitting room. "Where do I prepare my meals?" The same agent replied that she would share the kitchen with other families. "Twenty families?" He explained that the kitchen would be made into five separate units. "What about my coachman?" The group had not thought of him and looked at each other for advice. Finally the leader explained that if Tamara wanted to hire the man, he would have to stay in her suite. "But he has a room in the servants' quarters." The agents became aggravated. She had used the word "servant" too many times and they wanted her to know that there was no longer such a thing as servitude. "If I pay for his room in those quarters, may he keep it?" The mention of payment struck the correct chord and the agents agreed; however, they would let her know how much she would owe. Tamara asked one more question, "When will all this take place?"

"Tomorrow," the leader answered, adding, "We are in great need of housing." The group left feeling very satisfied.

Immediate work was necessary. Yakov did not understand what had happened and Tamara sat him down and explained. He only shook his head. She told him that she was going to look after him and that he should continue taking care of the horses and the coach. Fortunately they had not confiscated it, but that could happen at any time. He would no longer be doorman and could spend time in Tamara's suite. Yakov's eyes opened in disbelief. "I know it sounds strange, but our world has disappeared. We have to do what we can." The old man nodded.

Tamara walked around the salon and the study picking out some pieces that she helped Yakov carry to her suite. They exchanged them for furniture of lesser value. A pair of Louis XV chairs went into a corner and a pair of Louis XVI went out. A table that had belonged to Marie Antoinette replaced a table of 19th century inlay. Tamara was sure that the French Queen must have had the largest bedroom in the history of mankind. She knew so many grand hostesses who claimed to have furniture that belonged to the ill fated Marie. When they finished, she told Yakov that they would leave the things behind the panel on the staircase because it was probably the safest place. Also, instead of being the doorman at the main entrance of the mansion, he would be the watchman for her suite once the people move in. The old man agreed and thanked his mistress.

Arriving late in the afternoon at the hospital, the princess found that Shota was asleep, but the sheet over him was crumpled. She lifted it and, because his night shirt had scooted up during his slumbers, she saw real male genitals for the first time in her life. She could only stare. Before her was what gave Somi a son. It looked bigger than those on statues she had seen and she wondered how it performed. Suddenly she realized what she was doing and dropped the sheet, blushing.

A nurse came as she was working with papers and informed her that Shota had refused his walk in the morning because she was not there. "He kept asking for Tamarochka, and stayed in bed." Tamara smiled and said she would walk with him when he awoke. The incident recalled the doctor's remark about Shota's condition. He was now accustomed to a set routine and it should be kept for his equilibrium. Changing the pattern might cause a setback. Tamara decided never to be late again.

The next day Yakov was not waiting in his carriage outside the hospital when Tamara finished her volunteer work. She assumed that he was doing some shopping and waited a while. Since the medical facility was in an old Yusupov palace near the Dashkov mansion, she could walk without any problem and decided to stroll home. She had not noticed before how littered the streets were becoming in the finest area of the city. She walked over posters of "Bread, Land and Peace" and around piles of garbage. When she reached the Dashkovs', the courtyard was full of carts and wagons. People were carrying bundles and furniture into the edifice. Yakov was not at the doorway and anyone could walk in without being questioned. She entered and saw piles of luggage and boxes all over the grand entrance hall. She stopped for a moment and looked in disbelief, thinking, Oh, Lidia, thank God you are not here to see this!

At that moment a severe looking woman of about 60 came to her and asked if she was the Princess Zhorzhadze. She nodded. The woman introduced herself as Comrade Victory and explained that she was the House Manager. Tamara nodded again. "So, you won't condescend to speak to me!" the woman snarled.

"I don't understand," Tamara replied. "What do you want of me?"

"I want to search your suite. You aristocrats usually hide things that belong to the state. Would you please tell that old man to git away from your door. He has refused me your key and I'll have him arrested if he ever does it again."

Tamara quickly went up the stairs and had Yakov open the door. Comrade Victory, a name she had given herself after the great socialist revolution, a common practice among Soviets, walked in and began looking around. She searched in places where she assumed someone would try hiding valuables. Disappointed, she asked, "Are you hiding state property?" Tamara shook her head. "When I address you, you will please answer. I'll not take any condescension from your kind."

"No," Tamara replied and remained silent.

Giving them both an unpleasant look, she stated, "You must give me a duplicate key to this room. That's an order. We want no secret meetings in this house." Her mission completed, the house manager stalked out of the room

Tamara thanked Yakov for guarding the suite, but told him to obey the manager in the future, explaining that they had better cooperate with the unpleasant woman. Then she asked him to share some food with her. She had some pirozhki and apples from the hospital kitchen in her bag and they ate them seated at Marie Antoinette's table. While they ate Yakov related some bad news. He bowed his head while telling it. When the Soviets came to take over the building, they also confiscated the horses and carriages. His protests had been pointless and they had called him a "leech's leech."

Tamara assured him that it was not his fault and that they would survive with each other's help. Tears came into the old man's eyes and she comforted him by patting him on a shoulder. Since he had no duties anymore, she suggested that he come with her to the hospital. He could eat there at noon and help her with Shota. He was so touched, he merely nodded without speaking. So a team developed. They walked together in the mornings to the "Saviors of Russia," they ate together in the commissary and they walked Shota together. Yakov actually released other workers from certain duties and felt needed. He could not have been happier, feeling that he was still serving his masters.

In late December, during the holiday season, Tamara was shocked when Felix Yusupov came into Shota's room. She could not believe her eyes. His reason for making the long trip from the Crimea to Petrograd was to obtain more of their valuables in the Moika Palace. He had stopped in Moscow and hidden a cache of diamonds in a staircase and had come on to St. Petersburg for gold and more jewels. The Moika Palace had been confiscated, but not for housing. It was going to be a museum and he was able to enter it without problems. While watchmen were on hand, he knew where things were hidden and was able to slip into his clothing considerable jewelry. He also had a brief case full of gold coins which was very heavy. His purpose for coming to the hospital was again a plea from Irina. She begged Tamara to return with her husband to the Crimea. Tamara pointed to Shota and said, "He cannot be moved."

Felix Yusupov, handsome, effeminate and descended from Tartar princes, looked at the handsome, well-built prince of ancient lineage and said, "He's magnificent!" Shota's face showed confusion. He could not understand why this man was describing him in such language. "I don't think I've ever seen such a beautiful specimen. How is he?" Tamara explained, emphasizing the reasons he could not be moved. Felix said that Irina would be very disappointed, but that when he told her about Shota, he was sure she would understand.

Preparing to leave, Felix whispered that he was traveling under an assumed name and had used bribery to obtain railway passage. His final words were, "Don't wait too long. It's very possible they will start shooting our class soon. We would not want to lose you." He smiled, looked at Shota again and walked out. His last words had been very disturbing and she asked herself, What would she do if it became so dangerous?

Signs of on coming trouble for aristocrats were quite evident by the end of 1917. The banks had been nationalized and all valuables belonging to anyone of the old regime were confiscated from the bank vaults. Tamara regretted she had not taken Princess Dashkov's jewels, but how could she have known? Everyone had lost their valuables. The princess ran into Betsie Shuvalov in the Eliseev store once and the countess whispered, "I've lost all my jewels and three-forths of my house. I'm leaving Russia." It was the first time Tamara had heard someone in the city talk about leaving their homeland. She was shocked. Most had assumed that the turmoil of the present would pass and order would be restored. Privileges might be curtailed, but the end of their life style forever was not anticipated.

New laws were issued by the Soviets which also changed Russian mores based on centuries of tradition. Only civil marriages were officially recognized; having an illegitimate child was no longer to be considered a liability; divorce could be obtained by mail if each party signed a card; the ancient letters "Yats" and "iyod" were dropped from the Russian cyrillic alphabet, and the Gregorian calendar replaced the Julian except in ecclesiastical affairs. The most astounding change came in the separation of the church and state. Since the acceptance of Christianity in 988 A.D. the Russian rulers had been head of the church as well as the government. It was a centuries old duality adopted from the Byzantine Empire. The concept of the tsar as the intermediary between God and the citizens of the state was as old as the Russian Orthodox Church itself. Russians were told by the Soviets that their religion was ideologically pernicious and just an instrument of the exploiting aristocrats. Tsarist Russia was becoming a subject for history books.

At the Dashkov mansion Tamara found the first hint of the new government's attitude toward the Russian church. On the first Sunday after the mansion had been invaded by the new tenants, she went with Yakov to the small chapel in the left wing of the edifice. Its door was locked and a board nailed across it. They went to the house manager who now lived in the former study, but the chapel could not be opened.

For Tamara the holiday season of 1917 was not as bleak as the season of 1916. Her life style was worse, but she was content with taking care of Shota. He seemed somewhat better and she strove to keep a pleasant, normal routine. Yakov had become a lifesaver in many ways and with his help she was optimistic and started making plans. When Shota was able, the three of them would go to Tiflis. They would go home! She envisioned her grandmother's estate and the rugged Caucasian mountains. Her only despair was that her thoughts of the wild country of the Zhorzhadzes always led her to remember Somi. Shota was hers and if they returned there, Somi would take him from her. She whispered to herself, "Oh, Shota, if only we could go off to another world together."

CHAPTER 7

1918

Spiralling prices, shortages, lines in front of shops and overcrowding were a way of life in the Petrograd that welcomed in the new year, 1918. One heard only grumbling everywhere and most of the anger was legitimate. The old order had been destroyed, but the new order was worse in many ways. No wages could keep up with the cost of living; government allowances for draftees' families did not consider lodging and clothing; and food rationing was imposed. Survival depended on being registered with a local Soviet which judged the right of a citizen for maintenance by the state. Unfortunately for Tamara and Yakov, their local Soviet representative was Comrade Victory. When the new law came into affect, they joined the line in the entrance hall of the Dashkov mansion and waited their turn. Comrade Victory took one look at Tamara and said rather loudly, "Polnaia Lishchenka" (Completely Deprived). A young woman with a determined look sitting at a desk by the commander stamped a card and offered it to Tamara.

"What does this mean?" the princess asked.

"It means you are now deprived for having sponged on the great Russian people. No longer will leeches be tolerated. Next!"

"But I am working in a hospital."

"Are you being paid?"

"I am being given food."

"Then you don't need a card anyway."

"But—"

Comrade Victory looked around the princess and again said,

"Next!, but when she saw that it was Yakov, she said, "Worker's Rations" and the young woman stamped a card for Yakov. To show Tamara her power, Victory walked over by Yakov and said quite loud as she patted his back, "Don't worry, Comrade. The revolution will take care of you. No longer will you have to slave for the masters. All power to the people." With great aplomb she marched back and took her stance. "Next!"

Yakov immediately escorted the princess to her suite and told her that he would give her food. Tamara was so touched she almost cried, yet she knew it was a serious matter. Without the right for procurement, which was deemed by the authorities as just deserts for aristocrats, one could only depend on barter for existence. Suicide became common and an exodus started from the country of the most well-educated and knowledgeable class in Russian society. Many intellectual and political figures who were of bourgeois background were also denied sustenance and another wave of emigres began. Russia was losing much of its best and would suffer dearly for it in the future.

As if her despair were not complete, early in January Tamara received a letter from the countess in Tiflis with heart-breaking news. Count Vadim Trushinsky, her dearest uncle, had committed suicide. She dropped the letter without finishing and cried on Yakov's shoulder. The old man petted her as she told him what had happened. She sat down and continued reading. The count had been given a medical discharge from the military because of his hearing loss. It was a terrible adjustment for him and he could not contend with his distress. Then the communists started their madness in the city and he was roughed up a few times by brigands. The countess swore that she did everything she could for her husband, a fact that the princess doubted, but there was no helping his depression. To her horror, she found him with his revolver in his hand when she came home from a session of magnetism.

Tamara again dropped the letter and cried. "Oh, if only I had gone there," she said through her tears. "I would have been with him."

Other disparaging news followed. The countess revealed that Count Bagrov was now a Red commissar and was shouting their idiotic phrases continually. He was a member of a revolutionary "tribunal," which was the new name for a court of law. "He really thinks he's something in his uniform."

Then some more shocking news. The countess was so disgusted with what was happening in the city that she was going to Istanbul with a Turkish merchant she had met and would stay until things in Tiflis normalized. Again Tamara dropped the letter. The news was simply too incredible. Leave Russia?

A final paragraph mentioned that Luda was staying in their mansion and would be there when Tamara came. She also invited the princess to join her in Istanbul if she wanted. "The Turk has a lot of money and friends!"

Tamara felt nauseous. How could her aunt have become so cheap and obvious? And dear Vadim, if only you had not done it!

A few lines added under the signature drew the princess's attention. "Somi came with her son, Terial. He'll look just like his father someday. A beautiful child. She asked about Shota and you. Very glad that you're helping him. Auntie."

Auntie, indeed, Tamara thought. You drove Vadim to his grave with your seances and lovers. Oh, God, forgive him! I beg of you to forgive him!

The princess remembered her tutor of literature mentioning that Russians were suicide prone. Their obsession with God and the devil had driven them to challenging both. Russian roulette was a game of chance for the undecided. If one lived, God was on his side; if he died, the devil. Yet Vadim was above that, she contemplated. He was just worn down by his frustrations and the antics of the countess. Oh, dear man, forgive me for not being with you!

Sitting back in her chair while Yakov sadly watched, she thought of Count Bagrov. How typical that the scoundrel would join in with the riffraff taking over in Tiflis. Where is the dignity and honor that his title was supposed to represent? Oh, how shallow people have become!

In March all Romanovs were required to register with the central Soviet. Grand Duke Constantine Constantinovich and Princes John, Constantine and Igor were all arrested and placed in the Peter Paul Fortress. The Romanov nun, Grand Duchess Elizabeth was also imprisoned. News of the seizure of the royal family spread through upper class society and ignited another exodus of aristocrats and highly placed intellectuals. Tamara realized that she must move Shota south even if moving him was precarious. As descendants of royal blood, even though centuries ago, they could still be suspect. Already Captain Victory had shown that there was no place for her in the new Russia.

Preparations for leaving were difficult. Since she was on the best of terms with the doctors in the "Saviors of Russia," she consulted with them about what she should do. They suggested that she take Shota on a military train as far as could be arranged. She could go disguised as a nurse. When she asked about Yakov, they were not enthusiastic. After telling them about his service and how dependant he was on her, she begged that something be thought up for him on the train. They agreed and the head physician said he would start the paper work. The next hospital train South was in two days. Could she be ready? She asserted that she would be.

An administrator at the French Embassy appeared at the hospital and informed Tamara that a message had come for her through their courier service. He did not bring it from fear of being searched by Red guards who patrolled streets and harassed civilians. He suggested she accompany him to the Embassy and she did. How pleasant it was for her to enter a beautiful rococo setting like the waiting salon in the official building. The ambassador, Monsieur Conte de Ferney, came out of his office and bowed as he handed her a missile. Manners as his had disappeared in Russia and Tamara felt so relaxed in his presence.

The document was from Prince Vladimir Dashkov. He was

now living in Paris and serving in the French military services. He would not return home until conditions had normalized. He advised Tamara to join him in Paris for the same period. She could either travel via Finland or through the southern route, Odessa to Istanbul. He preferred that she close up the mansion and leave the Dashkov valuables in the bank as he had means of support in France. If she could accept his offer, he asked her for verification through the Embassy.

Tamara talked with the ambassador and he asked a clerk to take down the response the princess had for Prince Dashkov. She informed Vladimir that he obviously did not know the true conditions in Petrograd. The Dashkov mansion had been confiscated and the Dashkov valuables in the bank nationalized. She, herself, was accompanying Prince Shota Zhorzhadze, who was wounded, to Tiflis. If possible, she would join Vladimir in Paris later. She was amazed that she had added the last phrase because she had never thought of leaving her homeland, yet she had said it and let it be sent.

While dictating to the clerk, Tamara suddenly had an idea. She asked again for the ambassador and was escorted into his study. The apprehensive look on her face made him listen most attentively to her request. Her fine jewels, gifts from the deceased Duc de Crevreuse, whose mother the ambassador knew well, were behind a wall panel in the Dashkov mansion which had been taken over by the Bolsheviks for housing. Also, there were very famous French paintings by Boucher and Fragonard behind the panel. The ambassador's eyes opened wide. There was also silver urns and tureens and a bag of gold pieces. Could his honor possibly think of a ruse that would help her extricate those items from behind the staircase panel?

The elderly, distinguished man cocked his head and thought. Shortly he slightly nodded and said, "I think something can be worked out. When could it be done?" The princess explained that her train left the next afternoon. It would have to be in the morning. She also warned about Comrade Victory who kept her evil eyes open at all times. The ambassador nodded and had his chauffeur take Tamara to the "Saviors of Russia."

Yakov was seated with Shota telling him about wild and cunning horses he had used during his years of service. The stories had been repeated many times, but Shota enjoyed them over and over because of his equestrian prowess. Tamara had them walk in the courtyard with her while she explained what would happen in the morning. Shota did not understand, but she anticipated that. It was Yakov she wanted to inform without anyone hearing. Then she told Shota's head physician that they would definitely leave on the hospital train the next day and final preparations were made.

Tamara hardly slept. The next morning she went to the kitchen area she shared with five families and, after waiting a while, made a cup of tea for her and Yakov. They ate some rolls and waited in the princess's suite.

At 9:00 A.M. two large official cars pulled into the courtyard of the Dashkov mansion. The French ambassador himself entered with several aids. Someone must have run to Comrade Victory because she showed up immediately. The ambassador's aid asked in stumbling Russian if there was anyone who spoke French in the building? A look of disgust spread on Victory's face, but sensing the officious nature of the visit, she nodded and told a staring woman to fetch the princess.

Tamara was thrilled when she saw such a retinue of Frenchmen at the bottom of the staircase. Comrade Victory said in her usual gruff voice, "Find out who these men are and what they want?"

Tamara turned to the ambassador and presented herself and he did the same. The ambassador was considering the Dashkov mansion as a consulate for the French embassy. He had permission from the Supreme Soviet for an investigation of the building and would like a consultation with the house manager. The princess turned to Comrade Victory and translated the message, emphasizing the honor that she had been given for an ambassador himself to make such a call.

Victory was not impressed. "Does he think he can throw us out?"

Tamara asked and he explained that comparable housing would be provided for those under her supervision. He also whispered that it was imperative that she take him to her office. The princess assured Victory that her rights would be protected and that her charges would he given better housing. She added that the ambassador needed a private discussion with her.

Shaking her head in the direction of her office, she growled, "Come on!" and started walking away.

The ambassador told his aids to start their measurements. Tamara, having indicated to the Frenchmen that Yakov would show them the panel, followed Victory and the ambassador. In the office the cosmopolitan and sanguine diplomat seated himself with great care, pulling his sleeves down, straightening his collar and pulling down his vest. Comrade Victory, who looked as if she could not possibly live up to her name, waited impatiently. After the ambassador adjusted his shoulders as if trying to be comfortable, he asked, "May I smoke?"

Disdain spread on Victory's face, but she nodded.

It took at least five minutes for the visitor's elaborate preparations, during which he made trivial comments about the weather. Placing his cigarettes on Victory's desk, he took out his carved-ivory cigarette holder and accidently dropped it on the floor. It rolled under Victory's desk and she almost had a defeat in retrieving it. He thanked her and continued. Comrade Victory could have burned down Petrograd in the time wasted by the visitor.

Meanwhile, in the large entrance way, the French aids had blocked off with ribbon a large area of the hall and a section of the staircase landing on the second floor. Anyone wishing to go down the stairs was sent to other staircases which were numerous in the large edifice. In no time the panel was opened, Yakov put the sack of jewels in one pocket of his coat and the bag of gold in the other. The French carried out the pictures and several pieces of silver. The panel was restored and the measuring of the hall ceased. The mission was completed very quickly and no one witnessed it.

One of the French aids rushed to the office and knocked. When

Comrade Victory opened the door, she heard a fast phrase in a language she did not know and yelled, "What?" The ambassador stood up and said that an emergency had occurred at the embassy and that he must leave immediately. He asked Tamara to accompany him in case he needed an interpreter. Comrade Victory's mouth fell open. She was utterly confused. The diplomat told her he would return in two days and continue their most interesting discussion. They left Victory in defeat.

Yakov was in a corner of the large limousine when the princess and the diplomat joined him. The two cars drove off quickly and outside the courtyard, the ambassador started laughing. He had never seen such a "stick," as he called her and expressed his fear of what was happening in Russia. "There's going to be no one left that one can negotiate with! How could one ever strike a bargain with that dragon?"

At the hospital Tamara and Yakov dressed in white medical uniforms. His size was a problem and he still looked like an old peasant instead of a hospital orderly, but there was no choice.

The ambassador had waited for the travelers and took them to the train station. He suggested that an aide check the hospital list for their coach and had them wait in the car. Tamara tried expressing her gratitude for the Conte de Fernay's rendering such a service, but he said, "If the Duchesse de Crevreuse found out that I had not done everything in my power for you, I would be ostracized from society!" Tamara smiled. He added, "Besides, it is not often that a Frenchman has the opportunity of serving such a beautiful princess." She smiled again and blushed.

Their compartment was ready on the train and Yakov helped Shota walk through the crowds. Once seated, Tamara could hardly believe that everything had gone so well. She examined Shota, who was falling asleep, and he seemed normal. The many distractions along the way had not upset him and she was relieved. Yakov gave her the jewels, but left the gold in his pocket as a security measure. A basket of food had been brought by a French aide and when the train started moving out of Petrograd, the princess relaxed for the first time in days.

While the hospital train had priority, it took a week for the trip to Kiev. A major problem was clothes. They had not brought any changes because Comrade Victory would have suspected them carrying out suitcases. Fortunately Shota's hospital kit had soap and a comb, but after a few days they all felt in need of a bath. At the station in Moscow, Tamara was fearful that the police might have been informed about her departure and would be waiting for her. She sent Yakov into the station to buy food from the peasants who brought their produce in from the countryside. When the train finally pulled out of the ancient capital, Tamara closed her eyes and thanked God.

Occasionally Shota would say, "Tamarochka, let's stroll." Yakov would help him up and Tamara would walk with him along the corridor of the train. It was difficult because small tables with medicines and towels were along the narrow passageway, but they would manage a little exercise. Sitting with Shota in the car hour after hour Tamara felt closer to her beloved than ever before. She talked about their childhood and it sometimes seemed as if Shota remembered. One day he said, "Somi was there." Tamara quickly verified his remark and asked him, "Wasn't it you who put that snake on the patio?"

"No, it was our cousin Rustan," he answered.

Tamara could not believe her ears. The word "our" showed recognition. She quickly took his hands and looked into his eyes. "You remember me, don't you, Shota."

He looked at her a long time and said, "Yes, Tamarochka."

It was not Shota speaking and she knew it. He had come back for one second and then gone back into his clouded world. Yet that one second was worth all the anguish, vexation and trouble that she had endured.

The comfort of a hospital train with its sanitary facilities was taken from them outside of Kiev. When the train pulled into the small town of Neshin, it stopped. Thinking it was routine, Yakov prepared for another excursion for foodstuffs. However, a physician soon came by with a startling announcement. The train was going to turn around and go back to Moscow. It seems that White army groups had cut off the railway into Kiev. The civil war had started and Kiev was, at the time, in the control of the Whites. The doctor said that anyone could leave the train voluntarily if they chose.

Tamara knew that Moscow was too dangerous for them, but the idea of leaving the train was terrifying. What could they do? Then she remembered that the Dashkov estate Kholmka was not far from Kiev and that they might find refuge there. Springing into action, she had Yakov help Shota and she took their food basket and his medical supplies. It was the first time she was thankful that they did not have suitcases. They left the coach which they had settled into and went out into the unknown.

When the train pulled out, the crowd around the station gradually thinned. Tamara, Shota and Yakov went into the station house and sat down, wondering what they could do. Seeing that the station master had not yet closed the ticket window, Tamara asked if there would be a train into Kiev. He shook his head. "Looks like there will be a fight ahead."

The princess had not heard about the civil war that was starting. She had listened to rumors that opposition groups were forming against the Bolsheviks, but their stopping the train from reaching Kiev was one factor she had not considered. Since the station master was old, she thought his sympathies were surely with the old regime, so she said, "I'm transporting a wounded veteran to Kiev, is there any means of transportation?"

"None that I know. So many people have asked. They should have stayed on the train."

Tamara hesitated, then asked, "Have you heard of the estate Kholmka?"

He shook his head, but said, "There's some peasants out there by the tracks who are from this area. Maybe they know it."

The princess thanked him and told Yakov to wait with Shota.

She went out and approached the peasants who were selling produce. Because of her white, but soiled uniform, the seller she approached bowed. "Do you know an estate called Kholmka?"

Others had listened to the pretty woman, but no one answered. Finally one old man, scratching the back of his neck, said, "There's no Kholmka. There's Kholmiakov's place, but no Kholmka."

"Kholmiakov's place ain't Kholmka," another peasant joined the conversation. "His place's Raiska."

Another interrupted, "No, Kholmiakov's place is Roshcha, not Kholmka."

Tamara suddenly felt at ease. Her worry over what they should do left her for a few moments. She listened amused as the peasants argued over the location of Kholmka which they neither knew nor had ever heard of. When they had finally exhausted all their theories about the mysterious place, she thanked them and asked if any of them could drive her and a wounded veteran into the next town. No one answered. "For pay," she added and one man said immediately, "Wat town?"

Tamara waited out another conversation over the town which had not been mentioned, but which brought out again several names that it could be. When she had a chance, she said, "Kiev."

The group became silent. After a slight pause, the one who had volunteered replied, "Sfar as Nossowka, yeah?"

Tamara asked if that was the way to Kiev and he nodded. In a short while a princess, a prince and a peasant coachman were riding in the back of a cart toward Nossowka. They passed boys herding sheep along the road and an occasional cart going in the other direction. Sometimes the driver would yell a greeting to the passersby. Workers in the fields were cutting hay and women were gathering potatoes in summer gardens. Peasant girls in villages they passed would stare at the strangers and then go on with their weeding or tending their babies. It was another world and the princess thought, "I was nourished on illusions all my life. We never saw these people, they only saw us." She shook her head and wondered what it all meant.

Shota was thrilled at being in the open countryside and talked with the cart driver about his horses. He impressed the owner so much, he let him drive the team. Shota sat high and straight on the cart seat and loved every minute of the ride. Toward dark they approached the village and paid the driver with old rubles which he accepted.

An inn in Nossowka had only one free room. The three compatriots had slept in a coach together for days, so being in a room did not bother them. They went into the restaurant and ate soup with Russian dumplings and a piece of roast lamb. They could not believe their fortune. After days on the train with limited supplies and nourishment, they feasted. After dinner they collapsed on their beds and quickly slept in spite of the bed bugs. The next morning Tamara talked with the landlord and to her amazement, he knew Kholmka. It was famous in the area for its horses. However, he also had disturbing news. The peasants on the estate had confiscated it and had burned the manor house. Tamara winced and said, "Oh, no."

"You've been there?" the landlord asked.

Tamara hesitated and said, "I know someone there."

He looked at her suspiciously, but continued, "You want me to hire you a driver to Kholmka?" She nodded and the threesome was soon on the road again, bouncing on the back of a cart.

Again the open air and horses invigorated Shota. He occasionally let out an exclamation in Georgian or sang a ditty about his homeland. He was having a wonderful time and Tamara enjoyed watching him. Soon he was driving the horses and became even more merry. Suddenly he called, "Tamarochka, my little bird, come sit by me!"

"Shota!" Tamara screamed, "You know me?"

He turned around again, but when he opened his mouth, nothing came out. He quieted down and continued driving. Again it had been a moment of joy for Tamara and she was sure that he would soon come out of his dark, subconscious world.

As the card drove through the gates at Kholmka, an obvious

change was evident. The trees in the park had been cut down by peasants and sold the bushes needed trimming, the paths were filled with weeds and the manor house did not stand in the distance. It really had perished. The closer the cart came to the ruins, the sadder Tamara felt. She envisioned Princess Lidia Dashkov walking through the entrance way and old Prince Dashkov going out to his horses. "Oh thank God they're not here to see this," she thought and shook her head. They passed the few standing walls blackened by the fire and drove on to the stables. Stopping at the first building, Tamara asked some workers who was in charge?

One of the men shouted into the barn, "Oleg, git out 'ere!"

Suddenly, there he was, Oleg Dunatov, the very man who had reminded her of Shota; and here she was with Shota himself. The irony seemed incredible.

"Soooo!" Oleg's voice drew out the "o." "The beautiful princess has come back."

Tamara smiled and looked at him without turning away, "Hello, Oleg. So, you're now in charge?"

"Yes, the farm people elected me. I'm the master now."

The princess winced at the word 'master,' but said nothing.

"Who's the big Georgian?" he asked.

"My cousin, Shota." She explained his condition and hoped Oleg could help them with transportation into Kiev.

"Sure," he replied and winked at Tamara who pretended that she did not notice.

Oleg led them to a carriage house where he told a woman to prepare dinner and rooms. "I'll be back and join you," he commented and swaggered away.

Tamara had not known Oleg except as her brother's friend, but she had assumed he was mannerly. His wink and his attitude did not give a good impression and she wondered if she had made a mistake in coming to Kholmka. He did promise aid, so that relieved her anxiety for a while. At dinner, it returned. The new "master" seated himself across from Tamara and said, "Imagine. I'm eating with a princess!"

Tamara tried avoiding talking about the contrast between the past and the present and asked Oleg if he would show Shota the horse barns.

"Sure! Can he ride as well as your brother?"

It was obvious that Oleg did not know about Valery and the princess told him. He seemed sympathetic, but was soon telling stories about the peasants' take over of the estate. She saw more bragging in his tales than substance and was glad when the meal was finished.

After seeing that Shota and Yakov were settled in their room, Tamara started to hers. Oleg stepped out of a room and grabbed her. Before she could cry out, he had enfolded her in his arms and tried to kiss her. She scratched his face and broke free, calling out, "Help!"

No one heard her. She backed away from Oleg and said, "How dare you!"

"You're too good for me, eh?"

She backed farther away. "How dare you!" she repeated.

He stepped forward and she said, "I'll scream if you take one more step."

He stopped. "So, you haven't changed, eh? Still the princess, eh?"

She Looked into his eyes and wondered how she ever saw Shota there. "Losing one's country does not mean one loses one's dignity. The values I had before the revolution are the same I have now. I am still who I was and may God protect me!"

"The old rules don't apply any more."

"Maybe not to you, but they do to me."

"I've wanted you from the first time I saw you. Then you were a princess and I was a peasant."

"I'm still a princess."

"And you think I'm still a peasant?"

"No, I don't think you're a peasant. You're the master now, you've said so your self, but that does not mean that I have any obligations to you. There can be nothing between us and it has nothing to do with titles, princess or peasant. It's because I am in love with another man and will be all my life."

Oleg knew he was defeated. He could either use force or withdraw. Something about the beautiful lady before him would not let him try anything obscene. He bowed to fate and went into his room.

The next morning the "master" took Shota to the stables and let him ride a horse. Oleg had never seen anything like it. He himself was known as a great horseman, but he could not believe what Shota could do. Tamara was so proud of her cousin. She felt that he showed Oleg that breeding did make a difference even though she knew that masterful riding on a horse did not depend on one's bloodline. Yet she was fearful because she knew that Shota had not ridden a horse in some time; still he performed as if his talent was in his blood.

Before leaving for Kiev, Tamara bargained with some peasant girls for some clothes. She bought a pretty embroidered blouse and skirt and soon looked like a Ukrainian folk dancer. Oleg, who was pretending as if nothing had happened the evening before, said when he saw her, "She came as a princess and leaves as a peasant." Tamara laughed and climbed into the carriage that the "master" had provided. A coachman took the three travelers to the train station in Kiev.

Along the way the carriage stopped at a small village to water the horses. Another vehicle pulled in from the other direction carrying two merchants who were scurrying through the countryside for produce. Seeing Shota sitting on the high carriage seat, one of them said, "Good morning. Bad news about the tsar, wasn't it?"

A Maid of Honor to the Empress of All the Russias learned about her sovereign's demise while sitting in a peasant outfit in a carriage on the road to Kiev. Tsar Nicholas II, the Empress, the Grand Duchesses and the tsarevich had all been assassinated in Ekaterinburg, Siberia. Tamara closed her eyes and prayed for the souls of the departed. She envisioned the charming grand duchesses at the ball when they had their debut together. How stately and tall they had walked through the procession! She remembered how they had helped her when Valery was in their hospital. How sympathetic and benevolent they had been! She could see the proud and disdainful Empress during her presentation as a Maid of Honor; then she recalled how kind Her Majesty had been when she was studying in the grand duchesses' medical facility. She realized that the stern, unhappy look of the Empress was a cover for a woman in distress at the end of her tether. Surely she did not deserve such a fate, dear God! Surely not! Yet one thing was very clear. Russia was no longer safe for aristocrats.

The train station in Kiev was just as crowded and noisy as in Moscow and Petrograd. It seemed as if every Russian was on the move. Tamara waited in line for some time, dodging people's stares at her and her clothes. Fortunately there was an evening train to Rostov on the Don where cars for Tiflis would be attached to another locomotive. Since most people were heading to the Crimea, there were seats available to Tiflis. Tamara procured passage for her group in a compartment. The trip would take days so she left Shota with Yakov and went to the stalls of peasants for foodstuffs. It was all very wearisome and the wait for the train, which was late, added to their fatigue. Once on board they fell asleep in their bunks.

Tamara awoke the next morning when the train jerked as it stopped at a small town. She looked across the compartment and saw a well-dressed woman lying on the bunk opposite hers. After checking whether Shota and Yakov were still in the upper berths, she relaxed and closed her eyes. The sun shining into the compartment began sending in rays of light and the princess sat up. The woman was awake, but after examining Tamara's face and clothes, she looked away. The princess realized that her clothes had told the lady she was a peasant. She smiled, thinking that it was only the clothes that made the aristocrats different from the lower classes. She knew Felix would laugh heartily at that idea. Her friends stirred above and came down for some rolls they had brought with them. They raised their berths and fastened them to the ceiling making it possible to stand. A steward came by offering tea for kopecks and they purchased three glasses. The woman had observed them greet each other and prepare for a light breakfast, still she said nothing. Tamara broke the ice with, "Madame, may I offer you a roll?"

The lady, dressed in black silk, looked at the princess and said, "No, thank you my dear. I have something."

Since the woman used the Russian impersonal "you," and her tone was condescending, Tamara knew that she considered them peasants. The princess decided not to introduce herself and let matters be.

The horse riding the day before had invigorated Shota and when Yakov was in the water closet at the end of the train, he told Tamara in Georgian how amused he had been at Oleg whose eyes kept getting bigger and bigger as he performed. Tamara told him that she had been fearful he would fall, and he shook his head and said he never fell. Since he was so prone to accidents, Tamara smiled and was sure he'd fall the next time he was on a horse. She was thrilled that he seemed so well and asked him a question about Somi. He answered and she smiled, asking herself, Is he really all there?

Yakov returned and in his peasant Russian confirmed the woman's view of them. However, when Tamara and Shota responded to his questions, the woman became terribly confused. After a while she interrupted, "Excuse me, I simply have to ask. How is it possible that you speak such a cultured Russian. Did your master teach you?"

Tamara smiled and Shota looked at her with dismay. Yakov gagged on the roll he was eating and Shota hit him on the back. Tamara explained that they were not as they appeared. She did not mention their titles, but told about leaving Petrograd on a hospital train without luggage and about buying clothes from some peasants.

"It is obvious that I was mistaken about you and I ask your forgiveness. It's these times. One doesn't know whom to believe or what to do!"

Tamara introduced herself and Shota with their titles and the woman's face showed her surprise. The princess mentioned that Yakov was a family retainer of many, many years and was helping her take Shota back to their estate. The woman apologized again and introduced herself as the Countess de Tolly, a name famous in Russian history as General de Tolly had fought against Napoleon in the War of 1812. She explained that she had left her home in Moscow and had been stuck in Kiev for several days. Finally a train for Rostov on the Don was scheduled and she purchased her berth. She was going to her sister's. Hearing about Tamara's plight with clothes, she offered her a dress. Tamara was thrilled and offered payment, but the lady refused. In a short time, a peasant had become a princess.

The countess had news that was startling. She was leaving Russia with her sister not only because the tsar and his family had been assassinated, but because she had learned that the Bolsheviks had also thrown the Grand Duchess Elizabeth and several grand dukes into a mine shaft somewhere in Siberia. Tamara bit her lip. She recalled the kind, sweet nun who had blessed her and who had tried so hard to turn her sister, the Empress, against Rasputin. The lady could see by the anguish on Tamara's face that the news had shocked her and she added, I am also very distressed and am leaving this madhouse I used to call home while I can." As the train passed through the great open fields of the Ukraine, Tamara thought of her last trip in a comfortable first class compartment. Again she saw the workers in the fields and the cows and sheep being herded along the country roads. Talking with the countess was a pleasure and helped pass the time. Shota quieted down and only listened. He took his walks with Yakov and occasionally pointed out horses through the train window. At Rostov on the Don the countess bade farewell and told Tamara that if she should ever be in Paris to please call on her. The princess thanked her for the clothes and expressed her pleasure in having her company on such a difficult trip.

As the train started into the Caucasus Mountains Shota be-came excited. It was as if the fresh air over the rugged craigs and

precipices had instilled new life into his body. By morning they all
woke up in Vladikavkaz on the Georgian border, Shota looked
down from his bunk at the princess and said, "My little bird, what
are you doing here?"

Tamara stood up and looked into his eyes. The wonderful
sparkle that made his eyes so brilliant and beautiful beamed at
her. She cried, "Shota!" and went into his arms as he leaned over
the bunk. "Shota! My God, Shota."

"Why are you crying, my love?"

Tamara could not stop her tears. Yakov had arisen and tried
telling Shota that he had been ill. Finally Tamara controlled herself. Shota came down, sat on her bunk and she related his fate
during the last few months. He could remember only certain details and was amazed that he was near his homeland. He asked
questions about fellow officers, but of course Tamara knew nothing about his war experiences. He fell silent, remembering the
horrors he lived through; then he put his arm around the princess
and held her close. Looking into her eyes he said,

"You're still beautiful and you saved me. I owe you my life.
How can I repay you?"

Tears again came to her eyes. He leaned down and kissed her
on the lips. She cried.

Before the train departed Tamara managed to slip into the
station and send a telegram to Somi about their arrival in Tiflis
that evening. She bought some food and joined her companions.
The trip through the exotic mountain scenes added to their perfect day. Shota and Tamara reminisced about their grandmother
and their youth at the estate. Tamara told Yakov that she was sorry
they were speaking Georgian, but she thought it was probably
better for Shota's frame of mind. The old peasant who was used to
subservience all his life nodded his head as if it was all right. No
one had ever apologized for speaking French in front of him and he
thought they were speaking that language.

It was one of the most beautiful days in Tamara's life. Shota
often held her hand and several times embraced her to accentuate

a point he was making. They laughed, she cried, he comforted her. Yakov added some tales of his youth on the Dashkov estate Radnoe and when he talked about horses, Shota sat up and listened with pleasure. The three were so happy and the time passed quickly. When the train pulled into Tiflis it crossed the Kura and Shota shouted with joy at seeing the rushing waters so often described in great Russian literature. They were home for sure!

No one met them at the station and Tamara hired a carriage.

The coachman, who could not understand how someone coming from the train could not have luggage, drove them into the European section of the city and stopped at the Trushinsky mansion. Its windows were dark, but Yakov pounded on the door. Finally a voice asked who was there. "Oh, Luda, It's I, your Tamarochka!"

The door swung open and the princess fell into the arms of the old cook. They both cried. Shota and Yakov passed them and waited until they could control themselves. Luda had news. Somi had sent word that her son Terial was ill and so she had not met them. She awaited them at the estate in Mtsety and wished them God speed. They would go on the morrow.

Luda had food prepared and they ate. The old cook was surprised when Tamara had Yakov sit with them, but everything had changed and the princess knew best. Luda gave them bad news. The Bolsheviks were in power in Tiflis and on Thursdays soldiers had the right of entry into any home and could take what they wanted. They had already been in the Trushinsky mansion and took a phonograph and some silver. "I hid the good stuff," Luda said with a smile, "but they'll be back. It's every Thursday now."

Weary from their trip the companions retired early. Tamara went to her old room and found considerable clothes that she had left behind. Luda prepared rooms for the guests and asked about Yakov. "Should he have a guest room?"

Tamara nodded and said with a sly smile, "Give him the countess's boudoir."

Luda laughed.

The princess walked around her boudoir and remembered scenes from the past, especially her arguments with the countess. It was strange being back in Tiflis. She thought of Vadim and Valery. They should be there and they were gone forever. She undressed and found one of her silk night slips. It felt wonderful and she was about to slide into her bed when there was a knock on her door. She asked, "Who's there." Shota whispered something she did not understand. She hesitated. Should she open the door? Finally she went and unlocked it.

Shota's mighty arms pushed it open and he stepped into her room, wearing a nightshirt. "My love, I had to see you."

"Oh, Shota, this is wrong. You can't stay here."

He took her into his arms and held her close. She felt his strength pressing against her. It was a wonderful sensation. She looked up at him in the dim light and he said, "I have never loved anyone but you, my beautiful bird." He kissed her hard. Her mouth opened and his tongue blended into her. They held for what seemed an eternity. Tamara felt his strength rising and suddenly broke away.

"Oh, Shota, I still love you, I have to admit, but we can't do this. You know we can't."

"But we love each other."

"Yes, we do, but fate has separated us. If you only knew how many times during your illness I wanted you to run away with me. Anywhere, just so we could be together."

"Then let's do."

"Shota," she exclaimed with shame in her voice. "Think of what you're saying. You have a son. Would you let our Terial grow up without such a wonderful father? How could he imitate you if you're not there? And Somi! She loves you as I do. It's was grandmother who did this to us, but we must keep our dignity."

He grabed her again and held her close. His strength pressing into her was marvelous, sensuous and so desirable, but again she broke away."

"Shota, if our love is to have value at all, it must also have respect. How could we face each other if we continue?"

He hesitated and then stepped back. "My love, you are right, but I must have one more kiss before I leave."

She ran into his arms and they embraced so tightly it seemed as if their bodies had become one. When they were on the verge of falling back on her bed, she pushed him away and whispered, "Go now or we shall end up hating each other."

Again he hesitated, but slowly turned and went out the door.

Tamara fell on her bed burning with desire. Her tears did not comfort her, but she knew she had done the right thing.

The next morning Count Bagrov, dressed in a uniform of the Red guard with very shiny high boots, arrived at the Trushinsky mansion and asked for Tamara. She was surprised at his visit and asked how he knew she was back. "Oh, we commissars know everything that's happening in the city."

"So the coachman was an agent."

"Sure, but don't let that bother you. I've come to help you. you."

"In what way?"

"You need transportation to Mtsety and I shall provide it for you."

Tamara was leery of his kindness and she found it repulsive that a former noble had sold his soul to the Bolsheviks, but his help would be a blessing, so she agreed.

After a breakfast of cheese blintzes, which had caused Luda much trouble in procuring the ingredients, a car arrived and the travelers were on the road again. It was a lovely day and the ride brought back many wonderful memories. When they approached the ruins of Dvzhari Church on the hill overlooking Mtsety, Tamara asked that they stop so she and Shota could pray for their ancestors. After repeating a ceremony they had done often in their youth, they drove to the Zhorzhadze estate.

Somi came running into the court yard when they drove in. She was carrying Tariel and crying. Shota grabbed her, kissed her and took his son. Holding him high in the air, he tossed him a bit and made him laugh. Somi clung to Shota's waist and cried into his side. Finally she stopped and grabbed Tamara. The cousins embraced and cried.

Foodstuffs were still plentiful in the outer regions from Tiflis and Somi had prepared a feast of Georgian dishes: chicken in pomegranate juice, hochapuri cheese bread and chakhabilli chicken. They all drank the best Georgian wines and ate themselves full. When the evening settled down, their conversation turned to the crisis in Russia and what they should do. Somi insisted that Tamara should live with them, but she shook her head and looked at Shota. It would never do and they all understood. Somi felt sad. She knew grandmother had married her to Shota, but he was really destined for Tamara. It was a hopeless situation.

The solution came from the princess. Prince Vladimir Dashkov was in Paris and he had requested that she come there. Since she spoke French and had money there, she was planning on leaving for France as soon as possible. She assured them that she would return when things had normalized in Russia. Her cousins did not want her to go so far, but she emphasized that it was just for the duration of the chaos all over the country.

"And what about you? Shouldn't you come with me?"

Somi maintained that the landowning families in the Mtsety area had met and were sure that they would be left alone by the new order if they cooperated. They were under the assumption that the Bolsheviks did not hate the Georgian aristocracy and they would be incorporated into the new regime. Tamara was not sure since she had witnessed the disintegration of society in Petrograd, but her tales of confiscation and murder did not phase them. Mtsety was so remote they were sure it was not included in the Bolshevik plans.

Forgetting the disturbing politics and ceasing tales of the war, the family let the wine go to their heads and they sang and danced. It was like the old days with grandmother and they retired to their rooms content and happy.

Stretched out on her bed in the warm fresh air, Tamara thought of the wonderful night that Shota invaded her room and how angry it made their grandmother. She was dozing off when she heard a familiar sound. The rustle of leaves on the vine outside her window made her fully awake. "My, God! Surely he wouldn't do that again?" she questioned, but he would. In seconds Shota was in the window—frame and his beautiful body was outlined in the moonlight. He sprang toward her like a leopard and quickly had her in his arms. Before she could protest his burning kisses filled her mouth and she succumbed to his amorous embraces. He pulled himself upon her and she felt his strength pressing ever so tightly against her. It was a glorious feeling and she let herself wrap her legs around him. They kissed and kissed and kissed. She writhed in lascivious languor. When his lips went to her breasts, she burned with the anguish of desire. Finally, on the verge of surrendering herself forever, she summoned all the strength of her personal dignity and slipped out from under his embrace. Crying and panting, she whispered, "Oh, Shota, we promised each other last night. We mustn't."

He tried pulling her to him.

She sat up and said, "Shota, this is Somi's night."

"She will have me the rest of our lives. I want you forever."

Tamara slipped off the bed and he followed. They came together again at the window and embraced tightly. When she suddenly relaxed against him, no longer resisting, he picked her up and placed her on the bed. In seconds they were entwined together, kissing, fondling and finally giving way to the love that the ancient Rusthaveli epic heralded as pure and bonding for Nestan and Terial. The legend had become a reality: Tamara and Shota were one.

Tamara awoke from her sleep as Shota's shadow obstructed the moonlight pouring into the bedroom window. She realized that she had come to the family estate for another night with Shota. It had happened, and the memory would stay with her forever.

The next morning Somi took her cousin aside and revealed that she knew what had happened during the night and that she understood. Tamara embraced her cousin and cried softly on her shoulder. Somi escorted her to her bedroom and began helping her pack for the journey back to Tiflis.

It was arranged that Yakov would stay at the Zhorzhadze estate. Shota wanted his help in the stables and promised him care and security. The old man made a tearful goodbye with the princess and confessed that he thought he was deserting her. Tamara patted his shoulder and kissed his cheek in farewell, assuring him that she would be eternally grateful for all his service. She also started that she would come and visit when she returned to Russia.

When the car was ready, Somi and Shota, carrying Terial, hugged their cousin with tears and kisses. They followed her to the vehicle and kissed her again. Shota said, "Adieu, my beautiful bird." Tamara watched them through the back window as they became smaller and smaller in the distance and she wondered if she would ever see them again and in her heart she knew that she must.

It was Thursday in Tiflis when the car returned and some soldiers were in the Trushinsky mansion when Tamara arrived. Luda was bawling them out and using the word thievery. One of them pushed the old woman out of the way and snarled, "Listen you old bag, you want to be shot?" When they saw Tamara, they asked who she was and what she was doing there. The princess quickly surmised that a lie would take care of the situation and said that she had come for a visit with her grandmother. She nodded her head toward Luda, who quickly ran over and embraced her. The soldiers believed her and continued with their random searching. Tamara and Luda stayed together until the riotous group left, carrying out various articles.

Tamara had Luda sit down because she had made some plans and wanted her dear old friend to understand every detail. The princess was planning on going to Istanbul and then to Paris. When life in Russia was safe again, she would return. Luda could stay in the mansion and continue taking care of it. There would be no need for cleaning the whole edifice, just the rooms she lived in. If she wanted, she could have her grandchildren live with her in the

house. Luda begged her darling not to leave, but Tamara told her
how aristocrats were being shot in Great Russia and that such
events would eventually come to Tiflis. Luda finally agreed.

Amazingly a letter came from Irina in the Crimea. She was
writing in case Tamara had taken her cousin to his estate in Mtsety.
She had guessed well, but her news was alarming. The aristocrats
who had gathered at Yalta had learned that many of their relatives
had been killed in the Fortress of St. Peter and Paul in Petrograd.
They found out that Grand Duke George and Grand Duke Dmitry
had been shot while praying; that Grand Duke Paul, who was very
ill, was murdered on his stretcher; and that

Grand Duke Nicholas held a kitten in his arms and joked
with his executioners as they shot him. The tragedy made the
Dowager Empress realize that the group assembled in Yalta had to
leave Russia. A British dreadnought, the Marlborough, had come
to Sebastopol for the Dowager Empress Maria Fedorovna, but she
had obstinately refused departing unless all the aristocrats with
her could also leave. The British commander agreed that the
Yusupovs and other noble families could go with her to England
and eventually to Paris. Should Tamara be able to join them either
in London or in Paris, they would be ever so pleased. At the end
she asked that God should bless Tamara for her generosity in staying in Petrograd and helping her cousin. Irina prayed that one of
her letters would reach Tamara, either at the "Saviors of Russia" or
in Tiflis.

Having read the letter, Tamara again felt a sense of urgency. If
she was going to escape, it would have to be very soon. But how?
The British ship would have already left by the time she had received the letter. She thought of the countess who had left with a
Turk. Perhaps there was a black market running emigres out of
Batumi, the Georgian port on the Black Sea. She took a carriage
over to the old Georgian market where she walked with her governess as a child. It had not changed. Brass objects of countless
designs lined the walls and oriental rugs covered the floors of the
shops which had open fronts and ran one after the other for blocks.

The Georgian merchants, seeing the beautiful lady, tried enticing her into their establishments with compliments and offers of tea. She was not sure whom she should approach. Finally at one shop which appeared more substantial than most of the others, she asked a short, fat merchant if he had any Turkish cups. His eyes lit up and he invited her inside. The merchandise on the walls and tables shone brightly and looked of fine quality. He had her sit on a low ottoman and poured her a cup of tea. It was the typical service she remembered from her childhood. He started for some cups, but she stopped him, saying, "There's a matter I would like to discuss with you."

His eyes lit up again. "Ah, I thought so," he said and sat down across from her. "You want to leave Russia."

She looked around in fear and he said, "Don't be afraid. Most of the merchants along the street are helping emigres. We Georgians are not Bolsheviks. We can help each other and what a pleasure it would be to help you."

Tamara did not like his last remark, but she was amazed how easily she had made a contact. She wondered if she could trust him. Since she had no choice, she asked what passage to Istanbul would cost and how would it be arranged.

The little merchant started whispering. "No one wants money now. Do you have jewels or gold?" She nodded and he smiled. "Then I think you must meet Ahmed. He works with most of the merchants here. He pays us for our contacts." Tamara was impressed by the merchant's seemingly honest discourse and asked when it could all be arranged? "Very quickly, my dear. We know how dangerous things are becoming for those who must leave." It was obvious that he sensed that she was an aristocrat and desperate. "Come tomorrow morning at 10:00 and talk with Ahmed. Also," and he smiled again, "bring your—" She nodded before he finished and returned to the Trushinsky's quite satisfied.

That evening Count Bagrov paid an unexpected visit. He asked how life was in Mtsety and if Shota and his wife were happily reunited. Tamara assured him that they were. Then he explained the reason for his visit. He was in a very ticklish situation. As a Red official, he had access to important directives from the Supreme Soviet in Moscow. A crackdown on former abusers of the lower classes was soon going to intensify. Tamara laughed and asked if she was considered an "abuser" of the people. The count warned her that it was not a funny matter. He had come to help her and was doing it out of the respect he had always felt for her family. She did not believe a word of his dribble and was waiting for the ulterior motive. He suggested that she go abroad for a while until things—She interrupted and said the word "normalized!" He agreed and had worked out a plan. She listened. He would arrange for her to take the train to Batumi and he would meet her there. He would have a car meet them and they would go up to her family's dacha at Gagra. They could wait there while he worked out passage for her across the Black Sea to Istanbul.

Tamara saw the lies in his scheme and realized the depths of the aristocracy's fall in the twilight of their existence. Yet she did not accuse him; sensing that she should play him along until she had talked with Ahmed the next day. Consequently, she suggested he let her consider his scheme and would give him an answer the next evening. The count, who was expecting a refusal, was delighted at her reaction and said, "You know, I've always admired you so. It will be such a pleasure to help you."

Tamara thanked him while wanting to slap his face hard. She understood his ulterior motive quite plainly. They would be at Gagra through interminable waiting which he would arrange; in the mean time he would try every form of seduction imaginable. Her loathing of him was almost unbearable. That a man of noble background should have turned into a party hack and devise such a scandalous intrigue made her nauseous. She realized a painful truth: the elements of dignity inherent in the word noble, such as honesty, sincerity and honor were disappearing in Russia; the country was under the control of the worst elements of human nature, that is, deceit, falsehood and dishonor. When he left, he bowed and she smiled. She, too, could deceive.

The next morning Tamara arrived at the Georgian market in the ancient part of Tiflis at 10:00 A.M. as directed. The merchant, joyous as ever, welcomed her with tea and led her into a back room. Ahmed, a tall Turk, stood waiting. He explained that he could acquire passage for her on a Turkish ship leaving Batumi in two days. It would be necessary to depart Tiflis the next morning for the connection. The princess nodded. Then the foreigner stated that he did not take people who were in political trouble. He asked if the Bolsheviks were looking for her? She could honestly say no. The Turk seemed more interested and asked what she could pay for passage. She inquired what he would demand. He wanted jewels and she asked if he knew the Cartier firm in Paris. He did. At that she pulled out the diamond and emerald necklace the Duc de Chevreuse had sent her. It sparkled brightly amid the shining brass pots and urns. The Turk's eyes opened wide and he held it up to the light. His smile showed that he was impressed. He took out a small eye piece and examined the gems. "It is excellent."

"Will it do?"

"Yes."

Tamara held out her hand for him to return it. He said that he would take it now, but she objected. No longer did she trust so innocently. "No, I'll give it to you on the ship."

The Turk smiled and handed it back. "Then it is settled. You will take the morning train to Batumi and I shall meet you at the station."

The Turk started leaving, but Tamara stopped him. "There is one problem," she stated cautiously. He turned and listened. She told him about Count Bagrov, sparing no details. She was fearful of what the new commissar might do. The Turk was obviously disturbed. He had heard of this turn coat count and knew he was dangerous. He asked, "Did he say you were wanted for anything in particular?

"No. I'm not wanted or about to be arrested. I really believe he merely wanted to compromise me."

Ahmed nodded. After thinking a little, he devised the follow-

ing plan. Tamara must pack two suitcases; one with the things she
will take with her; the other a decoy that will stay on the train.
One of his men will pick up her real suitcase at her home late that
night. The decoy will go with her. The train from Tiflis cannot go
directly to Batumi because of the high mountains. It goes north
and then descends into a valley toward the seaside town of Poti.
From there it goes south along the coast to Batumi. The last stop
before the large sea port is Osurge. Tamara should leave the train
there. Since Bagrov might have men watching her, she should leave
the decoy suitcase at her seat and pretend that she is going to the
water closet. After careful observation, she should then slip off the
train where one of his agents will be watching for her. He will
bring her to Batumi and Ahmed himself will place her on the
ship. It all sounded so easy and Tamara wondered if it would be.

That evening Count Bagrov arrived at the Trushinsky mansion
in time for some vodka and pirozhki. Tamara was very kind and
gave him the news he wanted. She would go with him to Gagra
since he offered her a means of escape and she was leaving on the
morning train. He assured her again that he would do everything
in his power for her. When he was leaving, he put his arms around
her and looked into her eyes, "You'll see that I can be very valuable
to you, ma chere."

"Thank you," she sweetly replied and lovingly smiled while
trying to break out of his arms.

He held her tighter. "Your eyes are more beautiful than even I
could remember."

She smiled, but continued trying to free herself.

He leaned down for a kiss, but she turned her head and he
rubbed her cheek. Laughing, he released her. "We'll save that for
later, my pretty one."

Tamara smiled, wanting again to slap his face.

Leaving, his last words were, "I'll see you in Batumi, my dear
one."

Late that evening, there was a knock on a back door of the
kitchen area. The princess had warned Luda about the plan and

the old lady opened the door and handed the man the princess's suitcase. Nothing was said and the matter was settled in seconds.

Sleep would not come for a long time that evening. Tamara walked around the mansion in her nightgown and reminisced. She heard the countess exclaiming about the miracles she had witnessed at her last seance. Where are all those spirits now? Tamara asked herself. She could see her beloved uncle sitting in his leather chair in the library reading. Oh, how wonderful it would be to hug you Vadim, my dearest! Then her wonderful brother Valery's voice was audible as he excitedly described a new airplane. Oh, if only I had stopped him! she sighed. The ghosts of the past filled the rooms and halls. How could she leave them? What was ahead? Should she marry Vladimir? Would she make it to Paris?

The next morning a heartbreaking farewell was exchanged with Luda. Bothknew that the chances of ever seeing each other again were remote. They hugged tightly until time demanded they part. At the train station, Tamara bought a ticket to Batumi and had a porter carry her suitcase to the train. When she was seated in a compartment, she was joined by two men who looked rather suspicious, but she pretended that all was well. During the trip through the mountains the men spoke little, a sure indication, she thought, that Bagrov had sent them. Still she paid no attention and, surprisingly, they did not try talking with her. She had never been on a train before without fellow passengers making an effort to meet her. Again her suspicions were confirmed.

When the train started its descent into the valley toward the sea, she sensed a change in the air. It was heavier with humidity. She ate the lunch she had brought with her, avoiding the stares of her fellow travelers. At Poti there was a delay as the train took on water and coal. When it started up, she put a magazine and a hair comb on the seat next to her, giving the impression, she thought, of sorting her things. She knew that the distance to Osurge was short and listened for the conductor's call. Busily arranging things in her pocket book, she suddenly heard "Osurge!" She turned to the men, one of whom was asleep, and asked, "Excuse me, do you know in which direction the water closest is located?"

The man who was awake pointed to the right. Tamara thanked him, left her things on the seat, and went out of the compartment. Looking back she noticed that they did not come after her. She walked to the end of the coach and walked out on the platform between the cars. The train was slowing. When it stopped she stepped off and saw two Turks standing near the station. They ran over to her, placed a large black mantilla over her head and led her into the station. She asked them to let her observe the train as it pulled out. The two agents were still seated in the compartment as the train passed. She was free.

Admed had taken a midnight freight train to Batumi with Tamara's suitcase. He hid her during the day in a shop owned by a fellow countryman. That evening they slipped the princess onto a Turkish cargo ship and locked her in a cabin. She waited for a long time. Finally the door was unlocked and Ahmed entered. He winked at her and told her she was very beautiful. His attitude was disturbing and she sat back in the corner of her bed. "Oh, no!" he implored, "I would never harm you. I would want to, but I would never touch you unless you wanted me to. You don't want me to, do you?"

Tamara almost laughed. "No, I don't want you to."

He grinned. "Then we must part. You have—"

She was already taking the necklace out of a secret pocket in her dress.

When she handed it to him, he held it to the light and smiled. He thanked her and opened the door. A Turk in an officer's uniform entered and Ahmed introduced the captain. He was very cordial and the two men wished her a pleasant voyage.

The princess could not believe that everything had gone so smoothly. When the ship's motors started and she could feel it moving out of the quay, she left her room and went up on the deck. Thinking of Shota and Luda and Somi, she watched the port fade into the darkening distance. While the lights of Batumi disappeared in the deep grey horizon, she wondered about her future. Should she see the countess in Istanbul? Should she travel on to Irina and Felix in London or should she go to Vladimir in Paris?

As the lights dimmed in the dusk, so did her dreams and joys. She only knew one thing: she was parting from her Russia and her beloved. The depths of the twilight were immeasurable.

APPENDIX

1. The Rusthaveli epic "The Man in the Panther's Skin" is over 800 years old and is a centerpiece of Georgian culture. For generations young people learned it by heart and brides carried a copy of it at their wedding. Such veneration over so long a period shows that the story of the Panther-clad Knight presents an image of the Georgian outlook on life: its manifest joy, its capacity for love and its appreciation of God's generosity though the world be hard. Tariel, the Panther-clad Knight, is a hero who prefers an honorable death to a life of shame. For the heroine Nestan he feels a "love for which there is no cure" and to win her for his bride he triumphs over many adversities. Legend relates that Nestan represents the famous Georgian Queen Tamara whom Rusthaveli himself loved.

2. The titles "prince and princess" in Tsarist Russian society do not refer to children of the ruler, who were called "tsarevich and tsarevna." The title prince refers to old landed aristocrats of early Russian history who kept their titles after they no longer were in control of their ancient lands.

    The titles "count and countess" in Russia refer to the new aristocratic society created by Peter the Great to award outstanding military heroes or distinguished diplomats and other public servants.

3. Russian names follow a simple formula. For instance, in this book:

    In Tamara Borisovna Zhorzhadze's name, the "ovna" of the patronymic shows that she is the daughter of Boris Zhorzhadze. In Valery Borisovich Zhorzhadze's name, the "vich" shows that he is the son of Boris Zhorzhadze.